Sedona's Golden Secret

Sedona's Golden Secret

An action adventure of miracles, mysteries and wonders

Sharon O'Shea

iUniverse, Inc.
Bloomington

SEDONA'S GOLDEN SECRET
An action adventure of miracles, mysteries and wonders

iUniverse books may be ordered through booksellers or by contacting:

iUniverse
1663 Liberty Drive
Bloomington, IN 47403
www.iuniverse.com
1-800-Authors (1-800-288-4677)

ISBN: 978-1-4759-5279-7 (sc)
ISBN: 978-1-4759-5280-3 (ebk)

Library of Congress Control Number: 2012918032

Printed in the United States of America

iUniverse rev. date: 10/29/2012

Cover artwork, map and sketch of author were created by: Elizabeth Sullivan
Wild Spirit Artworks
www.ecsullivanart.com

Thank you to those who have been supportive of this endeavor,
and to those who have reviewed and proofed the drafts of this book.
In the end, however, this is a self-edited, self-published book.
Therefore, all errors are the sole responsibility of the author.
Comments, corrections and critiques
may be addressed to the author.

SEDONA'S GOLDEN SECRET

A novel of adventure and mystery as science
and rationality meet the metaphysical
and intuitive in the spectacular setting of Sedona, Arizona.

I have much to say to you,
but you are not able to grasp it now.

John 16:12

Soli Deo Gloria

Dedication

This book is dedicated to everyone who has ever helped me in any way
along life's journey.

A portion of the sale of this book goes toward the creation
and support of Merry Heart Ministries, a healing
and recovery center for abused women.

Author's note

This novel is written from Crystal O'Connor's viewpoint.
It is her experience, her voice, her exploration,
and her unique perspective that is presented.

Sedona is a real place, faithfully described,
used as a fictitious backdrop for this novel.
Kings Ransom is an actual establishment and used with permission.
The work of Dr. Emoto is real and, for the author,
has been life-changing.
Mr. Ilchi Lee's book *The Call of Sedona* is a real book,
as is his healing center, Sedona Mago Healing Center.
All other businesses and persons are pure fiction.
Names (unless used with permission), characters, places and incidents
are used fictitiously and/or are a product of the author's imagination.
Any resemblance to actual persons, living or dead,
or to actual events or locales is unintentional and coincidental.

At the core of this book are the contrast and clashes between
Dr. Katherine VanDyke's rational, scientific world view,
and Dr. Crystal O'Connor's spiritual, metaphysical perspective
as they search for the mystical orb of legend.

Prologue

Sedona

There's an old saying: "God created the Grand Canyon, but He lives in Sedona." On my first day in Sedona, I knew it must be true. Sedona felt like it truly was the divine, sacred land it was rumored to be.

The small, enchanting town of Sedona was nestled within the 'Red Rock Country' of Arizona. The town was named for Sedona Schnebly, wife of the first postmaster. Part of the Central Highlands of the Sonoran desert, Sedona was encircled by sandstone formations of layered shades of reds, oranges and golds—the major formations being Cathedral, Coffeepot and Thunder Mountain.

Native Americans believed that "great souls" lived in the rock formations around Sedona. Lore also said that when someone came to Sedona, Sedona awakened her to her true dreams and desires.

One could explore and appreciate Sedona, with her labyrinth of slot canyons and picturesque countryside, by foot, jeep or horseback. Or one could sit back and absorb Sedona's beauty and atmosphere from the comfort and seclusion of one's campsite or motel room.

Sedona was supported primarily by tourists. The older section of Sedona was called 'uptown Sedona' and was northeast of Highway 179. The old part of Sedona had been transformed from older buildings into a series of high-end shops and eateries—rock and mineral shops, metaphysical services, gift shops, art galleries, and clothing stores.

The newer section of Sedona was west of Highway 179. There one found markets, theaters, banks, a medical center, the library, a post office, many spas, psychics, rock and mineral shops, and a variety of eateries. Metaphysical and alternative healing services were scattered throughout Sedona.

Principal among Sedona's attractions were her vortexes, which were said to be created by the motion of energy as it rotated and spiraled around a central axis that, when it interacted with a person's inner self, was thought to be magical, mystical, and even sacred, and enhanced one's spiritual energy and psychic abilities. Sedona's vortexes were considered by many to be "hot spots" of positive energy that promoted healing and increased one's personal and psychic powers.

With her special ethereal feel, Sedona attracted the mystical and metaphysical who practiced psychic development, alternative and energy healers, and practitioners of magic. When Dr. Crystal O'Connor visited Sedona, it was a well-known destination for spiritual seekers of all kinds.

Sedona was also famous for her small pig-like residents, javelinas, hairy and smelly little beasts who were sometimes aggressive, but most often delightful and adorable. These little desert dwellers roamed about mornings and evenings in packs of six-to-twelve, then found shade for a siesta during the heat of the day. Their name referenced their long, sharp, pointed teeth which they used to protect themselves. As cute as they were, it was safest to observe them from a distance.

In addition to its natural beauty, gift shops, metaphysical atmosphere, vortexes and javelinas, Sedona was also home to a myriad of artists of all types and disciplines. The unique beauty and *feel* of the Sedona area also attracted those who simply loved the out-of-doors and the natural high desert allure that surrounded Sedona.

Like the feel of a summer breeze, or the scent of the first honeysuckle of spring, or the way watching an eagle in flight makes one's heart soar—it was almost impossible to describe Sedona with words—for Sedona had to be felt, seen, tasted and experienced first-hand.

Blended all together, one had the magical, mystical, mysterious Sedona!

July 4, 2011, Yosemite Valley, California

On July 4, 2011, the unthinkable happened. Archeology graduate students, Sam McDaniels and Michele Strathford, from the University of California, Berkeley, were hiking near Half Dome in Yosemite Valley when Sam slipped and skidded halfway down a steep slope. On her way down to help Sam, Michele spotted a half-gallon 1850's sky-blue glass Mason jar that had apparently been unearthed by Sam's mini-rockslide. After insuring that Sam was okay, Michele returned to where she had seen the jar, retrieved it, unscrewed the rusted zinc lid, and gently removed an old scroll that looked to have been made from some sort of hide. A hand-written message on the scroll appeared to contain clues to the whereabouts of the long missing ancient sacred golden sphere of Dunluce Castle in Ireland.

I Await

Not long ago, I resided in an Irish castle
Resplendent among my master's many other treasures.
Great power radiated from Me,
And ever more power I drew into Myself.
I was loved and adored,
And enjoyed great renown,
'Til I was stolen by the English
When they brought my master down.
In Sedona's sacred soil, I await.

In Sedona's sacred soil, I lie, I lie.
Nestled in her rock formations, I rest, I wait.
To those who have learned to listen,
The winds whisper My hiding place.
Though autumn breezes blow, and silent winter snow falls,
Though spring flowers bloom, and summer suns blaze,
I remain in one of the darkest places on earth,
Left behind, I glow alone
In Sedona's sacred soil, I await.

I await here alone for the one who will make Me her own.
For her I will once again glow.
To the evil and wicked I will appear not,
But to her my secrets and powers I will allot.
So search for Me if you will,
For I am eager to be free.
Leave Me not in this dark place.
Let Me not remain here for eternity.
In Sedona's sacred soil, I await.

At first, Sam and Michele thought the scroll was probably a prank. But later that night back at their camp they examined the jar and its contents more closely. The tall jar had been securely sealed so its contents survived in the changing temperatures and climate of Yosemite.

"It's amazing the jar was intact," Sam said.

"It is pretty incredible," Michele agreed.

Upon cursory examination, Sam and Michele decided the scroll could actually be the real thing.

They took the jar and scroll with them back to Berkeley and presented it to their supervising professors for authentication. Their professors agreed the jar was most likely from the 1850's, the scroll was made of doeskin, and it appeared to be authentic. They immediately dispatched the jar and scroll to the Smithsonian in Washington, D.C., to be authenticated by recognized experts. The results were expected to be made available as early as mid-November.

News of the mythical sacred scroll's discovery spread like a Texas wildfire through local academic circles. It had been over 500 years since the fabled magical sphere of Dunluce Castle in Ireland, along with the other spoils of that invasion, was taken by the British during their 16th century siege.

Legend says the golden sphere is slightly larger than a softball, but can shape-shift into just about anything. It is said to sometimes communicate with select people telepathically.

Lore says the sphere was once seen in London around 1650. Then it appears to have been transported to America in the early 1700's. Legend also says that a mystical sphere with amazing powers existed in Massachusetts around 1750. Reports fade until the 1850's when the sphere was rumored hidden near Sedona, Arizona, by a gold miner on his way to California. No one knows why he supposedly left the sphere behind, but persistent rumors abound. Most people discount the rumors, but some have taken them seriously, and have searched for the sphere.

In September, Katherine VanDyke, Ph.D., a professor of geology who lived and worked in Arizona, and who also led research expeditions in the California and Arizona deserts, was brought up-to-date on the discovery of the scroll by a geologist colleague, Jason Wells. Jason emailed Katherine a copy of the message that was written on the scroll, then called her with more details.

By the time Katherine VanDyke hung up the phone after talking with Jason, her heart pounded and her blood raced. The call of adventure beckoned loudly.

Katherine immediately contacted her former college and hiking friend, Dr. Crystal O'Connor, to share the information and ask for help searching for the sphere. She asked Crystal to meet her in Sedona in October, a month before results from the Smithsonian were to be made public, so that Katherine and Crystal could conduct their own search for the fabled mythical sphere before the public got involved.

To persuade Crystal, Katherine read the scroll to her.

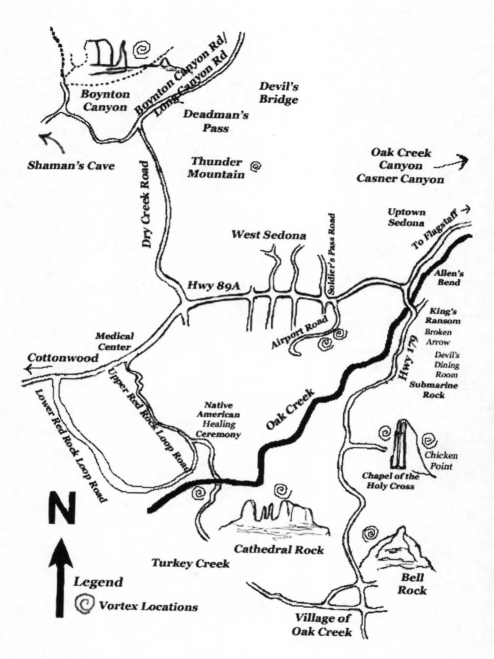

Map of Dr. Crystal O'Connor's and Dr. Katherine VanDyke's Search
for The Golden Sphere

Chapter One

"What do you say, Crissy? Will you join me? Let's do it! Finding that sphere would make my career. It would be the highlight of my life's work." Katherine was so enthused she almost yelled into the phone. "We can arrange for substitutes to cover our classes for a week, right? We can meet in Sedona in mid-October. That will give us time to research Dunluce Castle and the missing sphere. We can camp out. What do you say?"

"You haven't changed, Katherine," I replied, as I reflected that Katherine had always been in constant motion and displayed exuberant excitement by nature, whereas I had been a seeker of peaceful stillness and inward quietness. She was flush with the thrill of the hunt. The pending search for the mythical sphere caused her energy to peak beyond its normal hyper state.

I glanced up at our wall clock. It read 10:34 a.m.

Smiling to myself, I turned and walked the length of the dining room to our glass French doors and watched the sparrows, doves and finches eat and drink.

To my amazement, for the first time in months, a brilliant red Cardinal flew into our yard. He glistened in the morning sun. I watched as the Cardinal casually ate seeds. As he did, every now and then a sunflower seed shell fell from his beak. He stopped, looked up at me, picked up another seed, then repeated the procedure. I watched, mesmerized. Then he disappeared behind the Chinese Tallow tree.

As much as I loved Cardinals, and as long as I'd considered the sight of a red Cardinal *a sign*, I'd never had one stay in my yard so long, or look directly at me while he ate. Hypnotized by his presence, I heard myself say to Katherine, "There's a lone red Cardinal in my backyard. Maybe it's a sign I should join you?"

"You're kidding, right, Crissy?" Katherine said. "You don't really believe in that sort of thing, do you?"

I changed the subject, and said, "Let me check with Trevor and see what he thinks. If he's okay with it, I'll see if I can arrange coverage for my classes. *But only for* one *week, Katherine.* That would be my max. How's that? In the meantime, can you email me a copy of the scroll? I'll think about its meaning to see if I can intuit any clues from what the writer tried to communicate."

"Intuit? Since when do you 'intuit,' Crissy? That doesn't sound like the talk of a social-psychologist, does it?" Katherine said.

"You're still the energetic geologist always on the lookout for fun and adventure, I see," I replied, smiling, as I avoided her question. "Okay. I'll call you tomorrow evening with my plans. And, Katherine?"

"Yes?"

"I don't go by 'Crissy' anymore. I go by Crystal now."

After a pause, Katherine said, "Okay. Got it. Since we're updating one another, I go by Kat."

"Kat? You go by Kat?" I said.

"Yeah. Family and colleagues joked that I've used up seven of my nine lives. It just seemed to fit."

"I see," I slowly responded, wondering *why* people thought she'd 'used up' so many lives, but I didn't want to take the time to find out right then. *Besides, we'll spend a week together while we search and hike in Sedona. I'll find out then.*

Chapter Two

Sunday, September 18, 2011, 11:00 a.m.

I had no sooner hung up the phone after I had talked with Katherine when my husband, Trevor, walked into the room, and asked, "Who was that?"

"Katherine called. Seems she's excited and into planning another adventure."

"Really? What now?" Trevor responded.

"She said students at UC Berkeley found a scroll," I explained. "The scroll is at the Smithsonian for authentication. Katherine wants me to join her for a week of searching before news leaks to the general public and Sedona is besieged with treasure hunters. I've been feeling led to the desert, anyway, and to Sedona, in particular, so I think I'll go. What do you think? It won't be until next month, so I have time to get a substitute or reschedule classes, cancel appointments, and make plans."

"I know lately you've talked about feeling drawn to the desert, and that you're not happy about it. But is this a good idea? Should you just drop everything and dash off because Katherine called? What if others go to Sedona to search? What if there's competition to find it, if it even exists? What, exactly, is it you said Katherine wants to look for, anyway?"

"Don't laugh, okay? It's a sphere. Katherine says it's rumored to have come from Ireland by way of England, and then Massachusetts. It is supposed to have magical powers."

"Doesn't Katherine have enough spheres? Good grief, how many does she have, anyway? Fifty? Sixty?" Trevor said. "And 'magical?' Are you serious?"

"Katherine probably has somewhere in the neighborhood of a hundred impressive sphere-shaped mineral specimens. But, well, she *is* a geologist, and so for a lifetime she's collected unique and rare specimens, that's for sure. Actually, I think she's always collected rocks, crystals and other specimens. You knew that, right? But this is different. It's not a normal, common mineral sphere. There's a legend about this sacred golden sphere, supposedly magical and powerful, that was stolen from a castle and then stashed somewhere in America. The scroll that was found in Yosemite is a puzzle piece, or a poem, perhaps, and it says, if we're interpreting it correctly, that the sphere is or at least has been hidden somewhere in or near Sedona," I replied.

"You seem excited when you talk about it," Trevor said. "But you don't really believe it's real. Well, you don't, do you? And besides, do you have a way to know exactly where in Sedona this mythical sphere is hidden? If *you* do, then surely someone else does, too. Why hasn't someone found it already?"

"No. Not really," I answered, as our plump, friendly black cat, Zak, wrapped himself around my legs. "I don't think Katherine knows any more than I just told you. But while I talked with Katherine, a vibrant red Cardinal flew into our backyard. As long as Katherine and I talked about the sphere, the Cardinal stayed, fed on sunflower seeds, and watched me. When we hung up, he flew away. I'm sure it's a sign."

"Sounds like you've made up your mind to go?" Trevor asked.

"Yes, I guess I have decided to go," I responded. "Are you good with that? It can be a sort of tailor-made pilgrimage. It's nine days, like a Novena. I can think of it as a prolonged Vision Quest. Since I've felt led there, I'll go, and see if I can find out *why*."

"Sure. I'll be fine. The cats and I will miss you, but we'll be okay. Just be careful. Don't get lost out there in the desert with Katherine, or worse, hurt," Trevor cautioned. "Why don't you take my Expedition watch? It's rugged, and you can attach it to the strap of your backpack."

"Thanks. If you're sure you won't mind, I will take it. I'll also use my old Timex with the brown leather wristband. It's sturdy, and I think it can take the abuse of hiking. It will be good to have a backup."

Thinking about Trevor's concern, I added, "I don't think it's likely we'll get lost as long as we stay close to Sedona. But I'll check in with local law enforcement and forestry personnel when I get there, just to be sure they know we're in the area around Sedona. And I'll call you as often as I can so you don't have to worry about anything. Deal?"

"Deal."

Chapter Three

Wednesday, September 21, 2011, 9:31 a.m.,
near Austin, Texas

"How did it go with Trevor? Did you rearrange your schedule?" Katherine asked.

"Fine," I replied. "I was able to get substitutes for my sociology and social-psychology classes at the community college. And Rebecca has agreed to cover for my Thursday night Reiki and energy healing class, so I'm good. I just need to do some more research about Sedona, shop and pack. I ordered maps from the Sedona Chamber of Commerce. They should arrive soon, but if they don't, we can pick up local street maps when we get to Sedona."

After a pause, Katherine said, "What kind of class? And maps? Do we really need maps?"

"I can explain Reiki and energy healing when we're in Sedona," I said. "I could even give you a session, if you'd like. And I always need maps. I like to know where I've been, where I am, and where I'm going."

As I watched the Chinese Tallow tree's branches bend in the strong Texas wind, Katherine said, "I like to explore new areas without maps or preplanning."

I reached for my red rose-covered coffee cup and thought, *Yep, that sounds like the Katherine I remember.*

Katherine continued, "I thought we'd camp out. I have an ice chest, so we can stock up on food and drinks after we're in Sedona."

Instantly alarmed, I said, "You *are* kidding? That *is* a joke? Right? You don't expect *me* to sleep in the dirt with the spiders, snakes, mountain lions—not to mention human predators—do you? Besides, where would we shower? What would we use for bathroom facilities? Well . . ." as I continued to stammer, my heart raced and my face flushed. Finally, I paused, took a deep breath, and continued, "There's just no way I'm willing to camp out, Katherine."

After Katherine's long, loud sigh, I added, "Why don't I arrange a room for us? My treat. I've researched Sedona a bit. There are lots of lodging options. And even though with so many tourists hiking around the area it's almost impossible we will find anything interesting, let alone a magical golden sphere, we can still have fun, reconnect, hike, and explore Sedona. Right?"

"Alright," Katherine finally slowly responded. "But I plan to find that sphere!"

"Okay," I said. "When I checked out Sedona, I came across one motel that has large rooms and great views of the red rock formations that we can enjoy from the second story patio attached to the back side of our room. How does that sound to the geologist in you?"

After another shorter silence, Katherine replied, "Okay. I'll plan to see you in Sedona. You'll email me the details about the motel you settle on, and the time you'll arrive, right?"

"Right. I'll make the arrangements and let you know as soon as they are firm."

Over the next few weeks, autumn continued to turn the Austin landscape from green and lush to brown and barren. I was glad to learn that Sedona's colors changed later in the season, which meant it would be at its full fall glory during our visit.

Chapter Four

I decided to divide the drive to Sedona into two days.

The first day, Saturday, I left Austin at sunrise. Golden rays burst every which way behind huge fluffy clouds as I ventured north on H-35 toward Ft. Worth.

Clouds hid the sun as I drove west toward Amarillo late in the afternoon.

I had driven about 500 miles and had made three stops to rest and refuel my new red Jeep Liberty. I was relieved when I pulled into the Holiday Inn Express. I had a light dinner, took a refreshing shower, and watched TV.

The following day, I checked out at 5:00 a.m., and resumed my drive west on I-40. I made good time on the final 650 miles, which meant I would arrive in Sedona before 5:00 p.m.

Peace and confidence flowed through me. I looked forward to seeing Katherine again and exploring Sedona. As I made the long solo drive, I wondered what the Divine had in mind for me, and why I felt led into the desert. More specifically, as I drove toward Flagstaff, Arizona, I wondered why I was called to Sedona, in particular. I was glad the sun was behind me the whole way.

Sunday mid-afternoon, I stopped just before Flagstaff to rest and refuel. Then I headed south on I-17, and made the connection with H-179 west into Sedona.

I had long ago learned that often a "leap of faith" is necessary in order to experience revelations. I wanted to better understand the spiritual and the Divine. To do so, I knew I needed to follow my intuition.

Since I had felt led to Sedona, and had even had dreams about going into the desert, I had purchased a lizard necklace to hang on my bathroom wall as a constant reminder to be open and receptive to the idea of spending time in my least favorite place—the desert. One dream in particular kept recurring night after night, loud and clear, and would stay in my mind throughout the day. So when Katherine called and asked me to join her, it *felt* right.

After Katherine's call, I had researched Sedona. When I learned it was filled with magic and wonder, the mystical and the metaphysical, I was convinced I should go. In fact, Sedona seemed a sacred place in its own right. The mystery and lore of Sedona meshed perfectly with my metaphysical and research interests, which drew me to Sedona the way a gambler is drawn into a casino.

I didn't really believe the sphere existed, but Katherine did. To her, this wasn't just a fun adventure while we got reacquainted. She believed the sphere actually existed, and that if we searched hard enough, we might actually find it.

I had left Austin with a mixture of curiosity, excitement and a sense of daring. If it hadn't been for my intuitive leadings, though, I never would have left my comfortable and cozy life behind, not even for a week, especially during mid-term.

Although summer had slipped into fall, the weather remained hot and dry. So it was a pleasant surprise when, during my drive to Sedona, the temperature took an unexpected fifteen to twenty degree dip. Temperatures that had been predicted to be in the high eighties were now predicted to be in the high-sixty to mid-seventy degree range, which made the climate ideal for hiking.

Clear azure skies laced with willowy clouds greeted me as I turned onto H-179 toward Sedona. Gentle breezes of pure mountain air flowed over the desert landscape and sang softly through the open windows of my Jeep. The high desert foliage had turned to its fall colors of yellow, orange, rust and red. Red rock formations that stood sentinel over Sedona began to appear in the distance.

After the Texas drought, wildfires, and record-breaking heat the past summer, I was invigorated by the clean, cool high-desert air and natural peace and beauty.

Chapter Five

It had been years since Katherine and I had visited in person, so I was happy I'd see her again, and soon.

My research had indicated Sedona was not only filled with natural beauty, but it had a special quality that attracted mystics and artists. I looked forward to my own first-hand experience of all that Sedona offered. I didn't have much hope we'd find the sphere, but I did hope this trip would satisfy my spirit's pull toward Sedona.

In Oak Creek Village, I was awed by the change of scenery and foliage. There was a distinctive change in the atmosphere. The air grew heavier, more peaceful, as though I'd taken a mild tranquilizer laced with mind-expanding properties.

By the time I had passed Oak Creek Village, I was spellbound and curious. I pulled into the Bell Rock parking lot, and went for a short walk. I was wrapped in a soft blanket of peace and calm. Sunlight played on the gold, orange and red rock formations. A sense of safety and love, beauty and gentleness, permeated the atmosphere. I felt as if I had come home—to a very good home. Joy and enlightenment infused me like morning dew melding into a rose. The air felt liquid, heavy, as if I were moving in a buoyant sea of entrancing air.

After a half-hour walk at Bell Rock, I was in a mild euphoric state as I continued my drive toward Sedona.

I arrived at Kings Ransom in Sedona around 5:05 p.m., an hour before I was to meet Katherine. When I entered the lobby, it was empty. Shortly, the desk clerk came from the back office with computer papers in one hand and a cup of coffee in the other. A small Calico cat trotted alongside her and then glided upward, and settled next to where I signed in at the front desk. The clerk, Sandy, and the cat, Sophie, both welcomed me. The clerk oriented me to Kings Ransom and Sedona. Soon, I was in my upstairs room, number 247.

Once settled inside my room, I opened the heavy outer teal patio drapes, then the soft gauzy white inner curtains. Next, I opened the sliding glass door and stepped onto the cement patio. The view of the red rock formations streaked with gold and orange, with a backdrop of vibrant blue sky dotted with creamy white clouds stopped me in my tracks. The sun was dropping toward the horizon and its rays splashed golden color everywhere. In silent appreciation, I sat in one of the patio chairs and absorbed the scene that unfolded before me. As I watched the sun move closer toward the horizon, I knew I was in an atmosphere as spiritual and sacred as any church I'd ever attended.

After a few minutes, I returned to the room. The room felt dark and confining after having been outside on the patio watching the sunset and the activity of arriving tourists below in the parking lot.

I called Trevor. All was well at home, so I unpacked.

After I'd arranged my clothes on hangers and put some in the dresser, I arranged my toiletries on the sink. Then I placed the maps on the table. Having done all I could, I sat. I waited. I became restless. I was ready to see more of Sedona.

Since Katherine still hadn't arrived, I took a quick refreshing shower, then walked around the grounds. At 6:25 p.m., when Katherine *still* hadn't shown up or called, I began to worry. I decided to leave her a note, let the office know I was leaving for awhile, and go for a drive to get more of a feel of Sedona.

Chapter Six

B efore leaving the room, I stood in the middle, turned slowly, and took a much closer look. The colors were neutral. *Nice for a motel, but I love splashes of bright color. I'll get some flowers for the table while I'm out.* Then I realized I didn't smell anything. Nothing good, nothing bad. Not even the smell of cleaning supplies or disinfectants. So I walked to the sink, picked up my red can of Sexiest Musk, and lightly misted the air. *There. Just right. Much better.*

Before I left the room, I checked my backpack. First, I put my clutch-purse in one compartment, then checked to make sure my key chain with its various medallions of saints was in another zippered compartment. A Herkimer diamond was wrapped in a soft tissue and nestled next to my Beretta Tomcat. I pulled the backpack over one shoulder. On my way out the door, I grabbed my favorite old red sweatshirt. I picked up the room key, then, as I stepped onto the landing, I heard the door click closed behind me.

I stopped at the office to report a noisy fan and a flickering light in the bathroom. I was told the repairs would be taken care of while I was out. *Good. I'll have some peace and quiet and can sleep soundly tonight.*

While driving out of the parking lot, I decided, *I'd better check in at the local police department in the morning, especially since we'll be hiking in unfamiliar territory.*

Sedona was laid out like a divining rod. Highway 179 dead-ended into Highway 89. A right turn took me north, through the old part of town, which locals call "uptown," with its quaint tourist shops and the Sacajawea mall. Beyond uptown the highway turned into a narrow, winding mountain road that began to climb upward into Oak Creek Canyon.

Not wanting to go up into the canyon, I made a U-turn at the end of uptown Sedona and headed west on H-89, which took me to the newer shopping area. I passed the road to the airport, the spa where I planned to get a chakra-balancing massage, restaurants, a movie theater, and other businesses.

At the end of the main part of town, I turned left on Upper Red Rock Loop and drove slowly along the narrow winding two lane road. When I turned one corner, an unexpected sunset-bathed panorama suddenly appeared before me. I gasped. I pulled over onto the shoulder and parked. I absorbed the view of the highlighted multi-colored rock formations near and behind Kings Ransom the way a buttercup absorbs the morning sun. The last of the sun's rays bathed the red rock formations in a soft golden hue—a spectacular sight. I made a mental note to explore both this road and the formations later with Katherine.

I continued along the Upper Loop. It soon gave way to a rough, gravel road called Lower Red Rock Loop, which was narrow and full of pot holes, but eventually led me back to Highway 89-A.

I made a right, and headed back toward the newer part of town. Before going back to the room, I pulled into the Safeway parking lot to stock up on drinking water, bagels, apples, grapes, and other health-foods. I also bought a fortified health drink so I could take my vitamins and supplements with something more substantial than water, since taking pills with water almost always made me gag.

By the time I had loaded my groceries, the sun had fully set. Even so, streaks of sunlight still burst out from below the horizon to dance on golden clouds. The last dying rays of sunlight splashed in every direction through the darkening sky. As I watched, the blue sky turned charcoal. When the last of the sun's rays disappeared, and the night turned a deep charcoal-blue, I drove back to Kings Ransom. The lights in the shops began to come on.

I arrived back at the room just after 7:29 p.m., tired, but excited. *If Katherine hasn't arrived yet, I'll have coffee on the balcony while I enjoy the evening view from our room.*

There was no sign of Katherine, and she hadn't checked in at the office. So I unpacked groceries, put the perishables in the mini-refrigerator, arranged fruit, and found an empty plastic water bottle for the bouquet of Gerber Daisies and white long-stemmed roses I'd picked up at Safeway. I also opened a scented candle of lavender and vanilla and inhaled deeply of its fragrance.

While the Hazelnut coffee brewed, I clicked on the small table lamp and sat in one of the two upholstered chairs that flanked the table in the far corner of the room.

After I had explored Sedona's open spaces, it felt suffocating to be confined indoors. So when the coffee was finally brewed, I took my coffee cup and a power bar onto the patio to wait for word from Katherine.

Before long, I was ready for a walk and some fresh air. As I opened the door to leave the room, Katherine pulled into the parking lot. She looked up, noticed me, and waved while yelling, "Hey! Little Buddy! Nice to see you!"

Chapter Seven

Sunday, October 9, 2011, 7:51 p.m.

I made my way down the outside corridor toward the stairs. Katherine cheerfully yelled up to me again, "Hi! You been here long?"

Some things never change, I thought. I waved back, then responded, "Well, for about three hours now."

As I walked to meet her, Katherine gathered bags from the backseat of her deep honey-gold Land Rover. Her golden blond-streaked hair was pulled into a ponytail that cascaded down her back. Her snug navy slacks showcased her slender and toned body. Her yellow T-shirt matched her vibrancy. Navy flats completed her casual yet athletic look. Life and energy radiated from Katherine the way warmth radiates from the sun.

By the time I reached the top of the stairs, Katherine had bounded up all of the steps, as trim, tan and fit as when we were teens. *Apparently her energy level hasn't waned, either.* I began to feel a bit slow and tired in contrast to Katherine's speed and agility.

At the top of the stairs, Katherine and I hugged briefly. When I looked toward the end of the landing, I noticed Sophie, the office cat. She sat and groomed her right paw as she glanced up at us occasionally.

"You still wear jeans?" Katherine said, as I helped her carry her luggage back toward the room. "My family lived in Boston before we moved to Southern California." she continued. "We used to laugh at all those Southern Californians who wore jeans." As she marched forward, she continued to laugh heartily.

Speechless and feeling slightly insulted, I realized I had bitten the inside of my upper lip, something I hadn't done since high school. I struggled to hold back a defensive response. I paused on the landing for a minute, and looked at Katherine, not quite sure what to say, if anything.

After a few seconds, Katherine turned back to where I still stood, staring at her. "Right," Katherine answered my unspoken reaction. "Who were we to judge others? We didn't have much or my dad wouldn't have moved to Southern California for work in the first place. Even there, we lived a pretty sparse life."

Dazed, I didn't respond. Instead, I walked to the door and silently opened it.

"Actually," Katherine continued, as she walked into the room after me, "That's how I got involved in camping in the first place. My mom said we couldn't afford motels or restaurants, but we could afford gas. She said we could travel and go places in California if we packed our food and slept in the car or outside on the ground. That was the only way we could afford to take trips."

"So . . ." I slowly responded as I set her black suitcase on her bed, "Even though you're a college professor and pretty affluent these days, you still camp out and take an ice chest from home? Only now you lead students and other professionals on expeditions into the desert?" I asked, fascinated.

"Yeah. I guess so," Katherine said as she paused for a second to reflect on what I'd said as if that connection hadn't occurred to her before. "I suppose that's what made me comfortable hiking, camping and roughing it. I've done it my whole life."

"Not me," I said, as I put Katherine's other black bag down on the chair next to her bed. "I've always hated 'roughing it,' as you call it. I prefer to be clean and have a shower. I like indoor plumbing. When you first suggested we camp out, I thought it was a joke. I can't imagine it. Haven't you ever gotten into trouble out there?"

"No. Well, once," Katherine corrected herself. "A bunch of Hell's Angels biker-types roared up to my camp site. I was alone in the California desert near Death Valley. I told them I was the first of a wave of instructors who were posting signs for an expedition that started in the morning, and that the rest of my party would soon join me. They bought it. I was really just on my own. I wanted to spend a weekend in the desert."

"Back to your comment about my clothes," I said, still slightly piqued. "Yes, I still wear jeans. The older and more worn and comfortable, the better. I've always loved jeans. I try to break them in as quickly as I can. Speaking of clothes," I said as I turned to where Katherine unpacked hiking gear, "What are you wearing on your feet tomorrow? Tennis shoes or hiking boots? I brought both."

"I can't wear hiking boots anymore," Katherine replied.

"Really? Why not?"

"Yeah. My foot was mangled at a rock concert a few years ago. Now, I can wear tennis shoes, but not hiking boots."

"You hurt your foot at a rock concert? Did someone step on your foot, or something?"

"No. The lead singer invited me on stage. I was climbing up the metal bars that support the stage, when my foot got entangled in the scaffolding. The music and noise were so loud that he didn't hear me screaming in pain. He continued to pull on my arm, but I couldn't get my foot loose."

"But you still hike and dance, swim and travel? How do you manage it?" I asked.

"I don't let it stop me, or even slow me down all that much," she responded. "I just don't try to wear hiking boots anymore. I stick with tennis shoes."

"Okay. Tennis shoes it is," I replied.

I turned toward the patio and watched the view of lights twinkling in the valley below us and on the distant hillsides.

Katherine walked over and joined me as I slid the door open for some fresh air. "This view's amazing, isn't it?" I asked.

Temporarily motionless as she surveyed the outlines of mountains and the lights from town nestled at their base, Katherine added, "Yes, it is," and turned to dig her camera out of her backpack.

"You can take photos in the dark?" I asked.

"Sometimes," Katherine absently responded, as she walked outside onto the patio and clicked in first this direction, and then the other. "At least I can try."

"I like this spacious room, the attached private patio, and the view from here," I said to Katherine's back. "There were a couple of motels I checked out on the Internet that seemed plusher and newer, but the rooms were like small caves. And they didn't have a view of anything but a parking lot—and that view was out of a tiny window—nothing like the view of the distant rock formations we can see from this room, that's for sure. Why come all the way to Sedona and not be able to sit on a patio and enjoy the fabulous scenery?"

"Right," Katherine said as she strode the length of the patio and took photos with her digital camera.

As we turned to go back into the room, Katherine noticed my red plaid shirt and red sweatshirt. She paused, then said, "Hey, Little Red!" Then she smiled and added, "It really is great to see you again, Crissy."

Nope, Katherine hadn't changed much. She radiated a raw, almost volcanic energy. As she talked, she tapped her well-manicured, burnt orange artificial nails on the counter, desk, or whatever else was tap-able. I was fascinated that Katherine could be so athletic, and yet somehow so feminine. *What a combination.*

While unpacking her larger suitcase, Katherine tossed her tennis shoes onto the comforter. I paused, not sure what to say. Finally, I ventured, "Do they launder these spreads between guests?"

A quick glare told me she didn't care about future occupants and definitely didn't like being admonished.

Katherine tossed her purse next to her backpack and tennis shoes on the bed closest to the TV. Then she stood back and again scanned the room. By her expression, I guessed she was still not happy about my arrangement of a room instead of a campsite out-of-doors. But as Katherine continued to consider the size of the room, the view from the balcony, and the location of the motel, her displeasure seemed to slowly melt like snow in an Alaskan spring.

To change the subject, I reminded Katherine, "No one calls me Crissy anymore. Only you could still get away with that."

Katherine sat on the bed nearer the wall that separated the bedroom from the bathroom. She had apparently claimed that bed for herself since the television was positioned at the foot of the bed. With a short cord, the TV couldn't be easily moved. Her first order of business was to reposition the television stand. Then Katherine adjusted the TV's controls.

Who cares about a TV when you're in Sedona? I wondered. The more Katherine worked to position the TV, the faster my heart beat. Since I'm auditory, sounds and noise grate on my nerves like nails on a blackboard, so the thought of the television always on, with a continual string of programs and blaring commercials, caused my eyes to widen and my chest to tighten.

After Katherine repositioned the television, she told me *why* she had arrived later than our agreed upon time. "I was winning at the Cliff Castle Casino and just couldn't leave such a lucrative streak. You understand, right? Since my cell is in the shop for repairs, I couldn't call to let you know," Katherine added as she continued to nestle in and make herself comfortable on the bed.

I had driven for two long days, was up early, and was on the road before daylight to be on time. I was amazed Katherine was so casual as she told me why she was late. I sat in a nearby chair, silent, and watched her when she got up and continued to unpack. All the while, Katherine complained about the "tighter" slot machines at the casinos. *Am I supposed to be satisfied with this explanation? Does Katherine really think this is a viable excuse for being two hours late?* I wondered. *Oh, well. It's just one week.*

"I see," I finally said. My breathing had slowed and my face had warmed. I turned away from Katherine and looked across the room toward the patio, then changed the subject. In spite of her arriving late, I couldn't help but appreciate her energy, eccentricities and *joie de vivre.*

She rested for ten minutes, then Katherine was up and pacing like a puma (some things really never do change). As she walked, she rubbed a large clear Australian green chrysoprase that hung from a thick gold chain around her neck. The aqua color of the stone somehow made Katherine's green eyes look even greener.

When I commented on the stone's unique size and beauty, Katherine said it was a gift from her late husband, Walter, and the last gift he had given her before he died in 2008.

While I sat at the table and relaxed, Katherine moved around the room continuously. As she did, I followed her with my eyes, and asked, "Do you know the metaphysical lore about chrysoprase? It's interesting. Healers say it's a powerful stone that brings good fortune, prosperity and happiness. And I think . . ."

Katherine instantly interrupted me and, as she spun on her heel to face me, hands on slender hips, she snapped, "You know I don't believe in any of that metaphysical hype. That's just someone's way of making money by getting people to buy their stones. It's no different from ghost-watching, or tarot card reading, or horoscopes, or any of that other nonsense."

Affronted, but not deterred, I accepted the rebuff from my geologist friend and took a few long, slow, deep breaths. Then, when I looked across the room to where Katherine dug through her suitcase, I said, "Well, if chrysoprase improves friendships, I'm all for it. It certainly is beautiful. I've never seen a stone quite like it before. It's so clear. Aren't they normally opaque? And the black outlining around the stone is striking."

When she talked about Walter, sadness engulfed Katherine the way the sea engulfs a diver. She said they often camped out and explored the desert together. Obviously, it was a sad and sensitive topic for her, so I dropped the subject.

"Did you know," Katherine asked, "that 'crystal' means pure, clear thinking, and a universal healer? I think your name suits you."

"No, I didn't know that," I answered, amazed that Katherine, who didn't believe in the lore of stones, would know. "I have heard clear crystal quartz is often used to counter black magic and to enhance communication with the Other Side. But I hadn't heard what you just told me. By the way, thanks for the compliment," I added.

"So, are you beginning to consider that there might be something to the metaphysical lore of stones after all?" I added.

"Of course not!" Katherine said as she snapped her head around to face me with a startled look. After a deep sigh, she turned back around and continued to unpack toiletries onto the bathroom counter. "No way. But I know you're interested, so I thought I'd share that with you."

"Thanks," I responded.

"What sort of necklace are *you* wearing? Is that a gold medallion? And a diamond?" she asked.

"It's a Miraculous Medal," I answered. "I had it custom made. It's based on something I read in a Catholic book about novenas. It . . ."

"That's okay," Katherine cut in. "I don't need to know any more. It's all superstition to me. I went to a Catholic school for a year. A nun cracked my knuckles with a ruler because I was left-handed. I think that might be why I have arthritis today. I don't want to even hear about anything Catholic!"

"You were naturally left-handed?" I said.

"Yes," she said. "But now I write with my right hand."

"I see," I said, as I absorbed this new information, and how the experience at the Catholic school had affected Katherine. "Well, I don't think one experience at one school is reflective of all Catholic schools and practices," I ventured. "But if you dislike them, you dislike them. As for me, I love my medal and never take it off."

"You don't *really* believe in all that metaphysical and superstitious nonsense, do you?" Katherine said. "You're too well-educated for all of that. Well, aren't you?"

Taken by surprise at such an abrupt denouncement of my beliefs and values, I had to take a long breath before replying, "Well, actually I do believe in it. You've heard the old saying that we teach what we most need to learn, right? Well, perhaps I was drawn to study, and then teach, the metaphysical because that's what I most needed to learn?"

"I don't see *you* wearing any stones," Katherine challenged.

"I have some of my stones with me, though," I said. "I have a medicine bag of small stones I carry in my left pocket all the time. It's got a clear quartz crystal, among others." I smiled, mostly to myself, before I continued, "One is moldavite. Anyway, I have my medicine bag with me all the time."

Katherine paused, hands again on hips, and stared at me. The more she stared, the more I squirmed.

I changed the subject yet again, this time to food, since we were long overdue to have dinner, and if memory served, Katherine had an insatiable appetite.

Chapter Eight

Sunday, October 9, 2011, 8:17 p.m.

After a quick shower, Katherine changed into tan slacks, a short-sleeved peach-colored Angora sweater, and brown leather loafers. The sweater highlighted her deep tan and golden hair, and somehow brought out the gold flecks in her emerald green eyes. In contrast to her mostly athletic look, Katherine added a pair of elegant yellow-gold dangle earrings that boasted pear-shaped citrine stones that dangled halfway down Katherine's slender brown neck.

As I looked at Katherine, I suddenly felt too casually dressed in my plaid shirt, old jeans, and tennis shoes.

Katherine turned and faced me, frowned, then said, "You don't look the same, Crissy."

"What do you mean?" I said, confused and curious. "It has been years since we've seen each other, you know. People change."

"Don't you wear your hair down anymore? And no make-up? When did you stop wearing make-up?" Katherine asked, as she applied fresh blush, put on more mascara, and teased her long bangs that tangled with her eyelashes.

I paused and reflected. Then I realized my appearance probably had changed a lot. I began to explain, "Well, I've been really busy. I stopped messing around so much with my hair while I was in graduate school, and I just started to tie it back. As for the make-up, I still wear it, just not the mascara. Mascara made my eyelids itch if I didn't get all of it removed at night, and it smeared in the mist or rain. So I finally just gave it up altogether." *I guess I do seem somewhat understated by comparison*, I thought, as I watched Katherine finish getting ready.

Without further comment, Katherine put down her comb and headed for the door. "I'm ready. I'll drive," she said as she reached for the knob.

"I'll be there in a minute. I still need to check my gun. I want to be sure it's concealed, then I'll join you downstairs," I said.

Katherine stopped mid-stride, and spun around to face me, horror written all over her face. She almost shouted, "You have a gun! I hate firearms. Why do you have a gun?"

Surprised, I put down my backpack, stood, and responded, "I always have my gun with me, Katherine. I was law enforcement before going back to college, remember? It's a Beretta 3032 Tomcat. My size. Actually, since you go by Kat now, and you camp out alone so much in the desert, maybe it would be a good gun for you, too?" I added, trying to lighten the moment.

Katherine continued to stare at me unblinkingly.

So I added, smiling "In fact, I never leave home without my Tomcat."

My attempt at humor didn't lighten Katherine's mood or her obvious disapproval. Remembering Katherine's innate spontaneity and her tendency to tell everyone everything that was on her mind, I added, "Katherine, do *not* tell *anyone* I have a gun. Agreed?"

"Fine," Katherine spat, as she spun back around and stomped out of the room.

I locked the sliding glass patio door, then gathered my belongings. I sighed as I reached for my backpack. *Five days and I'm out of here*, I reminded myself. *I can endure almost anything for five days. But I think this week is going to be quite a bit longer than I'd anticipated.* I walked toward Katherine's Land Rover where she now waited and revved the engine.

As I climbed into the tall passenger seat, I continued my admonition. "I mean it, Katherine. *No one*," I said, as I settled my 100-pound body into her massive vehicle, feeling like a small child in a Lincoln Town Car.

Katherine responded to my comment with, "Alright, Mom!"

My jaw tightened. I realized I was again biting my upper lip. I took another deep breath and slowly exhaled, then I turned and silently looked out the passenger's side window. Regardless of Katherine's obvious disapproval, I planned to enjoy the scenery on the way to dinner. *Even at night Sedona's magic and majesty were palpable.*

Chapter Nine

Sunday, October 9, 2011, 8:23 p.m.

Katherine whipped in and out of traffic on the way to dinner. The drive was silent, yet strangely pleasant. When Katherine turned left on Highway 89, I continued to watch the moonlight from the near-full moon as it played on the surrounding red rock formations. I took deep breaths to calm myself. Before long, the sound of the wind as it rustled the autumn leaves combined with the liquid feel of the air had worked its magic. I felt energetic and revived, and yet centered somehow.

Katherine's head bobbed back and forth as she darted in and out of the lanes. She finally began to talk to me again. "About the golden sphere we're here to find," she said. "There are many places it could be hidden in or around Sedona. I want to start our search in Casner Canyon in the morning."

"That's fine with me," I said. "You're the explorer—the one who leads expeditions. It's your baby. I thought I'd follow your lead. Besides, you're the one with contacts in the geology and history departments. I'm just along for the ride, really. And to help you. I came mainly so we could get reacquainted while I helped you search. I had been feeling led to the desert lately, wanted to experience Sedona, and hadn't seen you in a while. So when you called, and I saw the red Cardinal while we talked on the telephone, it just felt like the right thing to do."

Although driving, Katherine gave me a long, hard look. I began to worry about an accident, but she suddenly turned her head back to focus on the road and the traffic. *I think I'm being evaluated and found wanting*, I thought once again.

After another uncomfortable silence, Katherine responded, "Good, then it's settled. I've already planned the days. Anything you want to do evenings?"

"Evenings? We'll probably be exhausted, don't you think?" I responded. As I answered, I recalled what happened when we would work the all night parties at Disneyland. After our shift, I would collapse on the beach and sleep. Not Katherine. She would body-surf and hike to the end of the jetty. "Well, one of us will be exhausted," I corrected myself. "While I'm here, I would like to investigate some of the metaphysical side of Sedona. This area is famous for her vortexes, psychics, energy healers, and metaphysical phenomena. Things like that. I find it all so exciting . . ."

"The whole desert's a vortex," Katherine cut in. "And the rest of that is just hype and superstition."

I guess there are some things I'll be doing alone. I turned and once again looked out the side window at the unique scenery that whipped past.

We'd settled on a quick, casual dinner at The Purple Moon, a fun 50's style diner where Katherine could get a meal of meat and ice cream, and I could order something vegetarian.

The Purple Moon's parking lot was full, a good sign, so we parked nearby and walked toward the diner.

Katherine, who never met a stranger, struck up a conversation with a man who introduced himself as Ryan Cho. He was an older, distinguished-looking gentleman who said he was a retired New York newspaperman turned prospector. He was dressed in well-worn high-end casual clothes. After introductions, I watched Ryan as he listened to Katherine's questions about the best places to hike in Sedona.

"You ladies here to search for the golden sphere?" he asked. His deep, slow speech revealed a thoughtful, well-educated man. His eyes were wise; his manner deliberate.

"Sphere? What sphere?" Katherine asked.

Apparently knowing Katherine's answer was not forthright, Ryan turned his gaze to study me more closely.

I fidgeted and took a step back, uncomfortable under such close scrutiny. I turned to the side and looked up at the nearly full moon, not wanting to contradict Katherine to a stranger, yet not wanting to lie to Ryan Cho, either.

Unbidden, Ryan began to slowly tell us a legend the locals talked about. It was of a fabled ancient and powerful golden sphere, supposedly priceless, that had been left in Sedona decades ago by a miner on his way to the California gold rush.

I noticed that as she listened to Ryan, Katherine's left hand reached up to touch her necklace and her eyes darted from the diner to the nearby trees and back. As soon as Ryan finished his story about the sphere, Katherine looked toward the café again.

I continued to watch him and listen carefully to what Ryan said.

Katherine asked Ryan, "If locals have always known about the sphere, why are people just now coming to Sedona to search for it?"

"Don't know for sure," Ryan Cho replied. "Local people have searched for the orb for decades. What I heard recently is that serious word has just gotten outside Sedona—to out-of-towners. The discovery of a scroll in Yosemite last summer, they say, got people interested again. There were rumors around here before that about the sphere, sure, but not many folks took those stories too seriously. Now, I can see that outsiders like you two have started to come to Sedona. When the news becomes even more public, who knows what's likely to happen? It'll probably be like the gold rush days, I suppose. People might trample down Sedona just to try and find a rumored golden sphere. Who knows if it even exists? And, if it does, if it's anywhere around here?"

Ryan Cho's thoughts about the sphere reflected my own. I listened as Ryan watched us, then I looked up at the bright moon. When I again turned toward the café, more people were entering the Purple Moon.

Ryan continued to watch me intently.

Finally, Ryan said, "My great-grandfather left me a cabin here in Sedona. He told my granddad that he'd talked with a reclusive man who said he knew of an old guy who told him he had hidden a golden sphere here in Sedona somewhere. My granddad said the old man had told him he would return one day to claim the sphere after he'd staked his claim in California. Seems he never returned, and he hadn't told anyone exactly where he'd hidden the sphere." Ryan added, "In fact, a friend of my father's died in a rock slide trying to find the sphere. That's how sure *he* was it existed. If there was such a sphere, and even if it didn't have any special abilities or qualities, but was simply made of pure gold, it would still be quite a find, wouldn't it?" he said, as he smiled wryly.

Without comment, Katherine looked toward the diner.

I replied, and said to Ryan, "Your father had a friend who disappeared while in search of the sphere?"

"Yes," Ryan replied. "Joseph Eagle Feather had searched for the orb around Soldier Pass the last anyone knew. Then he just up and disappeared. Years later, his remains were found. But no one knew for sure exactly where he had searched, or where he thought the sphere might be," Ryan added.

"Okay then," Katherine said, having obviously heard enough of Ryan's story about the orb. "You ready, Little Red? Time for food."

"Yes," I said, "But first, I have a question for Ryan. I've read about vortexes and that in Sedona they are referred to as 'vortexes' and not 'vortices.' Is that right?"

"That's right," he responded.

"I have maps from the Chamber of Commerce. I'd like to visit at least one of the four major vortexes while I'm here this week. Do you have any *insider information* about the vortexes? If I can visit only one, is there one that's better to experience than the others? Can you tell me anything that might help me understand vortexes better?" I eagerly asked.

Katherine rolled her eyes, gazed into the diner, and sighed deeply.

Ryan thoughtfully began to answer my questions.

Katherine turned and walked toward the diner. Then over her shoulder she said to me, "I'm hungry. I'll meet you inside."

"Fine." I said. I was so fully engaged with what Ryan Cho began to tell me, I said to Katherine, "Go ahead. I won't be long."

"Okay," Katherine answered, before she disappeared inside the café.

"Well . . ." Ryan said. He seemed to understand I wanted to know more than the usual printed tourist information, "Our vortexes are extremely powerful. The Native Americans referred to them as *power places* for a reason. People with a strong spiritual or supernatural bent seek them out. They say they can actually feel the power, the energy, of the vortexes. The average tourist, though, not so much. But vortexes are part of the reason Sedona attracts so many mystics and psychics. They feel at home and at peace here. Many say their supernatural abilities are heightened at the vortexes. Mystics often say it's like they put gas in their spiritual tanks. Are you one of those? Were you drawn here, too?"

"Well, yes, I have felt led to come here," I hesitantly admitted. "It's like Sedona has been whispering my name for a long time."

"I thought so," he said. Ryan looked at the ground as if he were listening to something before he turned and faced me again, stared directly into my eyes, and said, "I have a message for you. I have a notepad. Do you have a pen?"

I slipped my backpack off my shoulder, reached inside, then handed him a pen. Then he wrote:

> If you look for Me in a place that's not clean
> You will find Me when I give off a gleam.
> Five clues in all I will give to you.
> If you do what is asked, both our dreams will come true.

When I read the note, I began to feel lightheaded and confused. Questions flooded my mind. But Ryan continued, "You will not have to search for the sphere. It has called you. It brought you unto itself. When you go to Inner Light Spa tomorrow evening for your chakra-balancing massage, be sure you receive your massage from Elke Strauss, their finest masseuse. Listen for her message. I'm sure she will know who you are. She has another part of the message for you—the next puzzle piece, as it were. If you follow her instructions, they will take you one step closer to the sphere."

I stared at Ryan Cho. I had no idea how to respond. I wondered about his message, and how he knew about my appointment with Elke. When I had gathered my thoughts and started to ask how he knew my plans for Monday night when even Katherine didn't know yet, he cut me off with a look toward Katherine, who now stood, hands once again on hips, in the doorway to the diner.

"Just be sure you don't miss your appointment tomorrow night," he added, "And remember, *you* don't have to look hard to find It; *It* has summoned *you.* Somehow, clues are being given to certain locals to pass on to you. When you have all the clues, you will find the sphere. That's all I know. Just listen to Elke. Then you'll know what to do next. Go ahead and share this information with Katherine, even though she will tell others. It's okay if she does. Do you understand?"

"Yes, I think so," I almost whispered in response, not sure what to make of what he said. *Is this for real?* I wondered.

"Yes, it's 'for real.'" Ryan surprised me by responding to my thoughts.

Even though it was a warm evening, chills ran down my spine.

Ryan smiled, turned and resumed his walk toward the dark parking lot.

Dazed, I turned to join Katherine. When I looked back toward where Ryan had walked, he was gone. There was no sign of him anywhere.

In the entry to the diner, I told Katherine I had something exciting I *had* to tell her.

"Later," she said. "First—food!"

Chapter Ten

Sunday, October 9, 2011, 9:15 p.m.

Katherine darted between customers as she slipped back into the café. I paused at the door. Before I followed her, I turned to look again at the almost full moon and then turned to watch its light as it reflected off Lost Wilson Mountain. I could hear the gentle October breeze rustle through the nearby cottonwood and sycamore trees causing crisp fall leaves to crackle as they fell nearby. Then I took a long, deep breath of the cool, crisp high desert air before I turned and stepped into the café.

As soon as I walked through the door, I was assaulted by the noise of clanking dishes and the hum of a packed restaurant. Customers had to practically shout to be heard. The aroma of burgers and fries wafted through the air reminding me dinner was long over-due.

I looked for Katherine. She had made a quick detour into a large over-flow dining room. As she approached our assigned table, she quickly changed her mind, picked up the silverware and menus, and settled into a nearby booth. By the time I reached her, she was surveying her choices.

As I slid into the booth opposite Katherine, two rugged, handsome, clean-shaven men walked up to our booth and struck up a conversation. One had straight blond hair and clear aqua-blue eyes the color of the Florida gulf coast waters. The other had dark curly hair and eyes so dark brown they looked almost black.

Katherine perked up instantly. Her eyes sparkled, her voice purred, and a large smile finally appeared.

I was annoyed. *Oh, God. How can I get rid of these guys?*

I didn't want to get bogged down with men on this trip. But as I turned toward the two strangers to explain that Katherine and I wanted to be alone to get reacquainted, in a loud and cheerful voice Katherine said to them, "Hey. Why don't you join us?"

My breath caught. Shocked, my heart began to pound in my ears. I snapped my head around and looked over at Katherine, who was sliding across the red vinyl seat to make room for the sandy-haired man. "Crissy, why don't you slide over, too?" Katherine said—directing more than asking—when she noticed I hadn't budged. Before I could respond, she immediately turned back to the blond man and engaged him in blithe conversation.

Red faced, I reluctantly slid toward the wall. It was impossible for Katherine to go anywhere unnoticed. She thrived on public attention; I abhorred public attention.

As I fumed, the dark haired man smiled and moved in closer to me. I could feel my face turn crimson and perspiration formed on my upper lip. I glanced down at the menu to avoid eye contact.

When I looked up, I noticed the man had a warm smile that could melt the heart of the coldest woman. Increasingly uncomfortable, I said to him, "We're in a hurry. We just stopped in for a quick bite. Wouldn't you be more comfortable at another table?"

He smiled a little wider, and said, "Hi, Crissy. I'm Manny Branson." His friend then introduced himself as Joe Lombardi. "We don't mind a quick meal," Manny added. "You're really petite, aren't you?" he asked in a deep baritone voice.

Oh, God, spare me! I forced myself not to tell Manny what I thought about people who referred to my size. I had long ago learned that in order to accurately assess any situation, I needed to remain quiet, observe, and tune into my intuition. So I fought the heat that grew in my chest and spread down from my neck and face, and tried to control the redness that spread across my cheeks.

"Hello," I finally responded, while I slid even further inward and hugged the wall. I again looked up and glared across the table at Katherine. She avoided my gaze as she continued to chat with Joe. "I'm Crystal O'Connor," I finally said to Manny. "Not 'Crissy.'"

"I'm Manfred," Manny replied, still smiling, "But you may call me Manny. I didn't mean to offend you, but you are rather tiny, aren't you?"

"My size really isn't any of your business, is it?" I said, hotly. As I caught the rudeness in my voice, I saw Katherine suddenly look over and glare at me from across the table. I quickly added, "You know, Manny, I'm married. And I came here to spend some time outdoors and to get reconnected with my friend. In other words, I want to be alone."

"I see," Manny responded. He still smiled his slow Rhett Butler smile.

"So," Joe interjected after a tense pause. "What did you say brings you two to Sedona? The call of the wild? Shopping? Escape? What is it?" he said. "Or could you be here to search for the rumored golden sphere?"

Unnerved by Joe's comment, I suddenly sensed these men brought trouble with them. I didn't believe the 'salesmen on vacation' story they told us. Who were they? Why were they so quick and direct when they made our acquaintance? And why did they mention the rumors about the sacred sphere?

The waiter interrupted my thoughts when he came to take our order, which gave me time to think about how I would respond to Joe's questions.

Before she ordered, Katherine hesitated, looked at me across the gray Formica table, and said, "I don't feel right if I order meat and ice cream when you don't eat either one."

I quickly looked up in surprise, then replied, "Don't worry about me. Order whatever you want, Katherine. Whatever makes you happy. I'm fine. I'll find something on the menu that works for me. Besides, I do have desserts sometimes. Just not often."

When the waiter had taken our orders—a burger, fries and a chocolate ice cream root beer float for Katherine—a veggie-stuffed baked potato and water for me—cheeseburgers, fries and coffee for Joe and Manny—the laughter and casual conversation between Joe and Katherine picked up where it had left off.

"You're not having coffee?" Manny asked.

"No," I replied. "We're getting an early start in the morning. I need to sleep well tonight."

I became light-headed as I watched Katherine flirt with Joe. *You don't suppose Katherine's going to hook-up with Joe? She doesn't even know him.*

Manny commented on my wedding ring, then said, "So, you said you're married?"

"Yes, I *am* married. Quite happily, actually. I like my life just the way it is."

Joe's focus turned in my direction when he heard me tell Manny again that I was married. Then he turned back to Katherine and asked, "Are you married, too?"

"No," Katherine replied, as her joie de vivre faded. "My husband died suddenly a couple years ago," she added, tearing. I knew how much Katherine disliked any sign of weakness, so I watched her, concerned we might be headed toward tricky waters. Katherine quickly recovered, and changed the subject to tomorrow's hike.

As I watched and listened to Katherine, I began to absentmindedly scan the room. Suddenly, my discomfort increased as I realized that Katherine's animated conversation had attracted not only attention from Joe and Manny, but from other customers, as well. I became light-headed when I noticed how many people were paying close attention to our conversations.

My focus was quickly pulled back to our table when Manny asked, "Are you having any luck in your search for the golden sphere?"

"What?" I said, as my attention snapped back to our table and my heart began to beat more quickly. With their second question about the sphere, I realized they somehow knew we were looking for the fabled orb.

"*The* sphere," Manny repeated. "Isn't that really why you're here?"

It suddenly seemed obvious Joe and Manny had chosen us not because they were interested in us, but because they, too, were in Sedona to search for the sacred golden sphere of legend.

Instantly convinced that Katherine had told these strangers too much about us and our search for the sphere, any semblance of poise flowed away from me the way a river flows down a mountainside. Enormous red flags waved frantically in my mind. Angry, I turned to Manny, leaned in his direction, and said, "It's time for you to leave."

Manny seemed taken aback by my intensity, but made no sign of leaving, or of letting me out of the booth. Instead, he gave Joe and Katherine a glance, then said, "You must have heard that a scroll was found in Yosemite with information about the missing Dunluce Castle sphere? The scroll was cryptic, but clearly indicated the sphere is hidden somewhere around Sedona. Isn't that right?"

It was obvious Joe and Manny weren't to be easily deterred. They appeared to think Katherine and I had useful information about the sphere's location that we might share with them. My stomach churned. I suddenly felt seriously ill. I wasn't even sure there *was* a magical, mystical sphere, and I didn't want anyone to think that if there were such a sphere, we might know its whereabouts. *Should I get out of here? Or should I explain that we really are ignorant of any details about the sphere?* I sat in silence for a few seconds and tried to wrap my mind around what was happening. *How was it they knew to latch onto us? What was their real motivation in trying to befriend us?*

As their questions about the sphere grew, so did my alarm. My head began to spin. Manny sat so close to me it was hard for me to focus. His right arm rested on the back of our booth, and his woodsy cologne wafted in my direction. His dark brown eyes were warm and friendly. He was tan, and his thick hair perfectly cut and combed. As I listened to his soft, deep voice, I thought, *This must be how a rabbit feels in the presence of a boa constrictor.*

"Really?" I finally responded, as I tried to change the conversation away from the sphere, eager to end our evening at the diner.

"Hey, Crissy," Katherine said, as she broke into my thoughts. "Should we tell them?"

Oh, God! What now? "Tell them?" I asked, barely able to breathe.

"Crissy?" Manny said. "I thought you said your name was Crystal."

"It *is* Crystal. Like I said, Katherine, and *only Katherine*, calls me Crissy these days," I replied. The muscles in my back and neck continued to tighten. I looked for the waiter. "Where's our food?"

"Chill, Crissy," Katherine said.

"Crystal it is," Manny said, as he winked at me.

Both men and Katherine stared at me. I stared back. My eyes burned from the long days on the road. I was so tired I could no longer concentrate. When our food finally did arrive, the aroma from the burgers and my huge potato that dripped with butter and overflowed with veggies caused me to realize just how hungry I was.

Manny surprised me when he suddenly changed the subject and asked, "What color are your eyes, anyway? Olive?"

"They're hazel," I replied, as I sighed loudly in exasperation. "They just look olive when I'm wearing certain colors. You do remember I'm married, right?" The area between my shoulder blades tightened even more. *Oh, God! I don't think I can take very much more of this. I've got to get out of here.*

"Sure. I noticed that ring first thing. But there's no reason we can't be friends, is there?" he replied in his slow, deep voice. Then he added, "Speaking of friends, I can't believe you and Katherine are friends. You seem so different."

I didn't respond. *This guy's good looks and charm could disarm anyone,* I thought, as I looked over my right shoulder and wished I weren't hemmed in by Manny. *When, oh when, can we get out of here,* I groused to myself. "You know, Manny," I said, "The *only* reason I came here was to reunite with

Katherine, and check out Sedona. I'm not interested in anything or anybody else."

"And to search for the fabled golden sphere?" Manny pressed, as he studied my reaction.

"I'm not really up to chatting," I said. "It's been a *long* and tiring two day drive from Austin. I just want to have dinner and get back to my room. Besides, this café is getting busier, noisier, and more crowded by the minute."

Katherine gave me a withering look that let me know I had put a damper on her fun. I exhaled again, and resigned myself to whatever was to come.

As we ate, we chatted about the superficial things people discuss when they don't know each another well. Joe and Manny talked about their jobs as computer salesmen. I didn't believe they actually *were* salesmen of anything.

Although knowing I was eager to leave, Katherine ordered a banana split for dessert. My jaw tightened. My eyes blazed. Joe and Manny followed her lead. Joe ordered lemon meringue pie. Manny had cherry pie ala mode. I relented and selected the New York style cheesecake.

As I watched Katherine laugh and flirt, I felt frustrated and a little jealous. I thought, *Not much has changed. Katherine's still the life of every party.*

Just then, Katherine unconsciously reached up with her left hand and touched her Chrysoprase necklace, which reminded me that as a widow she probably especially enjoyed the company of a handsome and attentive man. *Perhaps I should ease up and give her this?*

My attitude mellowed. I relaxed back into the booth.

I sighed again in resignation and tried to be civil to Manny, who pleasantly peppered me with questions about my life, home, and career, none of which I wanted to discuss, especially with a stranger.

Even though Joe and Manny exuded charm, my intuition told me they were not who they presented themselves to be. Everything about them *felt* wrong, so I trusted it *was* wrong.

But what to do about Katherine? I wondered. *She appears to so deeply enjoy the fun and excitement of conversation with strangers about a mysterious sphere. This is just one more adventure to her. She obviously enjoys Joe's attentions. But what if they take her seriously? What if they think we really are in search of the sphere, and that we know more than we do?*

Katherine broke into my thoughts, "You're worrying, aren't you, Crissy? You worry too much. Worry, worry, worry."

My cheeks flushed red at Katherine's public admonishment. I quickly changed the subject. "We don't know much about the sphere. Right, Katherine?" I said louder than I'd intended. Then I added, "Katherine is a geologist and I am a social scientist. It's a fun and colorful tale about a powerful, mystical sphere, to be sure, but not something we take all that seriously. We have a copy of the scroll. So we'll hike and search, and keep our eyes and ears open. When the week is over, we'll leave Sedona, probably without anything, let alone a mythical sphere. Isn't that right, Katherine?"

"That's half right," Katherine responded. "Except by the time *I* leave Sedona, I plan to have that sphere!"

"I'm not sure they know you're joking, Katherine," I said, my face had grown numb and my breath was more shallow than ever.

The disruption when Joe and Manny joined us had caused me to forget all about Ryan's message. When I suddenly remembered it, I decided, *I'll have to tell Katherine, but definitely not now.*

I could tell Katherine wanted to spend more time with Joe, and that I had put a damper on her fun. Before I knew it, Joe suggested drinks at Mulligan's. I quickly declined. I was relieved when Katherine reluctantly turned down Joe's invitation, too. I began to relax, but too soon. Suddenly, it was as if I'd been hit with a bolt of lightening when I heard Katherine tell Joe and Manny where we were staying, and even our room number. I sighed loudly, and gave up on corralling Katherine.

Dessert had dragged on forever. When I finally looked around the dining room, shivers ran down my spine when I noticed at least half a dozen customers were listening to our conversation. Three men paid particular attention to everything Katherine said, right down to our motel and room number. Suddenly, I felt violated and threatened.

Two of the men sat opposite each other at a nearby table. They were huge. The first looked to be the size of The Incredible Hulk. He was about forty, had two prominent scars on the left side of his face—one above his left eye, the other at his jawbone. He stared at us unashamedly with intense deep blue eyes. Straggly white blond hair framed a balding head. His skin was pitted and appeared greasy. His blatant aggressive eavesdropping made my skin feel clammy.

His companion was just a little smaller. Dull medium brown hair stood straight up on top of his head giving him the appearance of a startled porcupine. He had a small head with weasel-like features—pointed nose, black eyes, small mouth—that didn't fit with his large body. His teeth were yellow and, as he shoved another handful of french fries into his mouth, I noticed he was missing a front tooth.

When they realized I was staring back at them, the two men stood, then shoved their chairs away from the table. The blond man said, "Come on, Hank. Let's get out of here."

"Sure," Hank replied, as he wiped his hands on the legs of his pants. His chair screeched on the tile as he shoved it away from the table. "Where are we headed, Rex?" he added, as he picked up the check and followed the blond man to the register. All the while, they continued to watch and listen to us. As they passed, I smelled the unpleasant mixture of sweat, dirt, urine and bad breath. Shivers continued to race up and down my spine. I involuntarily turned away from them and looked down toward my backpack.

At a different table, a small, black-haired man sat alone and discreetly listened in on our conversation. He sipped coffee while he absentmindedly tapped his spoon on the Formica table top. The tapping grated on my already frayed nerves. His jet black oily hair was slicked back. Large deep brown eyes glanced around the room, then returned to rest on our table. When he finally stood to leave, I realized how incredibly thin and small-boned he was. His deep blue suit, vest, bow-tie and hat seemed out-of-place at the diner, or anywhere else in Sedona, for that matter. His skin was porcelain-pale. He appeared elegant and rich, and yet frail somehow. His walk was more of a graceful strut, which made him appear arrogant.

As he passed our booth, our eyes locked. He smiled and turned his head slightly down as he looked at me. He moved the way an eel glides sideways through water—slithery. Every thing about him made my skin feel even clammier. As I watched him leave the diningroom and re-enter the main room, I sighed with relief.

Suddenly, I felt extreme exhaustion as if I had deflated and melted into the booth. My skin crawled; my pulse hammered; my breathing slowed. I *had* to leave. Immediately. I anxiously looked toward the nearest exit.

My attention snapped back to our booth when I heard Katherine say, "Maybe tomorrow night?" to Joe as we slid out of the booth and prepared to leave the diner.

Manny added, "I hope you'll join us, Crystal."

"I'm married," I said again, then looked away. "Besides, I'm used to turning in early. Much earlier than this, actually. And, besides, after a day of hiking tomorrow, I'm sure I'll be ready for a quick, quiet dinner, and then crash."

As I reached for the bill, Manny picked up the check.

"No!" I said, alarmed. "Absolutely not. I'll pay for my own dinner."

But I was too late. Manny, bill in hand, turned and walked toward the adjoining room to find our waiter.

I stood by the booth, deflated and disgusted, as Katherine sidled up to me and hotly whispered, "Loosen up, Crissy. They're just being nice."

"I don't like this," I angrily whispered back, as I grabbed my backpack with such force it almost flew out of my grip.

Katherine continued to talk in a low voice, "Oh, come on, Crissy. What's a drink and a little dancing?"

"I keep telling you, Katherine, I don't like it!" I repeated. "Manny is *too* smooth. And Joe? He seems nice enough, but I'm sure he's not who he says he is. Something's wrong. I don't like the feel of it. Besides, as I've said many times, *I'm married. Married, Katherine!* I don't go out for drinks or dinner or dancing with handsome, enchanting strangers."

"Crissy, Crissy, Crissy. The *feel* of it?" She mocked. "I'm sure Joe and Manny are fine. They're just different. Relax."

"'Different?' They're 'different' alright," I responded, much louder than I'd intended. "Okay, Katherine. Do what you want. Just never leave me alone with either of those guys. And I don't think you should be alone with them, either. Besides, how did they know about the sphere? Did you tell them?"

Katherine's jaw tightened and her eyes narrowed as she said, "It's just dinner and dancing, *Mom.*"

It was obvious Katherine was going to do whatever Katherine *wanted* to do, so I added, "We don't know them. They seem *off* somehow to me. But I'm not the one who wants to go out with them," I said, resigned. "Just do not get me involved in any of your plans—especially with slick Manny—so you can be free to go play with Joe. I'd rather be by myself."

"Okay, Crissy! Okay. I get it," Katherine replied, obviously annoyed.

I continued, "These guys unnerve me, Katherine."

Katherine's head turned as she silently studied me again. I recognized her stare that meant I was being unfavorably evaluated again. I began to squirm, but I was determined not to relent. I no longer cared whether or not Katherine liked my decisions.

"That look you're giving me makes me uncomfortable," I finally told Katherine.

"I wish you'd relax. The days are shorter this time of year, so we'll be back from hiking early. I rarely sleep more than two or three hours a night, so I'd like to do something fun in the evenings. Dinner and dancing with Joe would be perfect," Katherine added. "And, you know, it really wouldn't hurt you to go with Manny and keep him company."

"What?! Katherine! Do you not hear me at all? I'm *married*. Contentedly married. And I want to stay that way. I'm not going anywhere with any man for any reason. You can go. I will *not!*"

"Fine!" Katherine shot me a nasty look, then she turned her back to me, folded her arms, and dropped the subject.

I was glad. Angry, slightly lightheaded and disoriented, but glad. I couldn't wait to get some fresh air, and then go back to the comfort and solitude of the motel room.

Katherine moved toward the door like a Navy cutter moves through the open sea. I turned and slowly began to weave my way through the crowd as I followed in her wake.

I walked toward the door through the press of patrons. Suddenly, and as smooth as a snake, the man with the slicked-back black hair slid in front of me, blocking my path. He faced me and, looking at me from one side of his face, said in a smooth, low, almost guttural voice, "Hello. I'm Patrick Bailey. I'd like to talk with you if you can spare a minute." My chest constricted and chills covered my arms and back. I shivered.

"I don't have the time, Mr. Bailey," I responded after I'd blinked a couple of times. Then I took a deep breath, moved around and past him, and continued toward the door where Katherine now tapped her nails on the glass door as she impatiently waited

After I had squeezed past Patrick Bailey, a tall, slender woman, poshly dressed in black slacks, black flats, and a grey floral silk blouse, floated up to me and touched my shoulder. Puzzled, I stopped and turned in her direction. In a low, soft, conspiratorial voice, she whispered, "The aura of the man with the black hair indicates you cannot trust him. And the two large men who just left? They spell trouble for you, dear. They are dangerous. I would watch out, if I were you." Then, as quietly and unobtrusively as she had appeared, she turned and disappeared into the crowd.

Momentarily disoriented, I shook my head, then continued toward the door, wondering, *How could she know these things?*

When I reached Katherine, she asked, "What did that woman say to you?"

"That I should be careful," I replied, as I walked past Katherine and stepped into the cool, clean night air. The evening breeze still sighed through the trees while the light of the near-full moon continued to reflect off red rock mountains.

Chapter Eleven

Sunday, October 9, 2011, 11:32 p.m.

Once we had settled into Katherine's shiny new Land Rover, she popped a handful of Red Hots into her mouth, then surprised me when she said, "I'm not tired. Let's do something."

"I'm exhausted and it's the middle of the night! What could we possibly find to do now?" I replied.

"I'm ready for another dessert. Let's find someplace where we can review our plans for tomorrow over something sweet."

"I'm so tired I'm practically non-functional . . . But . . . Sure . . . I suppose we could do that if you can find a place that's still open this late on a Sunday night," I said.

Katherine made a quick U-turn in the middle of H-89, then we headed toward New Town Bar & Grill.

"Where did you hear of this place?" I asked

"I've brought groups here before," Katherine replied. "We'd stop-over in Sedona for fun and shopping. This restaurant is great. And it has lots of chocolate!"

"You and your chocolate," I laughed.

Fortunately, or unfortunately, the restaurant was still open. In fact, it didn't close until 2:00 a.m. As we entered, live country music flowed throughout the bar area. The music drifted into the dining room where we were seated at an old wooden table. "One of my favorites," I said. "Soft country music."

"Mine, too," Katherine said. She stood, her head bobbing this way and that, and looked around the dining room for a waiter.

Katherine's eyes widened and she smiled when she realized that the restaurant still served their famous deep-dish-triple chocolate fudge cake. "That's what I'm having," she said, then slammed the menu shut.

Just the thought of that much chocolate made my teeth tingle.

After she had joked with the waiter for what seemed an eternity, Katherine ordered the cake and a Coke.

I ordered the deep dish peach pie ala mode and water.

"I thought you avoided sugar?" Katherine said, as she reached for her cola.

"I do," I replied. "But tonight is different. I think I need another sugar boost to keep up with you." Then I considered the cheesecake I'd had earlier, and thought, *Oh, well. Why not? I suppose I can count on the sugar shakes later, followed by the sugar blues, I suppose.*

When the desserts arrived, Katherine said, "This is great cake, but it's not really sweet enough for me." When Katherine had eaten the last crumb of her cake, she asked the waiter for a Coke refill, only this time she wanted Root Beer. He obliged.

Since I rarely ate sugar, my pie tasted as sweet as if I were eating pure honey. "I don't think I can handle any more of this pie," I said. "I think it's just too much sugar and sweetness for me for one night."

"Too sweet?" she said. "Shove it in my direction. I'll finish it for you."

"Really? Okay. It's almost *too* good, isn't it? It's too tempting to come back and have another dessert, isn't it? I try to avoid trying new desserts, or anything that's not good for my body, actually," I added.

Katherine stopped surveying the room, and stared at me.

"I know. I'm a bit extreme when it comes to avoiding meats and sweets."

While Katherine finished the deep dish peach pie, I pulled the Sedona maps out of my backpack so we could discuss the best route to Casner Canyon. I could have saved myself the trouble. Katherine already had a good idea how she wanted to reach Casner Canyon, as well as how she wanted Monday's search to unfold. I tried to absorb Katherine's plans for the upcoming day. Next, Katherine mapped out her thoughts for the coming week. My eyes grew wide. My exhausted body rebelled. My head throbbed. But I said nothing.

Since Katherine wanted to start the search at Casner Canyon, I reviewed the map for the best route. Katherine seemed disinterested, so I refolded the map and put it away. Casner Canyon was up a steep, winding mountain road that curved along Oak Creek Canyon. It wasn't very far from uptown Sedona, so I thought it should prove to be a relatively quick drive.

Once the morning's plans for the search were decided, Katherine said, "Who knows? We might actually find that sphere in the morning."

With Katherine's extensive experience with geological and archeological expeditions, I felt confident in her decisions. But I didn't share her confidence or enthusiasm about finding the mythical sphere. I had assumed correctly that she had already mapped out her idea of the best plan of action for the morning, and for our entire week of exploration, actually. I sat back, content to follow her lead.

As Katherine talked, I could feel the last energy drain from my body the way water goes down a drain. My mind wandered. My shoulders slumped. My eyelids felt as heavy as if laced with lead. Engulfed by fatigue, I couldn't stifle a yawn. The bones in my face ached. As I slipped into sleep, I wearily responded, "Anything's possible, Katherine. And we might spot some flying donkeys while we're here, too. But I doubt it. I really do. Now, I must get back to the room and to bed."

"I'm finding that sphere, Crissy!" Katherine said.

"I hope you do," I replied.

I suddenly snapped half-awake. "The message from Ryan!" My bloodshot eyes flew open as I continued, "I don't know what to think of Ryan's note. It seems really strange, but there might be something to it. He even knew we have reservations for our chakra-balancing massages tomorrow night."

"Our what? You've planned massages?" Katherine said with a furrowed brow.

"Yes. I thought I told you. When I made our room reservations, I selected the package that included a chakra-balancing reading and massage. It's already scheduled and paid for. We have appointments at 8:00 p.m. tomorrow night. It's long after sundown, so we have time for a light dinner before we head to the spa."

Katherine's jaw tightened. Her green eyes flashed as she stared at me. "You know I'm not into that sort of metaphysical stuff, Crissy."

I sighed, then added, "By the way, Katherine, I don't trust Joe. Or Manny. I don't think either of them were being truthful about who they are, or what they do for a living. That worries me. But you're an adult. You can do whatever you want. As for me, after we hike, then do whatever else the clues might lead us to do, I plan to eat and go straight back to the room. And as far as the massage, I've never heard of a 'chakra-balancing massage' before, either, and I don't want to miss it. This will be a new experience for me. Besides, Ryan said I'll get another clue from Elke when I meet with her at the spa."

Katherine gave me another of what I was beginning to think of as *those* looks.

"You know, Katherine," I said, "We've been friends so long you don't have to say much for me to get the message. When I'm around you, I realize the experts are probably right—eighty-five to ninety percent of communications really are non-verbal."

"A massage?" Katherine repeated in a low voice while she continued to stare at me.

"Yes. A massage. Like I said, the sun will be down. We can't hike and search in the dark. Right? And, Katherine, if you think you can talk me out of going to the spa and experiencing the chakra-balancing, you're wrong. There is absolutely no chance I will change my mind. Especially after what Ryan Cho told me tonight."

"You don't really believe he was serious, do you?" Katherine said, as she scraped her fork across her plate to get the last remnants of the peach dessert. "Besides, I meant to tell you," she said as she turned her head and looked toward the far window, "Joe and I have plans for dinner then dancing tomorrow night. I don't know if I can squeeze in a massage."

I involuntarily looked down toward my backpack and sighed, realizing I would most probably be on my own the following night.

I looked up again when Katherine added, "And like I said, I have every intention of finding that sphere. Even if I have to search by moonlight, I plan to find it. It will make my career."

Katherine finished her third soda in silence as I picked up my backpack and prepared to leave. When I tasted blood, I realized I had bitten my upper lip again. I pushed my chair back and put my backpack over one shoulder, and said, "I don't think it's wise for us to talk about our search for the golden sphere around strangers, Katherine. What if Joe or Manny, or anyone for that matter, takes you seriously? Some people at the diner were listening to every word you said. What if they believe *we* actually *know* where the sphere might be hidden? It's a fascinating legend, I agree. But to talk openly to strangers about our search for a magical, mystical, powerful sphere here in Sedona could get us into serious trouble."

"You worry too much, Crissy," Katherine dismissively replied. She reached for the check. "You always worry. I'm *sure* the sphere exists and I *know* we can find it . . ."

I sighed again in tired resignation, then said, "Do what you want with *your* time and *your* life, Katherine, but leave *me* out of it. I don't want strangers anywhere near me. And I don't want people to think I have access to something of tremendous value they might covet. And I especially don't want to be anywhere near Manny."

"Crissy, that's ridiculous!" Katherine said. "Joe and Manny are a bit different, but I'm sure they're nice guys. And Manny is so gracious and gorgeous."

"Handsome and impressive, yes, they both are. No argument there. But '*nice*' guys? You don't know if they're 'nice,' or not, Katherine. They could be serial killers for all we know. You can go out with Joe. But do not include me in your plans. Deal?"

"All right, Crissy. I won't include you in any plans with Joe or Manny. Happy?" Katherine responded as she slammed her fork down on her plate, "But I think you're being ridiculous."

"Fine. Think what you will. It wasn't my intention to offend or alienate anyone tonight. But, Katherine, I thought this week was supposed to be about you and me getting reacquainted. Hadn't we agreed to spend the evening planning the upcoming week over a fun meal at a novel diner? I had no idea you'd invite strange men to join us, or that you would decide to share information about the sphere with them, let alone that you would give them the name of our motel *and even our room number.* If you want to be with them, fine. Be with them. But leave me out of it."

I reached into the zippered inside-pocket of my backpack and brought out the note from Ryan. I reviewed it quickly. As I passed the note to Katherine across the rickety table, I added, "Ryan seems to think the sphere really does exist and is around here somewhere. I don't know . . . Well, even if it *does* exist and *is* here, I think we have about as much chance of finding this mythical sphere as Carter did finding Tut's tomb."

"True," Katherine said. "But Carter *did* find Tut's tomb, remember?"

"Yes . . . ," I replied, "Carter ultimately found the tomb, but he searched for decades and was an expert in Egyptology and excavation. He also had a fortune in private funds to back his search. We have a week, no real leads, and no funds to speak of. And we both have real day jobs to get back to. So, this is fun—sure—but unless you have some more insider information that you haven't shared with me, I don't think we should be so sure about it, or count on finding the sphere. That's all I'm saying."

"Sure, Crissy. Sure," Katherine replied absentmindedly as she scanned Ryan's note. But I could tell by the far-away look in her eye that the lure of treasure had Katherine in its grip and she wasn't really listening anymore. Or was she thinking of Joe?

"You know, Crissy, I don't think I've ever seen you really angry before tonight, back at the diner. And I've known you how many years?"

"We all have our limits and dark sides," I responded, "And I'm keenly aware of just how dark mine can be. I don't get angry often, but when I do, it can be pretty ugly. That's why I work so hard to control it. Twice I've been slandered—one of those times was by Trevor's daughter—the other by someone to whom I donated a lot of time, effort, energy and money. Both times blew me out of the water. 'Candescent' is the word Trevor used to describe my response. He said he'd never seen me like that before, either. That's because I rarely get that angry. I shocked even myself. I work really hard on my spiritual growth and development, and I try not to let anger get the best of me. But it happens every once-in-awhile. When it does, I just lose it. Even *I* don't like to be around me when I do. I suppose the *up* side is it keeps things in perspective, and keeps me humble. I've learned to watch for those physical changes that take place right before I explode—the slipping concentration, narrowing focus, increased heart-rate, red face. Well, like Trevor says, 'Trucks and people have their limits, and I've about reached mine.' It happens. Sometimes I reach mine."

Katherine looked at me as if she were seeing me for the first time—*really* seeing me. I realized she was right. She had never seen me even close to angry before, let alone white-hot angry. I hoped this week wouldn't be the first time.

"Candescent?" she said.

"Yep. Candescent. It means white hot," I replied. "And I *was* white hot."

Katherine continued to silently stare at me.

"Let's get back to a decision about where we'll hike tomorrow," I finally said. "Ryan said he heard about someone who spent a great deal of time searching near Soldier Pass. Why don't we add that location to tomorrow morning's search?"

"I've planned on Casner Canyon for the morning," Katherine responded. "Maybe we can check out Soldier Pass in the afternoon?"

"Sounds good."

Chapter Twelve

Monday, October 10, 2011, 12:19 a.m.

It was after midnight when Katherine and I finally left the restaurant. A cool breeze wafted over us as we walked toward Katherine's Land Rover. The moon continued to highlight the surrounding mountains. A couple who seemed to have had too many drinks staggered toward a light blue convertible Lexus parked under one of the dim street lights. They hung onto each other, laughing and kissing as they stumbled toward their car.

That was when I saw him. He leaned on the front fender of a light-gold Cadillac Escalade EXT. Even in the shadows of the dimly lit parking lot, Patrick Bailey's greasy hair glistened. His three-piece suit, slicked-back black hair, and shifty expression made him instantly recognizable. He watched me. When he realized I'd seen him, he smiled that same sideways smile he'd given me in the Purple Moon. I slowed my pace and watched him. He turned and looked in the opposite direction.

My skin grew clammy and my chest tightened. I stopped and stared in his direction. Then I slipped my backpack off my shoulder and adjusted it so I could easily reach my Tomcat.

"What's the matter?" Katherine asked, when she noticed I was no longer headed toward the Rover, and was focused on something half-hidden in the shadows.

"It's him," I replied. "The same man we saw at the Purple Moon. Well, I'm not sure *you* saw him, but he spent a lot of time watching us and listening to you. He's watching us now. I wonder if he followed us here?"

"Crissy, you worry too much," Katherine said again.

As Katherine and I talked, Bailey slid into his car and drove out of the parking lot. I was left to wonder, *Had we simply bumped into him again? Or had he intentionally followed us?*

Chapter Thirteen

Monday, October 10, 2011, 12:20 a.m.

On the way back to Kings Ransom, we rolled the windows down so we could enjoy the fresh mountain air. We talked about our past, our present, and our plans for the upcoming week. Gentle breezes still rustled through the leaves of the nearby trees.

All the while, Katherine subtly grumbled that she'd rather camp outdoors in nature under the soon-to-be full moon than stay at a motel.

Finally, I reminded her of our agreement. Then I added, "*You* can still camp out if you really want to, but a room with a shower, bathroom and comfortable bed is my minimum requirement. These days, a motel room with a view is as close to camping out as I plan to get."

I'd already become enchanted with Sedona. The towering red, orange and golden rock formations stood sentinel all around. There was a unique liquid heaviness to the air. Oak Creek flowed through the Canyon, through the heart of town, and then beyond. Lush vegetation grew next to the creek. The changing colors of October in Sedona were hypnotic, even at night. The desert-like areas around Sedona still had plenty of vegetation. Wildlife in the form of rabbits, quail, birds and lizards abounded. There was a slow, peaceful pace to Sedona. Local residents were congenial and appeared contented.

I had researched Sedona while still in Austin and learned there was a unique metaphysical bent and artistic atmosphere in Sedona. The air was definitely charged with something I had never experienced before. I was excited by the promise of new paranormal experiences. I no longer wondered why, exactly, I had been led to Sedona. Whatever the reason, my curiosity had been stimulated and my senses heightened. Even though exhausted, I felt awakened and fully alive, yet at peace, in Sedona, as if I had stepped through an invisible curtain into a new dimension.

Chapter Fourteen

Monday, October 10, 2011, 12:55 a.m.

Once back in our room, Katherine quickly changed into a large oversized T-shirt. Then she tossed back the comforter and turned down the bedding on the bed nearer the television. As she clicked on the remote and turned up the volume, she said, "I told you I need to have the television on to sleep, didn't I?"

While putting my backpack in a nearby chair, I stopped, speechless, suddenly wide-eyed as the muscles in my neck and back began to tighten. Then I replied, "Well . . . you did mention it on the phone. But I told you I'm auditory and sensitive to noise. I can't sleep with any kind of noise. So . . ."

Ignoring my comment, Katherine turned her back to me and continued to adjust the angle of the television. Finally, with the TV aimed at the head of her bed, she said, "There. That shouldn't bother you."

I stared in disbelief at the flashing, noisy box. On-screen, a gangster shoot-out was in full progress. Resigned, I sighed, then picked up my nightgown and headed toward the bathroom to change. As I did, I wondered, *Who would come to the peace, beauty and serenity of Sedona and turn on a television?*

Without looking up, Katherine added, "Have you ever considered ear plugs and a sleeping blindfold?" as she turned her back to me and nestled between the sheets.

I looked at her back, speechless.

"No," I replied to her back. "I haven't. I like to be able to hear and see if something goes wrong in the night."

"That's you, Crissy. Worry, worry, worry."

"I do *not* worry needlessly," I snapped. "I'm just cautious," I added as I closed the bathroom door. I slipped into my pink floral cotton nightgown while I puzzled, *How can I possibly get any sleep tonight with the television blaring and flashing?*

By the time I left the bathroom, the gunfight had died down and Katherine was in a deep sleep, her back still toward me. I sighed loudly as I glared at the blaring television, then slid into my own bed.

I tossed.

I turned.

I flipped over repeatedly.

I fretted.

I finally got up and found some tissue to stuff into my ears. It didn't work. Nothing blocked the noise. The bright lights of the changing scenes on the screen flashed through my closed eyelids. Finally, I put my head under the covers. Even that didn't muffle the sound or dull the flashes of light. It just served to greatly reduce my oxygen supply and almost suffocate me.

Finally, thoroughly disgusted, I gave up. The red numbers on the bedside clock reflected 2:58 a.m. I quietly showered. When I emerged from the bathroom, Katherine hadn't stirred. I put on make-up and fresh clothes. Still, Katherine slept soundly. Finally, although normally cautious and reluctant to go out alone in the middle of the night, I decided to take a walk and get some fresh air—someplace where there was peace and quiet.

I scribbled a quick note for Katherine in case she awoke while I was out. Then, with my backpack over one shoulder, I quietly left the room. I walked down the flight of stairs. I was instantly relieved to inhale the fresh air and enjoy total peace and quiet.

Red-eyed, preoccupied and weary, I turned the corner of the motel and walked into the dimly lit front parking lot. I stopped abruptly when I heard banging, thudding and scraping, like metal against metal. Something was being pulled along the asphalt. Instantly wide-awake and alert, I stopped and listened more closely. Then I heard a loud snort. I flinched, then turned to face the noise coming from the shadows about twenty feet in front of me, slightly to the right, in a small alcove.

Now motionless, I reached into my backpack and wrapped my hand around my Tomcat. I continued to focus on the activity and sounds. As my eyes adjusted even more to the semi-darkness, I saw what looked like large hairy dogs with horns. They stood just a few yards in front of me. I looked at them. They turned and stared back at me. After about a minute, all but one of the strange beasts had turned back around and had resumed rummaging through the trash cans they had overturned. Using their snouts, they flung the trash around the alcove as they looked for food. They ate. I watched, transfixed.

But one animal hadn't turned back with the rest to continue foraging. I paid particular attention to him—the largest of the odd creatures—the one who that turned to face me head on, and that still stood motionless as he watched me. I stood equally motionless and didn't take my eyes off of him, either. Finally, he took one firm step forward, paused, then took another. I glanced from his horns, to his long canine-looking teeth. Unsure if he planned to charge, I took a step backward while I kept my right hand on my gun. My eyes remained locked on his. When I'd backtracked far enough, and he hadn't advanced further, I turned right, walked a few feet, and then quickly climbed back up the stairs to my room. My heart pounded so fast I could feel it throbbing in my neck.

Nerve-wracked and weary, I quickly and quietly slipped back into the room. Katherine continued to sleep as if in a coma. *What now?* I wondered. *I can't sleep, and I dare not go outside.* I walked on shaky legs to the nearby table and sat down. The television continued to blare and flash scenes of car chases, shoot-outs and loud confrontations.

I gave up altogether on any hope of sleep that night, and wondered what I'd do about sleep for the rest of the week. Then I remembered the novel I'd brought with me in the off-chance I might have time for reading. Not too happy about reading at 3:00 a.m., but not able to sleep or go for a walk, I decided to click on the small table lamp at the far side of the room. Once I had my book in hand, I sat down in one of the upholstered chairs and quietly clicked on the table lamp.

That's when Katherine shot straight up in bed, wide awake, and turned to glare at me.

Chapter Fifteen

Sunday, October 10, 2011, 3:05 a.m.

A s Katherine bolted upright in bed, she demanded, "What are you doing?!" Startled, I flinched, then said, "I couldn't sleep. The television blared all night and kept me awake. So I took a shower and went for a walk. But I ran into a herd of strange little horned creatures. That unnerved me, so I came back to the room. You were still sleeping the sleep of the dead, so I decided to read. I can't believe that with the television blaring and lights flashing all night, a little click of the desk lamp woke you. Especially since I'd taken a shower, dressed, left the room, then returned, and you didn't budge or even stir. Then the soft click of a table lamp woke you as if you'd been struck by a bolt of lightning? I'm amazed. But if it's bothering you for me to read, I'll stop. I can turn off the desk lamp."

"Don't bother. I'm awake now," Katherine snapped. "I might as well get up."

"It's just after 3:00 a.m.," I said. "Why get up if you can get some more sleep? There's nothing we can do now."

"I can't get back to sleep once I'm awake," Katherine barked. She flung the comforter aside, leapt out of bed, and stomped toward the bathroom. "Besides, I want to see those animals you're talking about."

Katherine quickly dressed. She grabbed her digital camera, then headed toward the door. Once outside, she charged forward. I cautiously followed, still on the lookout for the fierce little creatures with horns.

When Katherine spotted the animals she became even more animated. She clicked picture after picture as she chased the startled, frenzied little creatures around the outside of the motel and into the pool area. "These animals don't have *horns*," she said, as she looked back at me over her shoulder. "They have *tusks*. You're an educated woman. You should know better."

"I am a *social* scientist, Katherine. Not a *biologist*," I said. But Katherine had already disappeared around the side of the motel and didn't hear me.

Every time the camera flashed, the animals scurried in a different direction, with Katherine in hot pursuit. I gave up trying to keep up with her and walked back to the stairs to wait until Katherine had finished chasing the creatures. Before long, Katherine had chased the javelinas out of the pool area, across the parking lot, and into the nearby bushes.

That was when I turned around and saw a police officer's Jeep slowly drive into the parking lot.

Oops, I thought. I looked at the Jeep, then at Katherine and the fleeing animals, her camera still flashing. Then I turned back and watched the Jeep quietly roll toward where I stood. The officer looked from Katherine to me. I again tasted blood. I sighed, then slowly walked across the asphalt to where the policeman's Jeep had come to a full stop in the middle of the parking lot. As we talked, I learned the unsmiling officer's name was George Stampos. He said that some of the guests at the motel had called to complain about the unusual noise and commotion that was, "disturbing their peace and quiet" in the middle of the night. As he talked, he continually looked at the motel and scanned the rooms.

I left him in his Jeep and walked in the direction of the most noise, spotted Katherine, and signaled for her to make her way over to the parking lot where the officer waited, his Jeep's engine still humming.

Reluctantly, she put down her camera, looked longingly in the direction of the fleeing creatures, and began to march toward the Jeep.

Chapter Sixteen

Monday, October 10, 2011, 3:33 a.m.

Katherine finally joined me by the officer's idling Jeep. When she did, the officer politely yet clearly and firmly told us to cease our early morning javelina-hunting, as well as all other photo-op and noise-making activities. Still scanning the windows of the motel rooms, the officer then repeated we were to save our noise-making for daylight hours.

Admonished, I apologized, then sheepishly turned and began to walk toward the stairs which led to our room.

But I soon noticed Katherine wasn't with me. I turned and looked back toward the Jeep. Katherine had one foot on the running board and an arm on the window opening as she leaned in toward the officer and continued talking in a normal voice. As she talked, he continued to listen, expressionless, as his eyes surveyed the windows and surrounding area.

Before he left, Officer Stampos repeated yet again that *we* should be quiet.

Katherine and I were both wide awake now. We had nowhere to go. It was far too early to hike in unfamiliar territory, even with an almost full moon. So we decided to walk the half-block to the Circle-K. The early morning was hushed as we made our way across the street by the light of the moon and the street lamps. A cool breeze continued to blow through the silent town and rustle leaves. It refreshed me.

I purchased a coffee for myself and a hot chocolate for Katherine. As we headed toward the door, who walked in? The same officer who had just admonished us. I blushed and turned the other way. Katherine resumed their conversation and peppered him with questions. He listened. I listened. The clerk listened.

When the officer was finally able to break free, Katherine continued to visit with the clerk. I went outside and walked around for a few minutes.

Then I went back into the store and told Katherine I was heading back to the room. She decided to join me.

On the way back across the parking lot, she said, "You should have stayed. He's a really nice guy. He worked for the New York Fire Department until his wife died. He was so distraught when she died that he left the coast and moved to Sedona."

"I don't care who he is," I said. "I don't want to meet new people. I want to sleep, then hike and search for the sphere."

Chapter Seventeen

Monday, October 10, 2011, 4:11 a.m.

We continued toward the motel. I sauntered. Katherine stomped.

On the way, Katherine again told me how rude I was, and how annoyed she was, because I had turned on the light in the room while she slept. For some reason, it struck me funny—*very* funny. I began to chuckle. Then I started to laugh. The more I laughed, the funnier it struck me. As my laughter grew, I finally had to sit down on a nearby black metal bench and try to get my laughter under control. I searched for a tissue to catch my tears as I tried to squelch my laughter by covering my mouth with my free hand so as not to awaken any more residents at the motel. I had such a hard time trying to quell my laughter that I couldn't catch my breath. I began to feel light-headed. Once I had started laughing, I couldn't seem to stop. My laughter grew louder and louder as tears flowed down both cheeks.

Katherine, who stood nearby with her hands once again on her hips, looked at me in obvious disbelief. "I'm telling you off, and you're laughing!" she said hotly.

"It's all just too funny," I replied, as I tried to control my laughter. "It's all so ludicrous! You slept soundly while the television blared and all those television lights flashed—tires screeched, people screamed, there were even shoot-outs. Then you snapped wide awake when a tiny desk lamp was quietly clicked on. Now *you* are angry at *me* . . . and *you're* telling *me* off? It's just too hysterical. You're a riot!" I said, as I continued to try to get control of my laughter.

This did not bode well with Katherine. Scowling, she tapped her right foot louder and louder as she scanned the surrounding area.

Although she sizzled, I couldn't rein in my gales of laughter. Finally, after a few minutes, I did regain some control, although a periodic chuckle escaped now and then.

As she stomped back toward the room, Katherine didn't say a thing. Neither did I.

Chapter Eighteen

Monday, October 10, 2011, 5:30 a.m.

We were both wide-awake, showered, and dressed. Fortunately, I had recovered from my fit of laughter. Katherine was still speaking to me, but barely. We decided to take a night drive around Sedona and be back at Kings Ransom in time for their continental breakfast at 7:00 a.m. Katherine insisted on driving, so I grabbed the maps and my backpack then followed her to her vehicle.

I synchronized Trevor's Expedition with my wristwatch. They both reflected 5:30 a.m. I was careful when I placed my backpack on the floorboard by my feet since it had both Trevor's favorite timepiece hanging from a hook on the outside and my Beretta tucked securely inside.

As I reached for the door handle, suddenly tires screeched nearby. Katherine and I both jumped. We instinctively froze in place and looked in the direction of the noise. A six-point buck stood in the middle of the highway, motionless. His head was turned to face the traffic as he stared into someone's headlights.

We stood motionless, too, and watched him. After a minute or two, the buck calmly turned his head in the direction he had been heading and resumed a dignified amble across the highway.

Katherine and I decided to drive to Bell Rock near Oak Creek Village, then check out Chapel of the Holy Cross on our way back to Kings Ransom.

Once we got to Bell Rock, we surveyed the area and decided there was no reason to come back after daylight to search for the sphere since the scroll led us to believe the sphere was hidden closer to the town of Sedona, and not near Oak Creek Village.

We had practically passed the turnoff to the Chapel when we spotted Chapel Road on our way back to Sedona. "Jesus, Katherine!" I said as she made a last minute tire screeching, gravel flying, body jarring right turn.

"Relax. I'm not going to kill you," she said, as I bobbed around in the cab of her Land Rover the way an apple bobs in a tub of water.

Once I had recovered from the sharp turn, I marveled at the size of the huge cross built into the front of the Chapel.

We parked, then scouted out the parking lot area. Seeing nothing that indicated a possible hiding place for a sphere, we walked up the steep incline that was the walkway to the Chapel's patio. As we did, Katherine asked, "Are you into this Catholic stuff? Really? You?"

"Well . . ." I cautiously responded, "I'd say I'm a spiritual person, but not necessarily a religious one."

We continued to explore the area around Chapel of the Holy Cross in silence broken only by rare comments from Katherine about rock formations or food.

As we searched, I realized for the first time just how easy it would be to hide a sphere almost anywhere in Sedona. The task of finding the sphere seemed ever more insurmountable.

Not having found any sign of a hiding place near the Chapel, we headed back toward the town of Sedona. When the highway dead-ended at Highway 89, we made a right and drove the few blocks to uptown Sedona. Nothing was open at that early hour. We headed back to our room.

Chapter Nineteen

Monday, October 10, 2011, 6:15 a.m.

With still more time left before sunrise, and the continental breakfast at Kings Ransom not available until 7:00 a.m., we headed toward the newer part of town. As we drove down Highway 89, I located Inner Light Spa where we were scheduled for chakra-balancing massages that night. We also spotted a couple of rock, mineral and crystal shops we wanted to check out later, if time permitted. I was glad when I saw the medical center, although I hoped we wouldn't need to make use of it.

We pulled into a parking lot and found Thunder Mountain Road on the map. Katherine wanted to locate it so we could return and hike there later. She had heard from a colleague, she said, it would be a good place to hike and search for the sphere.

I was tired after a sleepless night.

Katherine was still upset because she'd been "jarred awake."

Since we drove most of the way in silence, I was able to absorb and enjoy the early morning peace and quiet.

At the far end of town, we made a right, and drove up toward Boynton Canyon Road. As we drove, the sky grew lighter, and changed from black to a misty cobalt blue to azure. *Ah. Morning won't be long in coming now. The sun's about to rise from behind the rugged rock formations.*

Just then, the sun began to peek over the towering red mountains in the east. We pulled off the road to watch the sunrise. As the sun gradually climbed over the tops of the formations, Sedona was soon bathed in liquid golden light.

Once the sun had risen, we returned to our room to prepare for a day of hiking and searching for the mythical sphere. We reviewed the map, located Casner Canyon again, and selected other areas we wanted to tackle that day.

Before leaving our room, I opened the thick drapes, then the sheer curtains. The morning view of Sedona as the sun lighted the red, orange, and golden rock formations was hypnotic. I stood for a moment and took it in. Before long, Katherine joined me. She too was spellbound by the natural beauty of Sedona in the morning light.

Grabbing her camera, Katherine returned to the patio. Together, we walked the length of the patio a few times, taking pictures as the day grew brighter. Once the sun was no longer casting shadows on the formations, we left to have breakfast.

Sedona at dawn. Definitely not disappointing.

Chapter Twenty

Monday, October 10, 2011, 7:05 a.m.

As we walked to breakfast in the coolness of morning, Katherine asked, "When did you change into this guru-type person? I don't think I even know you anymore."

"Well," I said, as I tried to think about how to respond in a way that didn't light a fire under a stick of already warm dynamite, "Like most things—there's the long story and the shorter version. Here's the shorter version. I've studied alternative healing and recovery strategies for years now . . ." I let my words trail off when Katherine's brow furrowed. "But that's probably a discussion better saved for later," I added.

The continental breakfast was more than anticipated. It included waffles. That translated into Katherine's decision to prepare two for herself. While the waffles cooked, she zipped around the counter and gathered hard boiled eggs, yogurt and juice.

Not wanting to be too full while I hiked, I had an egg, yogurt, and coffee.

I ate quickly, which was my norm. Then I waited.

Katherine's extensive breakfast took quite a while longer to consume. While Katherine finished her breakfast, I reached into my backpack and dug out a book I'd purchased at Safeway the day before. As I showed it to Katherine, who seemed far more interested in her food than the book, I told her, "I came across this book yesterday while I was out. It was published a couple of months ago. I looked through it. It looks like the perfect book to read to learn more about Sedona. It's *The Call of Sedona—Journey of the Heart* by Ilchi Lee. In his book, Mr. Lee said he had searched the U.S., and then decided to settle here and open a healing center. I think . . ."

Katherine cut me off with a piercing look, then said, "Crissy! Thanks for letting me know, but I'm not interested in that woo-woo stuff. I never have been. And I never will be. Unless the author has something to say about the flora and fauna, or the geology of Sedona, I'm not interested. I just want to find the golden sphere."

Realizing I was on my own, I said, "Fine. Okay," and put the book back in my backpack to read later. As I did, I made a mental note to postpone leaving Sedona at 5:00 a.m. Saturday morning, as I had planned, so I could visit Ilchi Lee's center before heading for home. Unless she brought it up, and I didn't think she would, the topic of Ilchi Lee's Sedona Mago Retreat was closed.

As I waited in the vinyl booth for Katherine to finish her breakfast, I checked Trevor's timepiece. It was shortly after 7:30 a.m.

When Katherine was ready, we headed for the police station in her Land Rover. I made the climb into her large vehicle and settled into the passenger's seat. Then I readjusted the height and back of the seat to better fit my smaller size. Even so, I couldn't get comfortable in such a large seat. *This must be how Goldilocks felt in Papa Bear's chair*, I mused, as I squirmed to get comfortable.

Chapter Twenty-One

Monday, October 10, 2011, 7:56 a.m.

Although Katherine said yet again she felt it was a waste of time, I insisted we check in and let officials know where we planned to hike each day, what areas we had decided to explore. I also wanted them to know that we might venture into normally unexplored areas in and around Sedona. Katherine wouldn't consider the possibility of our getting lost or injured. I wanted to be sure that if anything went wrong, someone would have a good idea where to start looking for us. And I wanted officials to know I carried a legal handgun in case we bumped into predators of any kind.

To save time, when we pulled into the parking lot, I said, "Wait here. I'll be right back," then jumped down and out of her Rover and quickly walked toward the double doors at the front of the station. I planned to make my visit quick, and hopefully minimize Katherine's annoyance.

But almost instantly I heard Katherine's car door slam, then the crunch of her footsteps as she strode to catch up with me. Katherine didn't try to hide her dislike of law enforcement and police stations. But she disliked directives even more than law enforcement, and she had interpreted my comment as my telling her what to do, so she insisted that she accompany me inside.

As we entered the building, a man with a name plate of Officer Rizzo looked up from his desk, then walked over to where we were standing. As he did, Officer Stampos walked by and recognized us from earlier in the morning.

I told Officer Rizzo our plans, filled out some paperwork, and was soon ready to leave. All the while, I heard Katherine in the background chatting with police staff.

Chapter Twenty-Two

Monday, October 10, 2011, 8:45 a.m.

O nce back in her Rover, Katherine jetted up the highway toward Oak Creek Canyon. As we headed toward the historic scenic route that connected Sedona to Flagstaff, my head throbbed with a mild headache.

The noise of morning commuters didn't diminish the natural beauty of Sedona. Green pines mingled with trees that displayed autumn colors of red, orange and gold. These were back-dropped by huge red, orange, and gold rock formations. The gentle clear stream gurgled quietly down the canyon, turned and crossed through town, then wound toward Oak Creek Village. Birds flew and chirped in the morning coolness.

After we passed the few blocks that comprised uptown Sedona, we left the town behind and started the climb toward Casner Canyon on a road that grew increasingly narrow, winding and steep. As we continued the climb on the two-lane road bordering Oak Creek Canyon, I became increasingly edgy from too much sugar, too much caffeine, not enough sleep, and the challenging driving conditions The cheesecake and deep dish pie from Sunday night felt as though they had morphed into lard and wrapped themselves around my waist and hips like a wet blanket. With every speedy turn up the winding road, I became more nauseated.

While negotiating a sharp curve, Katherine made another comment about her dislike of guns.

"Well, we come across predators all the time, don't we?" I replied, "Especially in the wild. Besides, the more I study human behavior, the more I think we're all just animals. Sophisticated, some of us, but animals. It behooves the prey to be prepared when the predators strike, don't you think?"

Katherine gave me what had become her signature disapproving glower. Suddenly, I noticed we were going quite a bit faster than before. *I hope we don't run into anyone coming down the mountains*, I thought. Katherine crossed the double line as she navigated another turn.

To take my mind off Katherine's driving and the winding road, I turned and watched the scenery fly past my window. "You know, Katherine," I said, as I measured my words, "You invited me to join you on this search for something that probably doesn't even exist. Our getting together and going on this search was *your* idea. Not mine. From my perspective, I'm here to help you. And about now I'm not feeling a whole lot of appreciation for my time, effort, input and expense."

Katherine was silent for a few minutes, then changed the subject, and said, "Since you like to read, there are a couple of bookstores in Sedona that the locals say are really good. One is The Sunset Read. Locals say it's dusty and musty, but full of rare and unusual books. If we have the time, we can visit it while you're here."

"Sure," I said. "If I have any steam left. We should be headed back to the room by sundown. We'll have the whole evening."

As we continued to drive upward along the canyon, I asked, "Tell me again what makes you think Casner is a likely place for the sphere to be hidden."

"Colleagues in Prescott said there was speculation among professional geologists and treasure hunters alike, as well as some credible local evidence, that a reclusive stranger from the east pitched camp there decades ago. No one knows what happened to him, but it's a possibility that he was the gold miner who went to California. If that's true, then perhaps he left the sphere somewhere in the canyon. It's a place to start. That's really all I know."

"So you think the recluse could be the same person who hid the sphere?"

"Could be," Katherine replied.

"Any idea where, exactly, he might have hidden it? It's a huge area," I said.

"No. That's about it. I thought we'd drive up there and see if we can spot the old abandoned mine shaft they were talking about," Katherine added.

Mine shaft? Katherine thinks I will agree to walk into an abandoned mine shaft? I thought. My heartbeat quickened and my head began to spin. Suddenly, I had trouble breathing. I ventured, "Is it safe to go into an old closed mine shaft?"

"Are you worrying again, Crissy?" she replied.

"I just wonder how safe it is," I answered.

Changing the subject again, Katherine said, "Last weekend, I checked out rumors with locals at the nearby casino. Some people who work there have heard the tale of a hidden powerful sphere. But most locals get pretty quiet as soon as you start asking too many questions. It's a good thing there's a free flow of booze at the casino or I wouldn't have learned anything," Katherine half laughed.

Katherine sped up the highway. I assessed the drop-off on one side of the road and the steep mountains on the other. As we zoomed around another curve, the slight buzzing in my ears became a low roar. My heart pounded faster as Katherine zipped around yet another curve. I clutched my seat belt with one hand, and thought, *I've got to concentrate on my breathing and make myself relax, or I'll lose it.* When I reached up with my free right hand to grip the grab-bar above the door I realized I had been squeezing the seatbelt so tightly my knuckles had turned white. I took another deep breath and continued to work to slow my heart rate.

As we flew forward, nothing calmed my frayed nerves. Not the beauty of the unique red rock formations, nor the bright yellow, orange and red of the changing autumn leaves. None of the natural beauty all around calmed me as Katherine raced upward toward Casner Canyon.

Chapter Twenty-Three

Monday, October 10, 2011, 9:33 a.m.

It had taken Katherine awhile to calm down after we checked in at the police station. But even the detour to the station hadn't dampened Katherine's spirit of an adventure-in-progress. It oozed from her every pore. She was bright and alive as she increased pressure on the gas pedal and charged upward.

Her eyes sparkled as she chatted about the history and geology of Oak Creek Canyon.

I watched the scenery zip past my window. The only thing I could see clearly was the larger, taller mountains. The rest was a blur.

I glanced at my watch. It read 9:33 a.m. by the time we reached Encinoso recreation site. Suddenly, we both realized we had passed the turn-off into Casner Canyon.

Without warning, Katherine looked in her rearview mirror, then spun the Land Rover around in the middle of the highway. Tires squealed. The Land Rover fish-tailed. Contents of the vehicle flew and slammed everywhere. I felt a flash of terror as I grabbed for the dashboard. Once the vehicle had righted itself, my wide-eyed shock and horror turned to nausea. Before I could even formulate a comment, we were headed back down Oak Creek Canyon at a speed even greater than when we were ascending.

Numb, I hung on even tighter to the grab-bar as I tried to right myself and regain my equilibrium.

Katherine spotted our turnoff, then found a place to park near Grasshopper Picnic Area. She spun into the lot with her characteristic gusto, then slammed on the brakes. I flew forward, as did everything else in the Rover that wasn't tied down.

Once I had time to regroup, catch my breath, and pick up my backpack, I joined Katherine. She leaned on a rock near a boulder she'd decided to use as a table. She unpacked bananas, Butterfingers and water from her backpack. After the briefest of rests, we began our walk to Allen's Bend.

I had to stop to catch my breath again. Then I rechecked and adjusted my backpack. By the time I had unscrewed the cap to my water bottle, Katherine was ready to take off again.

When we reached the incline, Katherine scaled the side of the mountain as easily as she'd hiked on flat ground. As I watched her take long deliberate strides upward, I began to feel even more tired.

I looked upward toward the entry of the mine shaft far, far above where I stood, panting. Then I took a long, slow, deep breath. I was as ready to begin the climb as I was ever going to be. Somehow, even the fall splendor surrounding me didn't lift my deteriorating mood.

We were at the innermost part of Casner Canyon. It was nearly 10:30 a.m., and I was already hot, sticky, dusty and coated in sweat. Even with October's soft cool breezes, it was too hot for me to hike, let alone climb a mountain.

I called out to Katherine that her goal of the old abandoned mine seemed an almost impossible-to-reach destination for me. But I knew as I spoke that the difficulty of the climb made it all the more of a challenge for Katherine.

"Fine," Katherine responded, before she turned back and continued to climb. "See you at the entrance."

By the time I had climbed to within shouting range again, Katherine was much closer to the entrance. When she noticed how much I not only lagged behind, but that I was soaked with sweat as I huffed and puffed up the side of the mountain, she yelled back down to me, "I thought you said you hiked and exercised?"

I used a shirt sleeve to wipe a rivulet of perspiration from my eyes, then yelled back, "I take morning walks around the flat countryside near Austin, and I do yoga stretches and floor exercises. That doesn't really prepare one to scale mountains, does it?" That used the last of the energy I could muster, so I paused to catch my breath.

As she watched me struggle up the mountainside, Katherine sat on a boulder, surveyed the canyon, then dipped into her backpack and dug out an orange and another bottle of water. "Join me," Katherine urged. There's room for both of us up here. And don't forget it's the desert. We need to stay hydrated."

I eyed the boulder suspiciously as I wondered what critters might call it home. I decided to just sit on the ground. I collapsed where I was, then pulled out a power bar and water from my floral backpack. While I ate and drank, I looked up at the far distant mine shaft entrance.

"Where did you find that backpack?" Katherine said, brow furrowed, as she more closely assessed my small, lightweight canvas bag.

"I'm not sure. I think I found it years ago in California," I responded, thinking, *I know. I know. It's not what a **real** hiker would use. But it's my size, and it serves my needs. Besides, flowers are fun and uplifting. Heavy-duty hiking gear is not.*

Katherine's limit for stopping and resting expired after a couple of minutes. She stood, secured her large backpack, and once again began to scale the side of the mountain.

I groaned as I stood, dusted myself off, and started back up the mountain. With each new step, I struggled to catch up with her.

I glanced upward. Katherine continued to all but lope up the scree-covered mountainside.

I had to practically crawl on all fours and use my hands as well as my feet to pull and push myself upward. My mood continued to plummet.

Sweat soaked through my red plaid shirt. My red sweatshirt was tied at my waist and felt heavy-laden. I was hot, weighted-down, and over-heated. As I struggled to follow Katherine, I heard her continue to scale the side of the mountain like a mountain goat. But I kept my focus trained on my next step.

I wanted to turn back, but knew I couldn't. So I concentrated on the few inches directly in front of me and, step-by-step, forced my protesting body upward.

Soon, from the ledge in front of the opening to the mine, Katherine yelled, "Come on, Little Red. You can do it. Let's go."

I took my eyes off the patch of scree immediately in front of me and looked up at Katherine. She stood firmly on the dusty flat ground at the entrance to the mine shaft and peered over the edge to where I struggled. Her hands were once again resting on her hips. White hiking shorts highlighted her deep golden tan. Her sun-bleached hair was pulled into a ponytail that bobbed as she peered over the side of the landing.

Suddenly, I felt even more weary and out-of-condition.

Unaccustomed to strenuous hiking, I struggled to reach the ledge where Katherine waited. With each attempted step forward, I slid backward on the loose pebbles. My jeans felt increasingly heavy and binding. As I inched my way upward, I began to envy Katherine's light-weight flexible shorts. Because of the increasing wind, strands of long auburn hair broke free of my hair-band and stung my face. Dust caked my nose and coated my mouth making it more difficult to breathe. I labored. I struggled. My arms ached. My legs rebelled. My eyes burned.

Yet I continued to follow Katherine upward, inch by painful inch, on an almost non-existent trail. Upward, I climbed. Around boulders, over logs, around junipers. I climbed, slid backward on the scree, and climbed again.

I came here to have fun, help Katherine search for a mythical sphere, and experience Sedona's natural beauty, vortexes, and her metaphysical magic, I grumbled. *Not to follow Katherine on one of her "extreme adventures."*

Before long, the enchantment of the canyon that had captivated my attention faded as I continued to labor up the mountain. I focused on monitoring my quickened heartbeat and shortened breath. I became lightheaded. Salty tears flooded my burning eyes.

Then it happened.

Chapter Twenty-Four

Monday, October 10, 2011, 10:55 a.m.

I paused and looked up to see if I could still spot Katherine and, before I knew it, I began to slide, then tumble, down the mountainside toward the gorge below. I grasped in vain for a shrub, or anything else to hang onto to stop my slide. I inhaled dirt and dust as I fought desperately to regain a foothold.

Almost instantly, I lost total control. I somersaulted downward on an avalanche of scree. Then I gasped as my body slammed sideways at the waist into a large pine tree. The air was knocked out of my already burning lungs. It felt as though something deep within me had broken, fractured. Pain shot outward in all directions. Terror flooded my mind.

Tears spilled down dirt-caked cheeks then dripped onto my torn and bloodied hands before falling onto the shale below. When I pushed against the tree and tried to stand, pain bolted up my arms and tore into my back. I collapsed again.

Through a hazy fog of mind-numbing pain, I heard Katherine call from far above, "Crystal! Are you alright?"

"No, I'm not alright!" I screamed. "I may never be alright again!"

"Don't panic," Katherine admonished. "I'll come and help you."

"No," I replied. "No use us both dying. Give me a few minutes." I looked down at the bits of glass protruding from my bleeding arm and my wristwatch that had been crushed during the tumble.

"You'll be alright, Crystal," Katherine said, concern tinged with annoyance. "Nobody's going to die here today. You know my motto: 'Bring 'em back alive.'"

My face burned with anger and pain. Blood ran down my left cheek. I had abrasions everywhere, but apparently no broken bones. I bit my tongue to stop from saying more to Katherine. I tried to calm myself while I took stock of my situation. After another long, deep, dusty breath, I coughed, then sputtered as I breathed in even more dust.

I struggled to avoid panic. I breathed deeply, then slowly counted backward from ten. The old habit I'd learned in a meditation class helped clear my mind.

Fatigue and exhaustion threatened. Shock was right around the corner. I trembled. I dared not look up for fear of falling. My terror of heights ensured I would never look down.

How could I have been so stupid? I groused to myself. *There's no way I can get myself out of here. I need help. I can hardly move. The pain is so bad I might pass out if I try to climb again. Or, worse, I could just bleed to death right here on the mountainside.*

I took another deep breath, then told myself, *You can do this. You can do this.* I grabbed a low branch and shoved against the tree trunk again. I steadied my wobbly legs. Finally in an upright position, I waited. I assessed my condition. My body seemed to work—not well, perhaps, and very painfully, but everything moved. Warm sticky blood continued to trickle down my face, arms and hands. My jeans and blouse were shredded. Scrapes and scratches covered my legs. My back was practically raw. I reached up with my left hand and felt a long, deep gash on my left cheek that ran from my eyebrow to the edge of my mouth. *If I make it out of here alive, I'm going to need a whole lot of stitches.*

I sighed, then I took another slow, deep breath. *How in God's name did I ever let myself get talked into this!? Adventure, danger, and pushing oneself past the max is Katherine's idea of "fun." Not mine.*

I continued to grumble as I slid backward into the tree yet again on the loose shale. My right shin was red, raw and oozed blood where it had scraped across the rough, dry bark of the old pine.

"*You* did not bring yourself to this place," a Voice said. "*I* brought you here."

Instantly alert and now even more scared, I began to shiver as I looked around. I saw no one. "Who are You? What do You mean?" I whispered into the air.

"You will heal totally, and quickly," the Voice continued.

A gentle warm breeze infused with glistening diamond-like vibrating confetti-looking particles began to appear from out of nowhere. They encircled and infused me, permeating my entire body. As it settled on me and began to soak into my skin, I was instantly injected with new energy. My body became light and buoyant. My mind cleared and became focused. Strength poured into me like a swift-moving waterfall. All pain vanished. The cuts on my hands, legs, back and face stopped hurting and quit bleeding.

Within a couple of minutes, I felt a gentle force like a huge, firm hand begin to softly push me upward, while an equally gentle force like an invisible rope tied around my back and chest softly pulled me upward toward the entrance. This time, the scree did not move.

"What's happening?" I asked the Voice.

There was no answer.

"Who are you talking to down there? Did I hear a man's voice?" Katherine asked.

"I'm not sure," I replied.

Baffled and light-headed, I soon found myself on the ledge. I said to Katherine, "So you heard it, too?" I collapsed onto the flat surface at the entry to the mine and stared first at Katherine, then out into the valley below.

"Of course I heard it," she replied.

I took a few ragged, deep breaths. I again counted backward from ten to one as I calmed myself, caught my breath, and gathered my thoughts. My body felt like it was made of soft, pliable, light-weight rubber. My mind spun. My eyes were glazed and I had to fight to focus. But I was alive.

Jeans torn, favorite blouse in tatters, auburn hair standing out in all directions, face caked with dirt and streaked with tears, I melted onto the ground. *Some teacher of the metaphysical,* I groused to myself. *If my students could only see me now!*

Katherine stepped closer to take a better look at my wounds. She turned pale under her perpetual golden tan, her eyes grew as large as green olives, and she took a couple of involuntary steps backward. For once, she was speechless.

"You're scaring me," I said. "Is it really that bad?"

"No. No. It's not that bad," Katherine responded. Then she blinked and shook her head as she looked from side to side. "How are you feeling? Those cuts, especially the one on your face, might need a few stitches. But I think the rest will heal okay. You have a lot of cuts and scrapes, but I think the swelling is already going down. Don't you? It looks like the wounds are closing and healing themselves, but that can't be happening. Can it?"

"How am I feeling!?" I shrieked, as my normal reserve crumbled. "How do you *think* I'm feeling? Horrible! That's how. The bleeding has stopped, but my eyes are filled with grit that scratches every time I blink. My cheek is gashed so deep it might be to the bone. I'm sure to have a deep and jagged, ugly scar. I can't even feel my hands anymore. And every fiber of my being is screaming and rebelling. How could you have led me here?!"

Katherine strode forward and helped get my dirt-covered and torn backpack off my shoulders. Then she began to open it. "I know you," she said. "You surely have something in here for first aid. Right? Don't worry. You're going to be fine. Don't move. Okay?"

"There's no chance of my going anywhere," I said. "I *couldn't* move even if I wanted to, and I don't want to."

I gasped when Katherine hastily dumped the contents of my clean and neatly organized backpack onto the dusty red ground, then tossed things aside as she dug through everything until she found gauze, Bactine, and safety pins. "Hold out your hands," she said nervously.

"I don't think I *can* move my hands," I slowly responded. My heartbeat skyrocketed as I realized my hands weren't responding.

"Sure you can, Little Red," Katherine coaxed.

As I continued to look down at my mangled hands, tears flooded my grit-filled eyes, and my anger turned to fear. Fresh tears began to flow down my dirty face and splash again onto my wounded hands.

Just then, Katherine whispered, "Look!" Then she slowly stood, Bactine in one hand and bandages in the other, and pointed toward the west.

I turned and looked where Katherine pointed. A warm breeze infused with brilliant colors like tiny multi-faceted jewels approached us and began to glide around me—soft and bright golds and yellows, citrus and mango, baby and vibrant pinks, pure and creamy whites, aquas and electric blues, scarlet, ruby and rose reds. They mixed with colors I'd never seen before as they glistened like sunlight on tropical water. The colors sparkled and danced as if alive. As they approached and enwrapped me, they formed a kaleidoscope of spell-binding color. Like before, one by one, they melted into my body.

The gentle warm wind continued to bring the colors to where I had collapsed. As the colors permeated my body, they moved in the same pattern as the center of a vortex. My body tingled as if I'd stepped into a swimming pool filled with liquid dandelions. Somehow I knew that softly and quietly, from the inside out, I was being miraculously healed. Not only of cuts and abrasions, but of fears and anxieties.

Katherine looked on in wonder. "What's happening?" she asked.

"So you see it, too? I don't know what's happening" I whispered as I continued to stare unblinkingly at the fluttering colors. "I only know that I can feel my body again, and it's being gently and quickly healed."

After a few minutes, the gentle breeze with the diamond-like colors began to float down into the valley. It quickly faded. In silence, we watched. Katherine stood with her hands on her hips. I sat cross-legged on the red dirt. We watched until the breeze and the living colors finally disappeared altogether.

Chapter Twenty-Five

Monday, October 10, 2011, 11:35 a.m.

When the breeze and the colors had disappeared, Katherine looked down at the bandages and medicine she'd retrieved from my bag. "I might as well see if you still need my help," she said. "Can you hold out your hands?"

"Yes. I think so."

"Okay. Then hold them out straight in front of you and I'll pour some water over them. You can wash off the blood and see if you still have any cuts or open wounds. If you do, I'll pour Bactine over them."

As Katherine poured the water over my hands, I rubbed them together. Most of the dirt and dried sticky blood washed to the ground. As I washed, I realized my hands and forearms had been totally healed. There were no scratches or cuts.

I looked up at Katherine.

She stared, speechless. As she examined my face, Katherine asked, "What happened to the cuts and gashes? What about that slice on your face that looked like it went clear to the bone?"

"I have no idea," I replied. "But the pain is gone. All of it. My legs feel fine now, and my lungs have stopped burning. I feel much better than I have in days. I feel like I could run a marathon, and I never run. It feels like even my soul has been healed."

I reached up and touched my face where the gaping wound had throbbed just a few minutes earlier. It felt fine. Katherine poured water into my cupped hands, and I splashed it on my face. Then I reached into the pile of my belongings Katherine had unceremoniously dumped into the dirt, and retrieved an old dishtowel I'd packed. I dried my face and hands. I picked up a compact and used the mirror to examine where the major wounds had been. With the exception of the ruined clothes, dirt still clinging to most of my body, and dried blood caked here and there, I looked healed. I felt many times better than I had when I left the motel room earlier that morning.

After I stood, I carefully steadied myself on the side of the entrance to the mine shaft. I tested my arms and hands. Then my legs. I bent. I stretched. I turned. I felt fine. All had been healed and restored!

Katherine continued to stand a couple feet away and stare at me. Her hands now hung loosely at her side. "I can't believe what I just saw. How were all those cuts and abrasions completely healed in front of our eyes?"

"I don't know," I said. "I have no idea." After a pause while we both tried to take in what had just happened, I told Katherine, "I need something to drink to wash the dust and grit out of my mouth. Is that my water bottle over there?"

Katherine spotted my water bottle that had rolled to one side. "Yes. Here it is," she said, as she picked it up, dusted it off, unscrewed the lid, and handed it to me.

To feel so good after feeling so bad was strange.

Disoriented and confused, I looked up at the drifting clouds.

Katherine reached into her backpack and pulled out a water bottle for herself. As she unscrewed the cap, she stood beside me at the mouth of the mine shaft. She, too, seemed to struggle to grasp what had just happened. She opened a box of Red Hots and began munching as she looked out onto the natural beauty of the valley below. Squirrels scampered around nearby scrub brush as if nothing had happened. Birds sang from somewhere nearby. We stood motionless and stared toward the adjacent mountainside.

I took a long, deep breath, then glanced over to where my empty backpack lay crumpled next to its former contents that were now strewn in the red dirt and covered in dust. I felt a wave of warmth and peace, and then was suddenly homesick when I spotted Trevor's timepiece. It had made it through the ordeal unscathed. I checked the time. It was around noon.

Chapter Twenty-Six

Monday, October 10, 2011, 12:30 p.m.

As if jarred into wakefulness, Katherine suddenly snapped her fingers, spun around in place, slapped her right thigh with her right hand, and said, "Well, Little Buddy, you are really something. I would never have believed anything like that was possible if I hadn't seen it with my own eyes. Time to check out the tunnel. Are you ready?"

"Actually, I feel fine," I said. "But after all that's happened, I assumed we'd forget the mine shaft and head back to the room so I could rest, shower and change."

Katherine shot me a look of concentrated disdain, then said, "No. We're not going back. You're fine. And it's too early to turn back, especially after such a steep climb. Besides, we've just started."

Mouth agape, I stared at her in disbelief for a full minute. I couldn't think of anything to say.

Katherine dismissed my surprise. She quickly donned her backpack, turned to face the entrance to the mine shaft, and dusted herself off. She looked around the landing, then peered into the mine as she prepared to go in. She turned, hands on the straps of her backback, brow furrowed, and waited for me to join her.

I closed my mouth, inhaled deeply through my nose, and glanced toward the side of the adjacent mountain.

Katherine thrust one hip outward, tapped her foot in the red dust, and tapped her nails on a rock that protruded from the side of the entrance. Her eyes darted around, then returned to rest on me.

Resigned, I slowly re-packed the contents of my backpack. Katherine looked on, now tapping her nails on the lumber that framed the entrance of the mine. When she realized I still had my old collapsible walking stick that I used when I was a teen, she said, "I can't believe you still have that old thing, or that you brought it with you."

"I've had it so long it's like a friend," I replied. "Besides I love it. When it's disassembled—see? The top screws off—then there's room for a small knife, or whatever else I want to put in it. It's good to have it along to fend off critters and other predators."

"I see," Katherine said, snorting in derision. When she turned, she added, "Okay, time to check out the mine."

My stomach turned and I again began to feel dizzy. My breathing slowed. I felt the color drain from my face as I looked hesitantly into the musty old mine shaft. "You know, Katherine," I said, "I've always been slightly claustrophobic. That hasn't changed. I'm not sure I can do this."

"Do your best. You always do," she said as she strode through the entrance and disappeared into the face of the mountain.

"Katherine," I called into the huge black hole as I watched her flashlight beam bob up and down, "Do people ever come across rattlesnakes or black widows in places like this?"

"Not often," Katherine yelled back. "Don't forget to use your flashlight. Follow me," she called. With that, the beam from her flashlight began to grow smaller. I was left at the entrance of the mine shaft—alone.

I slowly and carefully ventured into the dark hole. With each small step forward, I watched wide-eyed for anything that might move or crawl. As I moved forward, I began to remember, then softly sing, the old song, *Please Mr. Custer*:

> That famous day in history
> The men of the 7th cavalry went riding on.
> And from the rear a voice was heard
> A brave young man with a trembling word
> Rang loud and clear, "What am I doing here?
> Please Mr. Custer, I don't wanna go . . ."
> "Forward, ho . . ."
> "No, Mr. Custer, please don't make me go . . ."

"Are you talking to me?" Katherine yelled from far ahead in the darkness.

"No. I'm just singing an old song to keep my mind off what's going on," I answered.

Chapter Twenty-Seven

Monday, October 10, 2011, 12:35 p.m.

As I carefully worked my way toward Katherine's quickly fading flashlight beam, I sang the few verses of the Custer song I remembered. But before long, the musty dankness of the tunnel made it difficult to breathe. The cobwebs that covered the walls of the mine shaft seemed to close in on me. My heart rate increased. Every so often, I anxiously turned to look over my shoulder toward what was now a tiny dot of light—the mine shaft entrance. To calm my mind as I inched forward, I focused on even the smallest detail of the tunnel.

Katherine's light had become pinhead-sized as I continued to trip and stumble along behind her, not wanting to touch the sides of the shaft. With each step, my chest tightened and my breathing became more shallow. I was about to turn around and head back to the ledge at the mouth of the tunnel to wait for Katherine when I stumbled over something round and hard that sent me crashing to my knees. *Great. What's one more fall?*

But when I shone my flashlight beam onto what I'd tripped over, my disgust turned to delight. What I saw looked like a Shaman Stone. I tucked my flashlight under my right arm, and cautiously picked up the stone with my left hand. I turned it over in my palm to examine it more closely under the light of my flashlight. The tunnel was cool. Although I had felt chilled, the stone felt strangely warm in my hand. The longer I held it, the more my sense of peace and pleasure grew. As I rotated the dull brown-grey stone in my hand, I was engulfed by an unusual sensation of serendipity.

My focus was shattered when I heard Katherine yell, "Where are you, Crissy? Are you okay, Little Buddy?" Katherine's voice was so thin she was obviously far ahead of me in the dark interior of the narrow mine shaft.

"I'm fine, sort of," I yelled back. "I tripped over something. And I think I might have just found a Shaman Stone. Can you believe that?"

"Great. What's a Shaman Stone?" Katherine shouted in reply.

Surprised that my geologist friend didn't know what a Shaman Stone was, I yelled back, "I'll tell you later." Then I slipped off my backpack, wrapped the stone in a spare T-shirt, and gently nestled it in a zippered side pocket of my backpack next to my Beretta.

Suddenly energized, I smiled as I continued feeling my way deeper into the tunnel. I stopped when I reached Katherine. When my eyes had adjusted to the semi-darkness, I noticed Katherine stood, hands typically on hips, and puzzled over an obstruction.

"Oh. I see what stopped you," I said, when I realized Katherine hadn't waited for me, as I'd assumed. Instead, a cave-in had closed about 80% of the passageway.

I shouldn't have been surprised when Katherine said, "I guess we'll have to find a way over or through."

But I was surprised. "Katherine," I sputtered, "There was a cave-in. Right? That must mean this area is unstable. Unsafe. I don't think we should do this. We need to turn around and get out of here. Now."

Resting her flashlight on a rock, Katherine quickly opened her backpack, donned gloves, pulled out a small folding shovel that she assembled in a matter of seconds, and climbed to the top of the pile. As I watched in horror and dread, she began to energetically dig.

"This isn't safe, Katherine" I said. "You shouldn't be digging in this old shaft that's already had one collapse. Right?"

"Crissy, your constant worrying is really getting on my nerves," Katherine hissed.

"Wait. Stop digging. It's dangerous," I said.

From the top of the pile near the small opening, she continued to toss dirt, pebbles and debris down the side of the cave-in.

"We should just turn back now," I warned. For me, it was a no-brainer. Leave—and quickly. My head began to buzz and my ears began to ring.

Katherine ignored my growing alarm. She continued to move rocks and shove them down the side of the cave-in so she could create enough of an opening to see if there was a way we could squeeze through to the other side. Before long she said, "I think we can make it now."

We? I thought.

I watched Katherine dig a little more by the light of her flashlight. The dust stirred up from her feverish activity made it even more difficult for me to breathe. I began to choke as I inhaled the dust. Katherine continued to fling debris everywhere like a chipmunk digging a new home.

Dizzy, I looked longingly back at the mine entrance. My chest continued to tighten even more.

A strong desire to flee almost overtook me. But although concerned we could start another cave-in, my commitment to help my friend won out over my fear. I sighed, put down my backpack, and reluctantly prepared to help Katherine dig. *There goes nail number three. Oh, well. I suppose I can always grow more. That's if I make it out of here alive.*

I repositioned myself to move a large rock when I stepped on something that crackled. It looked like a long branch. I turned the flashlight on it to get a better look. Suddenly, I realized what it was. My eyes grew even larger, my breath caught, and my heart began to pound so hard I could feel it in my neck and temples. Nausea overcame me. I screamed to Katherine. "I've GOT to get out of here!" Chills coursed throughout my body. "There's a dead body in here!"

"There's a what? Where?" Katherine said, as she quickly half-skidded, half-crawled back down from the top of the pile.

"Right here," I said, as I pointed to where I had tripped.

"Really!" Katherine exclaimed, fascinated and energized. "Are you sure?"

"Of course I'm '*sure*,'" I said, hyper-ventilating, as I fell into the side of the wall for support. "Jesus," I murmured to myself.

"Okay. Okay," Katherine said as she quickly lowered her body to where I leaned for support against the wall of the mine shaft. The light from her flashlight made strange designs in the blackness as she waved it around the body. Shivers rippled down my spine. I grew more nauseated by the second.

"You're right," Katherine exclaimed. "It *is* a dead body!"

"Of course it is!" I snapped. Regaining my senses, I stepped closer to the remains.

We both bent down to take a closer look at the exposed parts of the body. Even in the dim light, we could tell the body had been there a very long time. It was little more than a skeleton. The brown skin had dried and shriveled, and appeared leathery. Some of the bone was exposed through rotted fabric. I gagged and gasped for air. An urgent need to get back outside overcame me.

Katherine poked around the body, fascinated. "Cover your mouth and nose," she said, while she continued to look around.

"Good God!" I said. "I need to get out of here—now."

"Where are you going?" Katherine asked when she looked up and noticed I'd grabbed my backpack and was heading back toward the pinhead of light that promised freedom and fresh air.

"Away!" I replied, as I groped my way along the tunnel.

Chapter Twenty-Eight

Monday, October 10, 2011, 1:55 p.m.

"Hey, wait up," Katherine said, as she reached for her flashlight, snatched her backpack, and flung it over one shoulder. She strode quickly in the dark tunnel to catch up with me. Her flashlight beam bobbed with every step. "The body's half covered in rocks and debris, but the arm that's protruding has a wedding ring and watch," she said from somewhere behind me.

"You shouldn't touch anything," I said as I walked and stumbled as fast I could toward the growing point of light. "It might be a crime scene. Let the authorities check her body out."

"Hey, it's not so bad, Crissy," Katherine added. "That body's been there a long time. It's not like it just happened. And besides, what makes you think it's a woman's body?"

"The size of the body is that of a petite woman, or maybe large female child. The remnants of fabric still clinging to the body are floral, which would indicate a female. The ring and watch appear feminine. From that, *my guess* is the remains are those of a small married woman, and not a man or child. But no matter what you say about this situation being benign, it's repulsive to me and my whole body is churning and cringing in revulsion. I need to get out of here. I'll see you at the entrance."

"Okay," Katherine replied, "I'm close behind you. Let's go." But then she suddenly stopped, turned back, and began to look around the body again.

My dust-filled eyes began to tear. I decided to leave Katherine in the mine shaft. For a minute, I had to stop and lean against the wall of the dirty tunnel to steady myself and gain my equilibrium. As soon as I was able, I continued toward the light.

When I had finally made my way out into the fresh air and sunshine, my legs trembled. I gasped and drank in the fresh high desert air. Then my legs buckled. I leaned my back against the mountain and looked out over the peaceful valley where critters scurried and birds sang. I took a half-bottle of water out of my backpack and drank thirstily. I tried to wash the dirt out of my mouth, but my mouth still felt gritty. *What **am** I doing here?*

I struggled to clear my mind, calm my nerves, and regain my composure. I reached into my backpack and pulled out a yogurt-covered raspberry power bar and the Shaman Stone I'd stumbled over in the tunnel. I unwrapped the bar, but couldn't eat. Then I examined the stone in the daylight. *This looks just like the Shaman Stone I have at home.*

"Katherine?" I finally called. "Are you coming, or not?"

"I'm on my way," she responded.

I fought the grim thoughts of the dead woman that flooded my mind. Finally, I gave up trying to erase the scene from my memory. I gently re-wrapped the stone before I slipped it back into the side pocket of my backpack. Fatigue and dread engulfed me. *That could have been us.*

"I wonder who she was?" Katherine loudly asked as she neared the entrance of the mine shaft.

"Who knows?" I called back. "What woman in her right mind would dig around in an old abandoned mine shaft alone?"

"I do it all the time," Katherine hotly replied.

I decided to stop talking. Any more discussion of the body could spark another explosion.

Just then, I heard a strange low rumble from inside the mine shaft. I jumped up, turned to face the entrance, squinted and peered back into the mine. As I did, Katherine jogged the rest of the way out of the shaft and into the sunlight. Billows of dust followed her.

"Good Lord, Katherine! You could have been killed in there!"

"I know," she said, as dust from the cave-in encased us.

"I hope we didn't start that cave-in when we dug around in the rocks and rubble," I said. "What do think just happened in there?"

"I don't know," Katherine replied, "But we'd better get out of here."

My ears began to ring again. I shuddered as more dust settled around us. When the rumbling stopped and there was no new dust emerging from the mine shaft, I turned away from Katherine and faced the horizon. My heart continued to jack-hammer and I felt faint. I was eager to get back to the Rover, and then to my safe, sane motel room.

As I looked downward, the thought of another fall on scree on my way down to the Rover caused chills to course up and down my spine. Goose bumps covered my arms. To calm myself, I focused on the changing gold, orange and red fall colors, listened to the birds, and watched the bushes and trees sway in the soft breeze. When I looked up, huge buttermilk clouds congregated and glistened against a backdrop of robin-egg-blue sky. I began to relax.

Then I heard a distant noise that caused me to jerk my head around and look back down into the canyon. As I did, Katherine squealed with delight. She had spotted what I had just heard. A vehicle was coming toward where we had parked on the remote gravel road. As I watched, it parked next to Katherine's Land Rover. *Oh, God, no! Please, tell me that's not Manny's black Hummer!*

Chapter Twenty-Nine

Monday, October 10, 2011, 2:15 p.m.

I stood and blinked into the bright sunlight. In the far distance, two men, one with light sandy hair, the other with dark curly hair, emerged from the Hummer and began to check out Katherine's Rover. Then they began to scan the surrounding area. They finally looked up and noticed Katherine and me standing on the ledge. They watched us. We watched them.

I groaned as Katherine waved enthusiastically and called down to them. *Joe and Manny!* I screamed inwardly. *How did they know we'd be here? What are they up to? Why did they come?*

Just then, a second thunderous noise from the mine shaft caused me to jump. My head turned back toward the tunnel. I shivered as I automatically turned full-body to face the mine entrance. When I did, a second cloud of dust enveloped me. "Good God! Katherine?" I gasped. "What just happened?"

"I don't know," Katherine answered. She, too, was covered in a new thick layer of red dust. She turned to face the canyon, and added, "But I'm out of here. Let's go!"

"I agree!" I said. I turned and reached for my backpack to follow Katherine down the mountain. When I turned back, she had already started downward. "When we get down we'll have to go to the police station to report the body," I called.

"That body's been there a really long time," Katherine responded. "It's not going anywhere. We're running out of daylight, and fast. The police report can wait until after dark."

Surprised, I paused, then decided, *I suppose she's right. Now the body is under even more rubble. What's one more night?*

Voices from below broke into our strained conversation. "Is that you, Kat and Crystal?" It was Joe.

Katherine's pace quickened, her eyes glistened, and she stood straight as she smiled and yelled back, "Yes. It's us. And we're on our way down."

Without another word, Katherine began to lope down the mountainside. As she zigzagged downward, dust and scree flew in her wake.

Oh, God! Say it isn't so, I thought wearily. While Katherine eagerly dashed down the slope, I began to cautiously work my way down the mountain. As I picked my way over branches and around large rocks, Katherine sprinted the last few yards to where the men waited. I could hear their laughter as she leaned on her Land Rover and talked with Joe and Manny.

I dreaded what I knew was to come. Trying to get rid of Joe and Manny seemed a daunting challenge. *Which is worse?* I mused. *The climb down from here? Or having to deal with Katherine's infatuation with Joe and Manny?*

As I slowly slid on the scree, Joe looked up and said, "Need some help, Crystal?"

When he did, Katherine turned and seemed to realize for the first time that I was only halfway down the mountainside.

"Thanks, Joe. I'll be fine. I just need to psych myself up for this," I called back. As the three of them now watched me, I felt even more self-conscious. My face burned. Sweat trickled down the sides of my face again and soaked my undergarments. My heartbeat quickened as I began to involuntarily slide down the mountain in slow motion. Somehow, I was able to regain my balance and arrive at the base of the mountain in a cloud of dust, unscathed.

Joe and Manny stood straighter and watched me as I walked closer to where they had parked. Their eyes widened and their brows creased. Joe looked at Manny. "Got it," Manny said, and turned toward the back of his Hummer. He emerged with a first aid kit.

Touched by their concern, I said, "Thanks. I'm fine. Really. I just had a bad fall. It's not as bad as it looks."

They continued to stare as Manny opened the kit.

I grew even more conscious of my torn jeans and my favorite blouse that was so shredded it barely covered my filthy, sweaty body. *What else could possibly go wrong?* I thought as my jaw tightened and I braced myself for whatever was to come.

Chapter Thirty

Monday, October 10, 2011, 2:39 p.m.

I soon realized the others had been drinking cola and eating the now-squished peanut butter sandwiches Katherine and I had made and packed that morning. "Hand this orange to Manny, will you?" Katherine said as I walked by toward the rear of the Rover.

"Sure," I responded, annoyed but not wanting to get into another confrontation, especially in front of Joe and Manny. I reached for the orange she had thrust in my direction and all but snatched it out of her hand.

Katherine glared at me. The yellow flecks in her green eyes flashed.

I glared back at her before I handed the orange to Manny. Then I picked up a sandwich, walked to the far side of the Rover, and sat in the passenger's seat. I used the dashboard as a table.

"Join us," Joe implored.

"No, thanks, Joe," I said, before I unwrapped my sandwich. I dug in my backpack for a water bottle and Fig Newtons, my comfort food.

It would be many days before I realized that in spite of what could only be called *miraculous healings,* my toenails would still turn black from the descent and ultimately fall off. *Just one of the many joys of mountain climbing with Katherine,* I would grumble.

Although Joe and Manny tried to downplay my appearance, I could tell they were concerned. The more attention they gave me and my appearance, the more agitated Katherine seemed to become. As they urged me to let them help, and offered their medicine and supplies, Katherine became restless. She tapped her nails on the Hummer. Then she paced. Next, she interjected herself when they asked me a question, and answered for me.

They looked at Katherine, then at me. I remained quiet and ate my sandwich, but I felt my face flush a little redder with each intrusion.

When I had eaten the last Fig Newton, I looked in the side mirror of the Land Rover. I quickly saw why Joe and Manny seemed so concerned.

Although my injuries had healed, dried blood caked with layers of dust still clung to my body from head to toe. My jeans were torn. My shredded blouse hung limply off one shoulder. My matted and bloodied hair stuck out in all directions. *Don't panic,* I told myself. *You can get through this. This, too, shall pass. You just need a shower, a nap, and clean clothes. You're fine.*

I poured water into a plastic bowl, then washed more of the dried blood and grime off my face and hands. I tried to repair my disheveled appearance, but didn't have much luck. As I worked, Katherine told Joe and Manny more about my fall, the tunnel, how it had caved-in, twice, and the dead body. The more I listened, the more lightheaded I became. I fought back tears.

"Have you called it in?" Joe asked Katherine.

"No. My cell's in the shop," Katherine answered. "And Crissy doesn't have one. Can you believe that?"

"Then I'll do it," he said, as he reached for his cell and dialed 9-1-1.

Chapter Thirty-One

Monday, October 10, 2011, 3:13 p.m.

J oe was told by the dispatcher that officers were being sent and, because of our remote location, would arrive in about thirty minutes.

Katherine looked at her watch, then at the sun that was edging toward the west.

I finished the last of my water. Next, I silently resumed repairing my appearance. Then I pulled a large towel out of the back of Katherine's Rover and spread it in the shade. I set my backpack down beside me, then lay back flat on the bed I'd made on the red earth.

"What are you doing?" Katherine demanded.

"Resting."

"You could join us and visit," she snapped.

I closed my eyes and tried not to listen.

"Let her rest, Kat," Joe said softly.

As I waited for law enforcement to arrive, I focused on recovering from the cave-in, and tried to curtail my annoyance at Joe and Manny's intrusion. Finally, I got up. I combed, then retied, my dirt-and-blood-caked hair into a pony-tail.

After I had repaired my appearance as much as possible, I dug in my backpack for more Fig Newtons. As I dug, the authorities arrived, accompanied by a K-9 unit.

Katherine explained to them what had happened.

They looked up the steep incline. "You were exploring *that* mine shaft?" Officer Ronald Reese asked. "No one . . ." He let his comment trail off as he looked at Katherine—who stood with her feet planted firmly on the ground, brow furrowed, serious stare. "Well, *almost* no one," he corrected. "No one should try to enter *that* mine shaft. Didn't you see the posted warning signs? That's a dangerous place. All abandoned mine shafts are dangerous. But that one is particularly bad. That's why it's posted."

"We didn't see any signs," I interjected from where I stood by the Rover.

"Who are you?" he asked.

"We were fine," Katherine said.

"Fine?" I said, as I turned and looked at Katherine in disbelief.

"I see," Officer Reese replied.

"There's a body about a quarter of a mile inside the entrance. It's mostly decomposed, and half covered—well, maybe now totally buried—in rocks and dirt," I said.

Officer Reese looked at Katherine again. Then back at me. I nodded, and added, "It's true." He looked back at Katherine.

The authorities asked a few more questions. They decided it was too late to arrange for someone to check out the cave. Because of the second cave-in, they were not hopeful of finding the body anytime soon.

I wonder if they'll ever find it? And if they do, how will they get it out of there? Helicopter?

The officers warned us to stay out of mine shafts, especially those posted with warnings, and left.

As I watched their Jeep disappear down the pot-holed gravel road, Katherine's laughter broke into my thoughts. I looked over toward her and the guys. When I did, I noticed that Manny's appearance was almost pristine—clean-shaven, neat, new clothes, well-put-together—right down to his manicured nails. *Right. Like he hikes regularly.*

Joe was different. He appeared to be relaxed and comfortable in his old dungarees, worn boots and faded blue plaid shirt, open at the neck. His ready smile and warm grey eyes were refreshing. When he looked at someone, he really saw them. I couldn't help but smile back.

It was almost 3:33 p.m. when Katherine handed me a Gatorade and said something about leaving Casner Canyon.

Manny commented that they'd have to take us to dinner to return the favor of such a "gourmet luncheon." Both men radiated a casual confidence that seemed to come from good looks and old money. For some reason, it made me even more uncomfortable. *Who, really, are these guys?*

"Thanks, but no," I said. "It's been an awful ordeal today, but we'll be fine. We don't need plans for dinner. We need to get back to our room to rest, recover and shower. Regroup. There's not much daylight left. Besides, we have plans for later tonight. Right, Katherine?" I hoped she'd agree.

"Well, we *did*," Katherine said coyly as she smiled at Joe, then looked away from me.

Oh, great! She wants to go off with these guys tonight. I'll be on my own. Well, I guess it could be worse.

Katherine made a point not to look in my direction.

My temples throbbed.

Joe broke into my thoughts, and said, "Come on. Join us Crystal. We'll have an early, light dinner."

"Well," I replied, "I'm on vacation. That is if you can call *this* a vacation. I came to Sedona to help Katherine. If she wants to join you, fine. Me? I'd rather not. What are you guys doing up here, anyway. How did you find us?"

Katherine quickly said, "Well! Time to go!" as she tossed her backpack into the Rover.

Manny changed the subject and asked, more to his real point, I thought, "So, how did you get involved with the search for the mystical orb?"

"I'm wondering that, myself," I replied. My jaws clenched. "This was supposed to be a fun reunion. I'm not quite sure how it turned into mountain climbing, a dead body, and a cave-in. As far as some mystical sphere, it's probably all just legend, right? Who would ever really believe such a thing existed? But when the scroll was found, it did give us an excuse to get together. Or so I thought at the time. We're mostly hiking, exploring and visiting. Neither of us really expects to find anything. Do we, Katherine?"

I could feel my face flush when Katherine replied, "This *is* a reunion, of sorts. And I *do* plan to find that sphere."

I fumed as I thought, *If I leave in the morning, I can be back in Austin by Wednesday night.* Then I decided it was ridiculous to leave after just one day. *She can do whatever she wants. I'm resting, then having a dinner alone before my session with Elke. God—what a misery of a day!*

My head snapped in his direction when I heard Manny say to Katherine, "Your search sounds interesting. We'd like to join you."

I glanced toward Heaven, took a deep breath, then broke in and said, "I don't think that's a good idea, Manny. I don't want to hike anymore today. And I really don't want to discuss it, especially now, and with you. I need to get back to the motel room."

Katherine glared at me.

Joe watched as I squirmed and shuffled my feet in the dirt. Finally, he said, "We understand. Maybe some other time. How about we meet for dinner another night while you're in Sedona?"

I shouldn't have been surprised, but I was, when Katherine sprang to her feet and said, "Just because Crissy is tired doesn't mean I am. Where else can we hike and search today? There's still daylight."

Both men looked at me, then back at Katherine. "Didn't you mention Soldier Pass earlier? That sounds like a good start," Joe said.

Chapter Thirty-Two

Monday, October 10, 2011, 3:38 p.m.

Manny asked, "Or how about Cibola Pass or Secret Mountain? I heard a lot of reclusive types hang out in both of those places. It's a thought."

"Soldier Pass sounds like a good place," Katherine responded. "We drove by it today, so I know how to get there. We'll meet you in about an hour."

"Wouldn't Secret Mountain be a likely place for someone to hide something? Something that's supposed to be a secret?" I added, realizing Katherine felt totally in charge of all decision-making and plans for this search.

"Probably," Katherine said, as she lifted her right hand and stroked her chin. "But we don't have much light and we all know where Soldier Pass is. Why don't we start there, then, if we have time we can move over to Secret Mountain?"

"Fine," I said. I sighed and looked down toward the valley in resignation.

Joe and Manny glanced at one another, then nodded their approval. I didn't think they much cared where we searched, as long as they were along for the ride.

Katherine turned toward the driver's door of her Rover, and said, "Well, folks, it's time to move out!" She shoved empty bottles and plastic sandwich baggies into a brown paper bag, then stashed them behind her seat.

Joe added, "Be sure to make a right on Soldier Pass Road. That will take you to where we'll park. Manny and I will meet you there."

"Okay," Katherine agreed.

Joe and Manny waved goodbye then took off.

Katherine and I stood and watched them leave. Katherine said, "You could be a little friendlier, Crissy," as she flung her backpack into the backseat of her Rover.

"Me? Friendlier?" I stammered. "What were they even doing here, Katherine? How did they find us? Who, really, *are* they?" I paused, caught my breath, then continued, more slowly, "Katherine, those guys are eerie. I don't think you should encourage them, not even a little. Besides, did you tell them where we were going to be searching this morning?"

"Crissy," Katherine sighed. "Well, no, I didn't tell them. I don't know how they found us. What's a little hiking, and then dinner and dancing with Joe and Manny? You might be tired, but I'm not. And they're both fun and interesting."

I was so alarmed about the unfolding plans with Joe and Manny that I temporarily forgot my questions about how they'd found us. "What do you mean, 'dinner and dancing'?" I said. "You're not going to the spa with me tonight? You've already made other plans with them?"

"I don't think I'm going to make it to the spa," Katherine said, looking away from me as she climbed into her SUV. "I'd much rather have some fun. I love to dance, and so does Joe. You should forget the spa and come with us."

"Okay," I sighed, resigned. "If you're not going, you're not going. I *am* going. Besides, Ryan said I will receive another clue tonight. Doesn't that interest you at all? But if you want to go dancing instead, fine. Just please don't joke about the sphere or tell them about last night's clue, okay?"

"You're not taking that nonsense about another clue seriously, are you?" she sneered.

"Just promise me you won't tell them," I said. "Don't give them any information that I wouldn't give them, okay?"

"Okay. Okay. I won't tell them," she replied. "But you could loosen up, Crissy. Relax. Have some fun."

"I didn't come here to 'loosen up,' Katherine, or to 'have some fun' with strange men," I said. "I came here to visit with you and help you search for a golden orb."

"All right. I won't say another word to them about the sphere or the clue. Happy, Mother?" Katherine said.

"Well, happier," I said, trying to ignore her sarcasm. My jaw clenched. My upper lip felt raw and I tasted blood again. Anger threatened to overtake my annoyance, and a mild headache threatened to become a migraine as it danced between my temples.

I soon became distracted by a rose-scented breeze that enfolded me. As the breeze melted into my body, so did a sense of peace. When I looked up, a vibrant red Cardinal flew directly in front of my windshield, and settled on a nearby branch. *It's a sign. But of what?* Soft waves of peace continued to wash over me. I sighed deeply, and relaxed.

"You ready, Crissy?" Katherine asked, as she slammed her car door shut.

"Sure. Yes. Ready," I replied. "I don't want to hike with Joe and Manny for long. I need to get back to the room and shower. I need to rest. And I want to change into something clean and fresh before my spa appointment," I insisted.

Katherine gave me another disapproving glance, then said, "Okay, but we should hike as long as there's daylight. If you want to go back early, maybe Manny can take you. I want to stay out and hike."

Of course you do.

Chapter Thirty-Three

"I don't like you pawning me off on Manny," I said. "From now on I'll drive my Jeep and follow you when we're out."

"It's a waste of time and gas," Katherine argued. "Besides, I don't see what you're so upset about. Manny seems like a nice guy. And he's handsome and fun. But alright. If that's what you want to do. But I think it's ridiculous."

"Of course *you* do!' I said. Then, slowing my breath and regaining control, I added, "But that's what I'm going to do." I dropped the subject and turned my gaze toward the fall scenery that flashed by my window. The breezes had died down. The shimmering yellows, oranges and reds of fall leaves, many of which floated gently toward the ground in the afternoon sunlight, were hypnotic. The sun reflected off Oak Creek causing it to sparkle as if laced with blue and white jewels. Birds flew, and critters scampered. The air . . . the air continued to feel heavy, as if infused with a narcotic. It felt alive, as though it had a mind and personality of its own. *Have I walked through an invisible, intelligent curtain of some kind?*

Katherine and I didn't speak as she darted back down the steep winding mountain road on her way to Soldier Pass. Finally, I broke the silence and said, "I feel like someone has been following us. Watching us. Have you felt anything unusual? Seen anyone unusual?"

"What do you mean? No," she said. "I haven't felt anything different. And I haven't seen anyone who looked like they paid particular attention to us. But, then, I've been occupied with the search. Are you sure you're not just imagining things?"

"I'm sure," I said. "I get this really creepy feeling that we're being watched. Haven't you noticed anything? Anything at all out of the norm?"

"No," she said. "I haven't seen anything or anyone unusual." Katherine turned to look at me. "You really do need to relax, Crissy."

"Okay. Well, I *have* felt like someone is watching and following me. It's rattled my nerves. I don't think we should talk to strangers. Especially about the sphere. No one needs to know anything about us. No one," I added.

"People will forever be strangers to us if you don't loosen up, Crissy," Katherine said. Then, mellowing, she added, "I like Joe. I'd like to get to know him better. You might not be interested in Manny, but I want to spend some more time with Joe."

I sighed deeply as I turned back toward the window and focused on the promise of a soothing warm shower and clean clothes. I wondered about the massage, the next clue, and how I would handle my meeting with Elke.

As we zipped back down Oak Creek Canyon, the sun moved in and out of clouds as it sank lower in the western sky. I hoped the bright sunlight wouldn't temporarily blind Katherine as she sped down the mountainside. I hadn't realized I'd been holding my breath until we reached uptown Sedona, and I began to relax. I took a deep breath, and let go of the grab-bar. I silently thanked God that we were finally safe and off the curving, steep mountain road.

We passed uptown Sedona and drove to the newer part of town, then made a right onto Soldier Pass Road. We parked at the trailhead. Joe and Manny were waiting. Joe walked to where we had parked and opened Katherine's car door. Manny smiled as he walked to my side of the vehicle to open my door, but I exited before he reached me.

As we hiked and searched around Soldier Pass, we stirred up more red dust that clung to our already dirt caked, sweaty bodies. Before long, we looked like living terra cotta dolls. When Katherine removed her sunglasses, I couldn't help but laugh.

"What's so funny?" she asked.

"With those circles around your eyes, you look like a red raccoon," I said.

Before she could reply, Joe quickly said, "Kat, you look adorable!"

Katherine smiled. They walked closer to one another. Then they resumed the search, side-by-side.

I think I've lost my hiking companion. And that's fine with me, I thought as Manny walked over to hike along side me.

It was around 5:00 p.m. when we agreed it was time to stop and rest. We sat on the dusty red soil under a pine tree that gave us some spotty shade and relief from the heat of the sinking afternoon sun. We drank bottled water. Katherine and I shared our power bars with Joe and Manny.

If he knew what we were doing here with Joe and Manny, Trevor would not be happy.

Sweat had caused Joe and Manny's black T-shirts to cling to their tan, well-muscled bodies. *They sure don't look or act like salesmen.*

Once we'd dusted ourselves off, I was ready to head back to the vehicles, and our room.

Katherine wanted to continue searching.

Joe, of course, agreed to hike with Katherine.

Manny watched me, then said, "I'd be glad to take you back to the motel, Crystal."

"No. That's okay," I said. "I'll wait for Katherine. It's almost sunset, so this can't go on much longer. Right, Katherine?"

Katherine ignored my question. She and Joe walked further down the trail.

Joe, though, looked back over his shoulder and smiled. He seemed to feel uncomfortable, but not uncomfortable enough to end the hike.

After another hour of fruitless searching, Katherine was finally ready to call it a day and head back toward the room.

As we put our backpacks in the vehicles, Joe and Katherine firmed up their plans for an evening of dinner and dancing.

Manny looked in my direction. "No?" he said, as he smiled.

"No," I smiled in response.

Chapter Thirty-Four

Monday, October 10, 2011, 6:05 p.m.

I was relieved when we headed back to the room. I wanted to rest before my appointment with Elke. I looked in the rearview mirror. The sky had turned a deep mango as the sun sank behind the wispy clouds that lined the horizon. As the sun continued to drop further below the clouds, fingers of silver and gold shot outward in every direction, bathing the landscape in a magical luster.

When we turned off Highway 89, and I could no longer see the sunset, I became more concerned about Katherine's tendency to talk freely to Joe and Manny, and anyone else who might be listening. *Will she talk to them about the sphere?*

Entering the motel's parking lot, I thought about my fall down the mountain earlier in the day. *What was the soft, warm wind with its clear colorful lights that glistened and danced around me, then soaked into my skin? How, exactly, was I mysteriously healed?* I was so deep in thought that I hadn't heard Katherine's question. I snapped out of my reverie when Katherine shouted, "Hey! Crissy! Did you hear me?"

I flinched. My hand hit Katherine's boxes of Red Hots and Good 'n Plenties that were open by the side of her seat. They fell and spilled all over both seats and the floorboard. Candies rolled, bounced and ricocheted everywhere.

"Sorry," I said, as I scrambled to pick them up.

"Don't worry," Katherine said. "Just put them back in the boxes. I'll eat them later."

I looked at the dirt and dust on the floorboard, then retrieved the candies and dropped them, one-by-one, back into their respective boxes. "I really am sorry," I said. "I was thinking about all that happened today. I didn't hear what you were saying. What was it?"

"Never mind. It's okay. It was about my plans with Joe. But we can talk later."

Chapter Thirty-Five

Monday, October 10, 2011, 6:39 p.m.

Dirty, rattled and shaky, I was relieved when we pulled up to the office at Kings Ransom. I glanced to the west and saw the last tip of the mango sun sink below the horizon, leaving traces of silver and gold reflecting off pink and orange clouds.

"Why don't you drop me at the office for a second?" I said. "I won't be long. I'll just check for messages and be right back."

"Crissy," Katherine said, "That's what I was telling you earlier. I'd like to take a quick shower, then take off and search some more with Joe. It's almost a full moon. I know you don't want to be out searching after dark, and that you plan to keep your appointment with Elke. But I have two hours before Joe and I are supposed to meet Manny for dinner. So I'll drop you off here at the office, take a shower, and leave. I'll probably already be showered and gone before you make it back to the room."

I sat for a minute in disbelief. Then I exhaled, and snatched my backpack from the floorboard with such force it banged into the door. Without replying, I slid out of the Rover. As soon as my feet hit the ground and the door had slammed closed, Katherine bolted toward the room. I watched her tail-lights turn the corner. I glanced up at the Heavens, then turned and walked into the lobby.

Red-faced and angry, I marched toward the front desk. *Fine. I'll walk to the room. She's an adult. Why do I care what she does? Why did she ask me to come here to help her, since she seems to resent my help? And why was I stupid enough to agree to come? If she wants to dump me off, climb rock formations at night with Joe, then go out to dinner and dancing with these guys, so what?*

As I stomped toward the front desk, all conversation and activity stopped. The room became hushed. I paused, furrowed my brow, and looked around.

Startled people looked back at me. I inhaled, slowed my pace, and continued toward the desk.

At the front desk, a wide-eyed clerk took a step backward, then said, "Are you okay? Do you need to go to the medical center?" Her concern made me glad the staff treated me more like a guest than just a paying customer.

When I finally stopped thinking about Katherine's treatment of me, and realized what I must look like—filth and dried blood still caked on my torn clothes and body, red eyes, wild hair—I suddenly regretted stopping in at the office.

"No," I said with a sigh. "I don't need to go to the medical center. But thanks for your concern. I just had a nasty fall, but now I'm fine. I need to shower, to put on some fresh clothes, and have something to eat. That's all. I only stopped in to see if I had any messages from my husband, Trevor."

"Okay. Your room number?" She said.

"Crystal O'Connor. Room 247," I replied.

She quickly checked, then said, "We don't have anything here for you. Just a minute. I'll check the more recent incoming messages and mail. No. Nothing there, either."

"Thank you," I said, now more self-conscious than ever.

When I turned to leave the lobby, I noticed Patrick Bailey sitting in one of the upholstered chairs. He was almost hidden behind an open newspaper. The hairs on my dirty neck stood up. His eyes darted to one side, then over the top on the newspaper, then back down at the page.

I took a deep breath, picked up my pace, and moved toward the door.

As I did, I heard the newspaper rattle. Then I heard, "Oh. Ms. O'Connor. Is that you? *Now* do you have a moment to talk?"

I turned and, when I saw Patrick Bailey slithering in my direction, said, "No. I don't. Not now. I need to shower, and I have an appointment tonight that I must keep." Then I turned and walked out of the lobby as quickly as my tired legs would carry me.

By the time I walked up the incline to the adjacent set of rooms, then climbed the staircase, and walked into our room, Katherine was just about ready to leave. Her dusty backpack was tossed in the corner closest to her bed. Her dirty tennis shoes were again tossed on the comforter next to her dirty clothes. Other items from her quick shower were strewn here and there. A heavy mist and the scent of Elizabeth Taylor's *White Diamonds* permeated the air.

"You beat it back to the room before I got out of here," she said. "What's wrong?" she added, as she looked at me in the mirror and watched me scan the dirty items on her bedspread.

"Nothing," I said, not wanting to get into another argument.

Katherine glared at me in the mirror.

I glared back. "Okay," I said. "It seems inconsiderate of the next guests for you to toss your dirty shoes and clothes on the comforter. That's all." I turned and plunked myself at the table. I was ready to be alone. I looked around, resigned, and reached for a bottle of water and an apple. There was only one apple left. *I'll go out and get more later, after the massage.*

While Katherine applied fresh make-up, I made more coffee and, while it brewed, slathered creamed cheese on a lavishly buttered bagel. My dinner. Then I checked the sliding glass door to be sure it was locked.

As she reached for her purse, Katherine asked, "What were you telling me yesterday about the message from Ryan? I forgot."

I turned to face Katherine, no longer sure I wanted to share anything with her, let alone my thoughts about the information Ryan had given me. My head throbbed. The bones in my face ached. I sat silent and considered what I would say.

Katherine had blow-dried her thick golden hair and now she pulled it back. She wore a soft, silky lavender blouse with a ruffle that cascaded down the front of a soft V-neck, along with sturdy brown shorts. She picked the dirty tennis shoes off the comforter, dusted them off, and put them on. Then she stuffed her clutch purse into her backpack.

I considered the message from Ryan. I wondered, *Is it a good time to review it with Katherine, who is obviously in a hurry to leave?* I slowly inhaled. Katherine walked to the sink and added a second layer of mascara to her already well-made-up eyes, combed her long golden bangs out of her eyelashes, and ran a comb through her long glistening ponytail.

As I tried to think of the best answer to Katherine's question, I turned toward the television and groaned inwardly at the blaring sound of the international news. "You don't mind, do you?" I said, as I reached over and clicked off the television.

I added, "About the message, I meant to tell you . . . Katherine . . . would you please hold still for one minute and listen so we can discuss it?"

A sharp look from Katherine was quickly followed by, "Can't you just tell me, Crissy? I'm in a hurry."

"Yes, I can, but I won't. This is too important, Katherine. It will have more impact and be clearer, and you're more likely to remember it, if . . ."

"Okay, *Mom!*" she said again. Then she plopped her fanny down in the chair opposite me, and said, "I'm sitting. I'm looking at you. I'm paying attention. Better? Where is the message?"

When my upper lip stung I knew I'd bitten into it again. Offended, I fought growing anger, and said, "Ryan said it's okay to share this with you. But don't tell Joe and Manny, Katherine," I added "Alright?"

"Alright! Alright, Crissy. Would you just read the note to me again and tell me whatever it is you want to say?" As she talked, her left hand reached up to clasp her necklace.

"You know, Katherine, I'm sorry I even mentioned the note to you now," I said, as I retrieved the note from where I'd tucked it the night before—the side pocket of my backpack. As I reached for it, I saw the Shaman Stone. Suddenly delighted, I pulled it out, too, and set it on the table. *I can rinse it off and examine it later.*

Katherine tapped her nails on the table as I reread the cryptic message to her. Then I handed it to her across the fruit and flower filled table. The pungent scent of aging roses wafted in the air. As she glanced at the note, I told Katherine that Ryan had somehow known I was scheduled for a massage at the spa that night. "He said I should make sure to be there if I wanted more information about the sphere," I concluded. "What do you think?"

Uncharacteristically still for a moment, Katherine stopped flipping her foot and tapping her nails, and responded, "Hum. That *is* strange. But I've known lots of weird characters—desert rats, I call them—old prospectors. Ryan's probably just one of those," she said, dismissing the note. She let go of the note and I watched it float onto the table. Katherine got up, grabbed her backpack, and strode toward the door.

I retrieved the note and tucked it back in its spot inside my backpack. Then I reached for the Shaman Stone and began to examine it more closely. When I did, I noticed Katherine, whose left hand was on the doorknob, stopped and watched me.

"What?" I said.

"What's that?" she asked.

"It's the stone I told you about. The one I found, well, stumbled over, in the mine shaft this morning. I think it's a Shaman Stone. I have one at home. It looks almost exactly like this one."

"I've never seen one before. That's odd, isn't it?" she said. "I thought I'd seen just about everything in the field of geology. Well, okay then," she added.

As I gently placed the stone down amid the fruit and flowers in the middle of the table, I told Katherine about the old saying, "If you want to hide something, put it in plain sight."

"No one's going to want your dull-looking little stone," Katherine said. "But if it makes you feel any better . . ."

"It does."

"Okay, then. I'm off," she responded as the door clicked behind her.

"Bye," I responded to the closed door as a film of tears burned my red eyes.

Chapter Thirty-Six

Monday, October 10, 2011, 7:15 p.m.

I stared out the sliding glass door into the darkness, thankful for the quiet and peace. Finally, I took my coffee and the rest of my bagel onto the balcony.

When I returned to the room, I clicked on the table lamp to reread Ryan's message. When I did, I remembered how the lamp's soft "click" had awakened Katherine that morning. I started to laugh all over again.

Before I showered, I locked the patio door and closed both sets of drapes.

When I saw my reflection in the mirror, I froze. *My God! No wonder people stared.*

After a few more minutes of delicious silence, I dragged my filthy, weary body into the bathroom for a long, hot shower. Red dirt and dried blood washed down the drain at my feet. As I stood under the running water, steam filled the bathroom and over-flowed into the dressing area causing the mirrors to fog over.

I put on fresh jeans, a white cotton V-neck pull-over T-shirt, and navy flats. The smell of over-ripe bananas mixed with the scent of roses permeated the room with a pleasant smell. I ate a banana, then finished my coffee. Then I put on fresh makeup and pulled my still damp hair back into a ponytail.

I found a laundry bag for my filthy and torn clothes. *Should I just throw them away?* I stashed the bag under my suitcase that sat open on the suitcase rack. Then I headed back to the small round table to reread Ryan's note.

I should have felt tired, but I didn't. I felt invigorated and alive. Even so, I didn't dare lie down on the bed for fear I might fall asleep and miss my appointment with Elke.

Chapter Thirty-Seven

Monday, October 10, 2011, 7:45 p.m.

The red numbers on the clock reflected 7:45 p.m. when I left the room to make the short trip to the spa.

I walked to my Jeep, my dusted-off backpack flung over one shoulder. Two large men loitered in the shadows. I slowed down to get a closer look, but they were too far away to be clearly seen. And I was in a hurry.

When I drove past them, one turned sideways and glanced my way, then stepped further into the shadows. The other moved behind the trunk of a large pine tree.

I continued to watch them as I drove by slowly. Their behavior was so suspicious that my heart pounded. A shiver crept over my shoulders and crawled up my neck. As if I were in a life-jacket a size too small, it was hard to breathe.

Now I was certain I was being followed. *But why? Who would want to follow me? Was it the sphere? Did someone overhear Katherine in the restaurant? If so, why weren't they following her? Or were they following her, too?*

Unnerved, but in a hurry to get to the spa and be on time for my appointment with Elke, I locked the doors of my Jeep and continued out of the parking lot toward the spa and, I hoped, to my next clue.

Chapter Thirty-Eight

Monday, October 10, 2011, 7:55 p.m.

D riving to the spa, I wondered, *What, exactly, is a chakra-balancing massage? What will Elke be like? Does she really have another clue to give to me, or was Ryan just playing with me?*

At the front desk, a large wooden wall clock behind the counter reflected I was just two minutes early. Once I had signed in, the receptionist explained their policies and procedures. Then she led me through the spa toward the dressing room. I breathed in the aroma of berry and vanilla scented candles that flickered in an alcove.

On the way to the changing area, the receptionist took me through a large public lounge area with sofas and magazines. There was a gently glowing fireplace and a large table that overflowed with fruit, tea, and candles.

In the dressing room, I was given a thick, fluffy teal robe that smelled mildly of lemons. The spa's representative pointed out the shower area, hot tub, and private lounge where I could wait for my therapist to fetch me. She then gave me a key to a locker and told me where I could store my belongings.

Naked under the soft, thick bathrobe, I went to the private lounge area. I wore white disposable flip-flops, listened to soft new-age music, closed my eyes, and waited.

I had been anxious about my meeting with Elke. But after a few minutes at the spa, I relaxed. Then I felt an unshakable certainty sweep over me. It melted into my being the way hot candle wax melts and flows.

A slow transformation took place. My nerves began to relax. My mind calmed. Before long, my spirit began to sing.

I had left my Beretta inside my backpack, which I had placed in a locker with my clothes. I now checked to make sure the locker key was still in my pocket. It was. Then I leaned back into the chaise lounge and nestled on soft sea-foam green pillows. The music was hypnotic. I began to feel drowsy.

Soon, Elke Strauss entered the lounge. I was pleasantly surprised that she, too, was petite. I wondered how she managed to work with larger clients. She had a soft, natural blond beauty, and was as fair as a Scandinavian. Her medium length almost white hair was pulled back into a casual bun at the nape of her neck. She wore what looked like a nurse's uniform—white shoes, white slacks, white blouse. She was slender, and her sea-foam-green eyes were almost the same color as the soft pillows upon which I rested. Her eyes reflected warmth and caring, while at the same time she looked at me so intensely she seemed to see right through to the core of my being. Her smile exuded a peaceful self-confidence. Her voice was soft, low and gentle. I felt even more tension and stress drain away.

I followed Elke up three flights of stairs into a large massage room. Soft music continued to soothe my soul. Sensual aromas from open jars of oils and scented candles filled the air. Diffused lights from behind huge crystals and colorful jars filled with oils gave the room a soft, warm glow.

When I first arrived in Sedona, I felt as if I had stepped into an alternate world. Now, it was as if I had stepped into yet another parallel world within that world.

In her soft, slow voice, Elke explained how we would proceed. As she talked, I noticed a soft light spotlighted an enormous quartz crystal that rested atop a large desk in the center of the far wall. On a counter along an adjacent wall were arranged bottles filled with fragrant and colorful oils that contained not only herbs, but crushed flowers, as well. She took off the lid of one of the capped bottles so I could smell and appreciate the exquisite aroma. As I inhaled, I continued to unwind and slip further into that other world.

The massage table, covered in warm off-white flannel sheets, stood on a hardwood floor in the center of the room. On top of the sheets, crystals of various colors had been carefully arranged in a semi-circle.

One small round table was placed near the door with a chair on either side. Elke moved the two chairs away from the table, and placed them next to the massage table, facing one another.

Then she asked me to take off all jewelry and sit in one of the chairs. Next, she quietly left the room and gently closed the door behind her.

As I removed my necklace, two gold and diamond rings, and gold earrings, my eyes slowly adapted to the semi-darkness. I continued to unwind as I inhaled the pleasing aromas. My spirit seemed to feed on the soft, gentle music.

For the last time before my reading and massage began, I wondered, *Is there any chance Katherine will make her appointment?*

Breaking into my thoughts, Elke softly knocked on the door, entered, then sat in the empty chair facing me.

"So, are you a psychic? Or are you a massage therapist?"

"Both, and more," Elke softly responded, as she used her hands to direct my gaze toward the crystals on the massage table. I felt increasingly relaxed. My eyelids half closed.

As part of the chakra-balancing reading, Elke cautioned that I should stay focused on living a life of gratitude, whether or not I was facing troubles and trials. She also said I should appreciate the sacredness of the moments that make up my life, and really, truly, deeply enjoy my life, not just work, labor and rush through it. There was much more to what Elke had to say, but I was so groggy that I didn't consciously hear all of it.

When the reading was over, Elke removed the crystals from the massage table, then she gently placed them near the oils. She turned back the top flannel sheet. Next, she told me she'd step out of the room again while I disrobed and slipped between the sheets.

The massage was so totally relaxing that it seemed over far too soon. First one limb, then the next, received Elke's expert attention. Then my back, neck and head.

As the heavenly session ended, Elke said, "I have a message for you. It might not make sense to you now, but when you have all five messages that Spirit wants you to have, it will lead you to what you're looking for. In addition to giving you this message, I'm to tell you to be sure to attend tomorrow night's Native American healing circle. I'll give you the flyer. Your next clue will be given to you there. Do you understand?"

Although in a dreamy state, I replied, "Yes, I understand. But how do you know all this? I haven't even told Katherine that I want to attend the healing circle."

Ignoring my question, Elke continued, "Last night, I received a message for you. I've written it down so you don't have to remember it. Here it is," she said, as she handed me a piece of lemon-scented pastel yellow paper. In a neatly handwritten note, it read:

> You have done well so far, this I know,
> For you now have two clues in tow.
> Continue to go where you are asked to go,
> And you will soon learn where I was hidden long, long ago.

I silently read the message. When I looked up at Elke, she answered my unspoken question, "I don't know what it means, if that's what you're wondering. I just do as Spirit leads. I do feel there will be a woman at the healing circle tomorrow night who will want to talk with you. She will have the next clue. If you don't get every one of the clues, the line will be broken, and you will get no further instructions. So it's vital you attend. And if a woman asks you to follow her tomorrow night, do as she asks. Alright?"

I nodded.

Elke quietly led me back to the changing area. I took my second hot shower of the evening. This time, I used a cucumber-scented luxury soap. I was reluctant to wash off the exquisite oils Elke had used during the massage. But I needn't have worried. Even after the shower, the softness and fragrance of the oils remained.

I had planned to stop at Safeway, then get a light meal on the way back to the room. But after my session with Elke, I changed my mind. I decided to go directly back to the room and get some sleep.

The Jeep's clock reflected 9:57 p.m. when I drove into the parking lot at Kings Ransom. Katherine's Land Rover was nowhere to be seen. I reached for my backpack and headed for the room. When it dawned on me I might not see Katherine until morning, if then, I sighed deeply. I was too relaxed to care.

Once in the room, I gently set my backpack on one of the two chairs, placed my Tomcat next to my pillow, and turned down the bed. The fabric of my soft flannel pajamas felt wonderful against my fragrant skin. I inhaled deeply of the scent of roses from the bouquet I'd purchased the night before that now mingled with the scent from the oils Elke had used. *So this is what heaven feels like?*

I called Trevor and told him all was going well. He didn't need to know every detail about the ins and outs of the day. What I didn't say was I was getting mysterious clues, and that I was being watched and followed. *Why worry him? There is nothing he can do.*

The call was quick. I was exhausted. Relieved that all was well at home, I smiled as I snuggled into a soft pillow. I fell into a deep, peaceful sleep.

Chapter Thirty-Nine

Tuesday, October 11, 2011—4:30 a.m.

Heart pounding and sweat beading on my face and neck, I bolted wide awake. It took a couple of minutes before I realized I was safe in my room and had just had an incredibly vivid nightmare.

The nightmare seemed so real. Am I losing my mind? What's happening to me?

I continued to shiver as I sat, stiff and upright, eyes wide open. As I looked around the room, I replayed it in my mind.

In my nightmare, I saw the image of a beautiful, but crazed, young woman who ran toward me, screaming something I couldn't quite decipher. She had long flowing auburn hair that flew out behind her as she raced across the parking lot. She waved a jar. Her wild deep brown eyes stared in my direction as she used her right hand to unscrew the lid of a jar that she tightly clutched in her left hand. I was on the upstairs landing and had turned to watch her. When she reached the stairs, she ascended them two at a time. When the woman was close enough to me, she jerked the lid the rest of the way off the jar, then tried to throw the contents on me. In my vivid dream, I had quickly slipped my backpack off my shoulder, grabbed it with both hands, swung it at the woman's mid-section, bent my knees as I swung, and made solid contact. The woman yelled as she doubled over at the waist. She slipped backwards off the landing, and began to tumble down the stairs. Her arms flew out in front and above her. As she fell, the jar flew upward into the air. I tried to duck away from the contents, but a drop splashed onto my forearm, burning it almost to the bone. When I looked back at the woman, the jar had landed on her upper back. The contents had spilled down her neck, shoulders, and arms. Some of the liquid had splattered onto her legs and burned through her slacks. I watched spellbound as she wailed in agony.

That was all of the nightmare I remembered. Now, safe in my room, I wondered what prompted such a horrific dream.

Time passed, but I couldn't get back to sleep. I finally tossed back the covers and decided to dress. The clock on the night-stand reflected 4:51 a.m. I started the coffee maker, then made notes about the dream.

After an invigorating cold shower, followed by coffee and a yogurt, I poured myself a second cup of coffee and stepped onto the patio to watch Sedona come alive in the first golden rays of morning.

Chapter Forty

Tuesday, October 11, 2011—5:34 a.m.

I'd no sooner settled in at the patio table and was rethinking the nightmare when the unexpected commotion of Katherine bounding into the room caused me to flinch and spill coffee down the front of my blouse and onto my clean forest green shorts. As coffee soaked into the front of my white blouse, I pulled it away from my damp skin. I left the patio and stepped back into the room.

"Hey, Crissy!" Katherine said. "I'm glad you're up. We can get an early start. Just let me take a short nap for a couple of hours," she added, as she deposited her belongings on the floor near the table. As quickly as she had entered the room, she dashed into the bathroom and closed the door. In a couple of minutes, she reemerged. She had slipped into an over-sized T-shirt. She marched over and flipped on the TV, then bounded into bed.

I sat at the small table, coffee in hand. I had opened my mouth to tell Katherine about the new message from Elke, and my nightmare, but Katherine had turned her back and was already sound asleep, snoring softly.

I looked down to survey the damage of the spilled coffee. Then, blouse and shorts spotted with brown, I returned to the patio and continued to sip coffee as I enjoyed the sounds and sights of a new day dawning in Sedona.

"The massage was other-worldly," I said softly to myself as I watched the sky turn from charcoal to a deep navy blue. "I'm sorry you weren't able to experience it, too, Katherine."

The early morning air was thick and heavy. As I breathed in the liquid energy and peace, I was energized yet somehow relaxed.

Chapter Forty-One

Tuesday, October 11, 2011, 6:30 a.m.

As Katherine slept, the television blared. To the sound of an anchor reporting the latest traffic fatality, I changed into tan shorts and a fresh green and yellow floral blouse. Then I quietly left the room and went for a short walk in the cool morning air. Birds sang. Critters scurried. Motel guests began to stir and leave their rooms.

When I returned, Katherine was still sleeping soundly, so I took the map onto the patio to study it. A few minutes later, Katherine snapped wide awake, then said, "Crissy? You here?"

"I'm on the patio," I said softly so I wouldn't wake the other guests.

I heard the sudden flurry of movement inside as I picked up my schedules, flyers, and maps, and headed back inside. By the time I reentered the room, I heard the shower running. I clicked the television off.

Once Katherine was out of the shower, I asked, "Did you say Thunder Mountain looked good for this morning?"

Katherine continued to apply blush, then donned fresh red hiking shorts and a tan stretch-fabric blouse. "Yes. I think it's northwest of here, right?"

"Right. It's not far," I replied.

A couple more minutes of preparations and Katherine was ready.

While she finished repacking her backpack, I said, "You know, Katherine, a couple things happened last night that I need to tell you about. First, I got a new message while at the spa. It's really exciting. I think there's something to these messages. I also had a really vivid and awful dream last night. It was more like a nightmare, really. Maybe it was prophetic?"

"What was the message and what was the dream," she asked as she continued to work with her backpack while scanning the room for another water bottle and fresh fruit.

"Well . . ." I started to respond.

After she put a water bottle, a box of Jujy Fruit candy, and a couple of power bars into her backpack, Katherine cut me off and said, "I'm ready. Let's go." Then she grabbed a few other items, shoved those into her backpack, too, and headed out the door.

I stood and looked out the front window for a second. *I've been looking out a lot of windows in silence lately,* I mused. Then I put on my tennis shoes, picked up my backpack that I'd already repacked the night before, locked the sliding glass door, and followed Katherine to the parking lot.

"I'll drive," Katherine said.

"Thanks, but I'll drive my own vehicle," I replied. "I'll follow you. But don't worry if you lose me. I've reviewed the map, so I can find my way there. If we get separated, I'll meet you at the site."

Katherine stood and looked at me for a minute, one hand on the strap of her backpack, the other on her hip. Then, without comment, she spun around, got into her Rover, and sped out of the parking lot. Dust and gravel flew in her wake.

I carefully placed my torn floral denim backpack on the adjacent floorboard, got into my Jeep, then headed toward Thunder Mountain.

By the time we reached the parking area, it was well into morning. The sun was up, and all of nature seemed to embrace the new day. Birds sang; breezes blew; colorful leaves gently floated to the ground; quail scurried. It was magical.

"Does it feel like the wind is picking up?" I asked.

"I don't think so," she replied.

I breathed deeply of the fresh mountain air as Katherine rummaged around in the back of her Rover for her sun visor. When she found it, she said, "Ready, Little Buddy?" then spun on her heel and walked toward the rock formations.

"Ready," I responded, more to myself than to Katherine, since she was already out of ear shot.

Soon, my legs rebelled. My back began to ache under the weight of my backpack. My arms throbbed. My eyes felt gritty, although I'd flushed them with cool water repeatedly the night before.

We were dwarfed by enormous red, orange and golden rock formations. The morning sky had turned a light ice blue. Wispy off-white and butter-cream clouds continued to form and grow larger and more numerous as they softly pedaled across the sky.

"Are you coming?" Katherine yelled as she crunched ahead at warp speed on the red desert sand as she wound her way around shrubs and rocks. Before long, she had disappeared up Teacup Trail. Then she reappeared. When she did, she was so far ahead of me that she looked about an inch tall. I watched her stop to make sure I was still following her. When she spotted me, she waved widely and called, "How are you doing, Crissy?"

"Fine," I yelled back, as I continued to pant up the trail.

"Good. I'm making a left here," she yelled. "Don't make a right. That will take you to Coffeepot Rock and Sugarloaf. We want Thunder Mountain. Right?"

"Right," I responded, as I continued making my way, step by painful step, toward the divide in the trail. By the time I reached the place where Katherine had been, I could see she was already quite a long way up Thunder Mountain Trail and about to disappear around a shrub encircled boulder.

It's absurd to try and keep up with Katherine. I might as well enjoy the scenery and hike at my own pace. The best I can hope for is to stay within yelling range.

Two hours of hiking around boulders, over hills, and down gullies did not reveal any sign of a sphere. It had just left me tired and hungry.

Chapter Forty-Two

Tuesday, October 11, 2011—10:44 a.m.

I stopped and listened. Someone was coming up behind me on the path. The crunching of sand and pebbles was unmistakable. Slipping my hand inside my backpack, I wrapped it around my Beretta. When I turned around to face whomever was following me, I saw him.

A bone-thin medium-sized dog who appeared to be part Australian Blue Heeler was quietly following us. He looked ragged. His head was bent down toward the red earth and his fur was dirty. He cautiously took one step, and then another, in my direction.

I called for Katherine. She appeared and bounded down a small hillside. I pointed to the dog. She stopped. We both stared at the dog. He looked back at us, then lay down on the path.

"What do you think?" I asked. "If he's a stray, I think we should help him."

We looked at each other. Then we dug into our respective backpacks for food and water. I came up with a small plastic bowl and poured water into it. Katherine tore a peanut butter sandwich into bite size pieces. We set the food and water on a smooth rock, then backed away to watch the dog.

He stood and inched forward. He lapped the water, splashing it all over the rock. Next, he practically inhaled the food. As he ate, he watched us. When he'd eaten the entire sandwich, we inched closer to him. His tail wagged. He walked closer to us. I poured more water. He drank.

"Tell you what," I said. "We've been at this quite a while already today and have had no luck finding the sphere. It's time to turn back, anyway. So let's take him with us. We can drop him off at a veterinarian's office in town. If he's been abandoned, I'll assume financial responsibility. I'll pay whatever charges are incurred. And I'll take him home with me."

"You will?" Katherine said, still watching the dog.

"Cattle and sheep ranchers often use these sorts of dogs as work dogs," I explained. "They are often left to fend for themselves when they're not of use. Some of the men think it strengthens the dogs, weeds out the weak ones. Years ago, I was hiking on private wilderness property. A dog wanted to leave with me, but I left him at the ranch because I felt he belonged to someone else. Later, I learned the rancher just left the whole pack on its own, without food. He let the dogs fend for themselves and many of them died. I've felt guilty ever since. I still get depressed over it. Maybe if I help this little guy, I'll feel better."

"I see," Katherine responded, looking from me, then back to the dog. "Sure. It's your call. No dog should be left to roam around and starve. But I hope he doesn't slow us down."

"He won't. I'll call him Pedro. I'll board him until I leave," I said.

Pedro followed us back down the trail to my Jeep. He walked by my side the entire way. He readily hopped into the backseat of my Jeep. We took him to the first veterinarian's office we came to on Highway 89. It was 11:30 a.m. No one who worked there recognized him. I left a deposit with Jody, the assistant. She said the vet would check him out, and they would board him. I told Jody that if Pedro hadn't been claimed by an owner who was kind and responsible, I'd be back Friday afternoon to pick him up.

Chapter Forty-Three

Tuesday, October 11, 2011—12:19 p.m.

O nce Pedro was settled in with Jody, Katherine asked, "What do you want to do for lunch?"

"Any place is fine," I replied. "I can always find something on the menu, like a baked potato or salad. If you're up for a sandwich, I saw a Subway in the main part of town. It's not far. I live on Subways for lunch when I travel. Most of the Subway shops offer veggie patties now, and they're great."

"Okay. Subway it is," Katherine responded.

We bought sandwiches to go at 12:30 p.m., put them in our backpacks, and by 1:00 p.m. we had turned east on H-179 toward Baldwin. As we gathered our gear and started the hike, Katherine told me Baldwin was an area Joe and Manny had suggested.

"So now Joe and Manny are deciding where we hike and search?" I said.

"No. Just a suggestion," Katherine replied.

As we hiked, I continued to soak in the magical quality of the Sedona vortex. I lagged behind, which had become the norm, and tried not to miss any of the peace and beauty that engulfed me.

What Katherine didn't know was that Baldwin and Cathedral Rock were near one of Sedona's main vortexes. I didn't tell her about it because I didn't want another argument. When I had first mentioned that I wanted to visit the vortexes, she had said she didn't believe in the vortexes, then added, "Besides, the whole desert is a vortex."

After we hiked for a few minutes, we found an ideal place for lunch. We enjoyed our sandwiches surrounded by a view of colorful rock formations. The red desert earth was dotted with various types of shrubs and succulents. A warm gentle breeze played through the desert vegetation. After our sandwiches, an orange juice for me, and cola for Katherine, we donned our backpacks and resumed our search.

The area was magical.

Autumn scenery was enriched with a thick energy that permeated the air. It was as though I had again stepped into another dimension. As we trekked all over the Baldwin area, I felt a distinct increase in inner peace as well as increased mental clarity. The desire to stop and soak it in almost overwhelmed me.

Not Katherine. "Are you coming?" she yelled.

"Yes. I'm coming," I answered, as I hiked on behind her.

I had quickly tired of our hike over red dusty rock-strewn trails and pathways. The climb up into uncharted areas bothered me. Thoughts of snakes began to creep back into my thoughts.

Suddenly, Katherine screamed and jumped off a three foot boulder onto the path almost in front of me. Then she dashed over to the side of the road and tossed her backpack on the ground. She quickly dug through the contents, grabbed something, and dashed off again.

Alarmed, I reached for my Tomcat and ran after her.

When I reached her, I asked, "Katherine, what is it?"

Katherine had taken a magnifying glass from the jumbled belongings in her backpack. With the glass in her left hand, she had then run back around the boulder. All the while, she talked about "babies." Then she said, "Find my camera, will you? It's still in my backpack. Bring it. Fast." And with that, Katherine disappeared from sight.

"Babies?" I puzzled, confused. I put my gun away and relaxed somewhat. Katherine was apparently not in any danger. What constituted danger for me, and what constituted danger in Katherine's mind, were two totally different things.

Finally, I found her camera. Then, with camera in hand, I cautiously made my way around the boulder. I half walked, half slid, down into a minor gully where Katherine was astride an opening, one leg braced against a small boulder, the other foot wedged against the trunk of a shrub. As I walked closer, Katherine peered at something through her magnifying glass. When she heard me approach, she held out her right hand for her camera.

Curious, but not feeling too sure it was safe, I asked Katherine, "What is it?" as I handed her the camera.

"A tarantula with her babies," she loudly whispered. "Thanks for the camera."

"Do you think it's a good idea to disturb them? I hear they can give a foe a nasty bite. Not poisonous, perhaps, but plenty painful."

"They're just too cute," she replied, ignoring my caution. "Did you bring your camera, too?"

"No," I said, as I slid my backpack off my shoulders then sat some distance away on the warm red earth.

After she'd taken a few pictures of the mother with her babies, Katherine stood and checked her camera to make sure she had at least a couple of good photos of the spiders.

I waited.

Katherine was more charged than ever. I hadn't thought it possible, but now she had even more energy. As we left the spiders to continue searching the area for any sign or mark that might indicate a hidden or buried treasure, she almost jogged ahead of me.

"Have you ever considered you might be hyperactive?" I cautiously asked.

"Sure. I know I am," she said, as she dashed on in front of me.

It must be nice to have the energy of ten people, I mused.

The area around Cathedral Rock was quiet and peaceful. The red of the tall rock formations against the darkening blue sky had a captivating, tranquilizing effect. Large white clouds drifted across the azure sky. The air seemed even more liquid and heavy. I felt like I had been mildly drugged. I walked slowly while I experienced and absorbed the ever-changing atmosphere and panorama—nature's kaleidoscope—of ever-changing temperatures, vegetation, rock formations and colors, animal life and changing color of sky.

We didn't find anything that might relate to the sphere, so we had no reason to investigate further.

It was 3:31 p.m. when we paused to discuss our next move. Then, out of nowhere, a loud rumble caused us to turn and look toward the west. When we did, we saw a charcoal-gray wall of clouds with lightning ricocheting inside quickly approaching.

"Did you hear anything about a storm predicted for today?" I asked, wide-eyed, as I stared at the lightning that flashed onto distant rock formations.

"No. Nothing," Katherine replied, as she, too, watched the black cloud race in our direction.

Thunder shook the valley.

I had never seen Katherine frightened or even alarmed before, so her reaction surprised me. It also made me want to get back to the room as quickly as possible.

Her eyes widened. She stood, frozen, her eyes fixated on the advancing darkness. Then, as the storm intensified before our eyes, Katherine snapped to and almost yelled. "We *must* head back . . . *now.*" She turned and began to jog down the path toward where we had parked.

"Right," I said. "It's headed our way. More like racing our way."

By the time we reached our vehicles, the storm was upon us full-force. Lightning flashed all around; booming thunder jarred my spine. I shuddered with each new clap of thunder that immediately followed a bright flash of lightning.

Torrents of rain pelted us as the storm washed over the Verde Valley. Within seconds, we were soaked. As we climbed into our vehicles, water poured off us into our driver seats. I was relieved when we made it back to the main paved road. As I drove, my windshield wipers worked at maximum capacity, but it was still difficult to see the pavement and lines in the road.

I could barely make out Katherine's tail-lights ahead of me as I squinted to see through the pouring rain.

I glanced at the passenger side floorboard of my Jeep where water trickled from my saturated backpack. In an effort to dry off, I flipped on the heater. The heat didn't do much to dry me or my backpack, but before long drying mud caked my body. My backpack began to emit a foul odor. The inside of my Jeep grew warm and foggy.

Chapter Forty-Four

Tuesday, October 11, 2011—4:17 p.m.

Once I had sloshed back inside our room, I saw Katherine was in no better shape than I was. We both showered, Katherine first, then we changed into fresh, warm clothes. As I sat on the bed and listened to the thunder and pouring rain, Katherine said, "Did I tell you I'm meeting Joe later?"

"No," I replied. My back tightened and I again tasted fresh blood. "You did not." Then I realized why Katherine was so willing to cut the day short. Even in a severe storm it wouldn't have been out of character for Katherine to continue the search.

I sank into the bed and looked toward the sink where Katherine blow-dried her hair then pulled it back into a ponytail.

"I shouldn't be surprised, should I?" I said. "You know, Katherine, when you asked me to join you in your search for a mythical golden sphere, I agreed, even though it would require days of driving for me to get here, and then home. And I had to arrange for someone to cover my classes. All of this has disrupted my normally quiet and peaceful life, and it cost me a couple thousand dollars. But when I agreed to help you, I felt there was an unspoken agreement that you would at least be present. Not only to hike and search during the day, but for getting reacquainted in the evenings, as well. I thought we could catch up. Spend some time together. I didn't expect to be left behind days while you jetted around, or left alone nights while you played with Joe."

I took a breath and was about to continue when Katherine interrupted me and said, "Don't be upset, Crissy. I really like this guy. Okay?"

"Okay, Katherine." I said. "But you will be back for the Native American healing circle tonight, though, won't you? I'm sure the storm will have passed by then, and if there is something to these messages, I will get another clue tonight. I would rather not do this alone. I mean, it is *you* who wants to find the sphere, right? I'm just here to help. I don't want to risk missing part of the clues. I was told that if I missed one, that would end the clues, and I'd never find the sphere."

"Probably," she said.

"Probably?" I replied. "You are the one who wants to find this thing. I'm just here to help you." Catching myself, I slowed down, lowered my voice, and added, "Okay. The healing circle is at 8:00 p.m. I made a copy of the brochure for you. I'll leave it on the table. If you're not back by 7:00 p.m., I'll go ahead and take off, alone. I'm not sure how to find this place, especially in the dark. But I'll try. How's that sound?"

"Why did you schedule these activities for 8:00 p.m.?" Katherine asked.

"I didn't schedule the time for the healing circle," I replied. "It's a prearranged group event. That's just when they're meeting. For the rest of the activities, the times vary. It depends on who can fit us in, and when. I sent you an email, right? You told me to decide. I felt that after a day of hiking, it would be fun if we could shower, have a light dinner, and then rest. Then in the evening we could find something fun and novel to do. But that was before the first clue. And before you hooked up with Joe and Manny. Oddly, most of the activities I'd wanted to experience, like the massage, happen to be places I've been told have clues for me."

"Right," she responded. Then without looking in my direction, she said, "I'll try to be back by 7:00 p.m."

I inhaled deeply as Katherine strode to the door. "You know, Katherine, Elke said I'd get a third clue tonight."

"What?" she said.

"A third clue," I repeated.

"Oh, right. The clues. That's all pretty strange, isn't it? I can't believe you're taking such nonsense so seriously," she said.

"Speaking of strange," I replied, "I still feel someone's been watching us. Are you feeling that, too, now?"

"No. No. I'm not feeling anything like that," Katherine said, distracted. "Besides, who would want to follow us?" she added.

With thoughts of the men at the Purple Moon coming to mind, I thought, *I don't know who, but I'm sure someone is watching us.*

To lighten the conversation, since Katherine was eager to leave and almost to the door, I said, "Well, back to the clues. This whole thing about getting clues is really fascinating to me." I wanted to continue, but I'd already lost Katherine's attention. Her mind was on saying goodbye so she could leave to meet Joe. *What are the odds she'll be back in time?* I stopped talking when I heard the now familiar "click" of the door.

Chapter Forty-Five

Tuesday, October 11, 2011—5:33 p.m.

After Katherine left, I picked up the Shaman Stone from the table and again looked at it closely. The more I examined it, the surer I was it resembled my stone at home. It was almost identical in size and was shaped like a large lemon. I wondered why the Native Americans had called them Shaman Stones. I decided I'd look it up on the Internet when I got home. I put the stone back on the table by the fruit at the base of the flowers.

The storm had passed as quickly as it had come. I opened the patio door and let in the fresh, clean air. Then I decided to lock up and take a walk. I could go to the office to check for messages. Water dripped and splashed from the pines and sycamores. Pools dotted the pavement and reflected the golden glow of parking lot lights.

There were no new messages. The clerk and I chatted briefly. Sophie jumped onto the counter and purred loudly as I petted her.

I took a short walk to the Circle-K, shopped, and brought back a magazine to flip through while I waited for the healing circle. Sophie raced across the damp pavement to meet me, then darted in and out in front of where I walked. Once on the landing, she settled at the end of the walkway and cleaned her right paw.

As I slid my key-card in to the slot to open the door to my room, a man's deep voice broke my reverie. I quickly turned left to where he stood. He said, "Hello. Looks like we're neighbors. What did you think of that storm? Something, wasn't it?"

I studied him for a second. He was handsome. His had light golden brown eyes and his wide smile could be seen from two doors down the corridor. *Could he look any more like Rufus Sewell?* I wondered. *Men shouldn't be that gorgeous.* His wavy brown hair was perfectly trimmed and neatly combed. He had just a hint of five-o'clock shadow.

I paused.

He didn't go into his room, but walked closer to where I stood.

"I'm Ralph Siegel," he said, offering me his hand. His eyes danced with warmth and a hint of mischief. Something about him caused me to smile in return. *I'll bet wherever this man goes, fun follows.*

"Crystal O'Connor," I slowly replied. "I'm exhausted from hiking all day. I've got to go."

He continued to smile. His hair glistened in the evening parking lot lights. He was about a foot taller than me, lean and fit. His charcoal slacks and black shoes were topped by a black polo shirt open at the neck. He struck me as someone from a place like New York who was on vacation in the "wilds" of Sedona.

He paused, took another step toward me, then watched as I opened the door to my room. I felt uncomfortable with a stranger standing so close as I entered my room. I hesitated. When I did, I heard something crash inside my room. Instantly alert, I reached for my Beretta. Then I slowly opened the door as wide as I could.

As I eased the door open, I heard sounds on the patio. Then it was quiet.

Ralph reached for his cell to dial 9-1-1.

It took my eyes a minute to adjust to the dim light that filtered through the open sliding glass door as I cautiously stepped into the room. I flipped on the light switch. I had locked the patio door, yet it was wide open and the gauzy curtains floated inward on a gentle damp breeze. My heart hammered; my pulse quickened. My body rigid and alert, I peered around the edge of the door.

Ralph eased in behind me.

The room appeared vacant. I slowly checked out the bathroom and closet. Then the patio. No one was in sight.

I stepped back into the room to survey the damage. The entire room was in shambles. It hadn't just been searched, it had been totally torn apart. Clothes were strewn everywhere. Make-up and toiletries had been tossed into the sink. The contents of our suitcases had been dumped onto the beds, and our suitcases thrown to the side. Even the food from the small refrigerator had been pulled out and strewn on the counter and floor. The fruit on the small round table had been tossed around, and the flowers overturned. Water trickled around the Shaman Stone before dripping onto the carpet.

I stood, speechless, and surveyed the room. Finally, I heard the siren of the police car that pulled into the parking lot. I put my gun back in my backpack.

I waited. I listened. I didn't hear any nearby footsteps or other activity except for the officer who knocked, then walked into the room through the open door. His right hand rested on his weapon; his eyes surveyed the scene.

I stood in the middle of the room and assessed the mess the intruders had made of our belongings. Ralph stepped closer to me. The officer rechecked the bathroom and shower, closet, and patio. Neither Ralph nor I had seen anyone. The officer said he hadn't seen anyone suspicious when he drove into the parking lot.

Sophie walked in, jumped onto my bed, settled on my pillow, and resumed licking her white right paw. I had to smile as I watched her fearlessly make the room her own.

As I talked with the officer, I began to feel dizzy. I sat down and absentmindedly reached for the Shaman Stone. When I thought about Katherine out playing with Joe and Manny while I contended with a break-in, especially since it was most likely her openly sharing of information to anyone within earshot had caused it, my face began to burn and my breathing grew more ragged.

Ralph asked, "Are you okay? Is there anything I can do to help?"

"I'm fine," I said. "And, no, there's nothing you can do to help. I appreciate your offer. I just need to finish the police report. Then I'll pack and see if I can change rooms. I don't want to stay here after what happened tonight."

"Perhaps I can help with the move?" he said.

"Well, maybe," I said, still dazed. "If you're sure you don't mind. Maybe the police would like to talk with you, too."

Ralph talked with the second officer who had arrived. When we had both given complete reports, I called the motel office. I was relieved to learn they had a room we could move into, and that they were able to spare someone to help me transfer our belongings. They quickly sent a staff member with a wheeled cart to help ease the move. I was grateful for the company and the help.

Officer George Stampos arrived soon after the reports had been completed. Like before, he didn't smile. Officer Stampo's grey eyes remained flat and expressionless as he processed the scene. His six-foot body moved purposefully around the room as he examined each inch of the damage, taking photos as he talked.

When he got to the patio door, he said the glass had been cut near the lock, and that was most probably how the intruder had gained access. The patio table and chairs had been upturned. The officer concluded that the reason no one noticed or reported the break-in was probably because of the noise and damage caused by the storm. In his mid-forties, with light brown hair that had greyed at the temples, Officer Stampos had an air of distinction and authority. However, the more he talked, the more nervous I became.

The two officers who had taken the reports left. I was relieved that Officer Stampos stayed until the office staff came to help me change rooms. He then escorted me to the new room, checked it to make sure it was safe and secure, and stayed with me as I got unpacked and settled.

Before he left, Officer Stampos told me I should stop by the station before I left Sedona. "By then,' he said, "we might have some news for you about who did this."

The office personnel had been quick and kind when they helped me change rooms. Room 247 was somewhat secluded. The new room was also upstairs and had a nice view, but it was near the lobby at the front of the motel, which felt safer.

Chapter Forty-Six

Tuesday, October 11, 2011—6:22 p.m.

When I had completely removed all of our belongings out of room 247, it was locked and sealed by the officer. Katherine would have to go to the office to find out what had happened, and where to find me and our new room.

Ralph joined me as I quickly unpacked my, then Katherine's, belongings. Not wanting to be left alone in the new room after what had happened, and since there was still time before the Native American healing circle started, I took Ralph up on his offer of coffee and cheesecake. I followed him to the restaurant in my Jeep.

I began to feel better after a few minutes of sipping strong hot coffee and having comfort food in the form of rich and creamy New York cheesecake topped with boysenberries that oozed down the sides. As I ate, I thought, *With all these desserts, I think I'm going to return to Austin a bit plumper than when I left.* I enjoyed the diversion and time with Ralph. He was warm and witty. As we visited, he asked "So, Crystal, what brought you to Sedona?" Then he asked, "And why are you alone tonight? Where is your friend?"

Suddenly alert, I wondered, *How did he know about Katherine? Had he seen her around the motel?* "She's out with friends tonight," I said. "I've come from Austin to help her for a few days. For me, this is more of a pilgrimage, like a novena or vision quest. For her, I think it's half work, half play."

"Really?" he said, as he urged me on.

But I didn't want to say more, or to delve into my personal motivations for being in Sedona. I certainly wasn't going to discuss the fabled golden sphere with a complete stranger. So I changed the subject and asked what brought *him* to Sedona.

"A long over-due vacation," he answered, as he leaned back in his chair, coffee cup in hand, and smiled.

I thanked Ralph for the coffee and cheesecake, said goodbye, and, in spite of his objections, returned to the motel in case Katherine had shown up while I was gone.

She hadn't. *Great. I am in this alone . . . totally alone.*

The clock on the table reflected 6:57 p.m. *If Katherine isn't here in five minutes, I'm going without her.*

As I looked around the room, I wondered why anyone would ransack our belongings. *Was it a thief? A thrill seeker? What?* I wondered, unable to sit down and relax. When I reached the small dining table, I picked up the Shaman Stone and turned it over and over while pondering all that had happened.

I held the stone as I walked the length of the room and then turned and walked back again. Finally, I decided Katherine wasn't going to make it. So I set the stone back on the table and picked up my backpack.

When the phone rang, I jumped, and looked at it as if it were a diamondback. Then I set my backpack on the bed.

I took a deep breath, collected myself, and slowly picked up the receiver. It was Trevor. I exhaled. We talked. I didn't tell him half of what was going on because I didn't want to worry him. He said I sounded stressed, then asked why I'd changed rooms, I told him what had happened.

He was upset.

"I'm really tired, and I'm late for a Native American Healing Ceremony. I've got to go. Don't worry. This room is close to the office. I'm sure we'll be fine."

I picked up my backpack and headed toward the door. *Better a short chat than let Trevor know the details of all that's happened. He'd want me to come home immediately. But I promised Katherine I'd stay the whole week and help her.*

I stopped at the door, and took one last look around the room. I checked and rechecked the patio door. I looked into the closet. I went back to the patio door, pulled back the drapes, and looked to see if anyone was lurking outside. Finally, I decided to leave for the ceremony.

Chapter Forty-Seven

Tuesday, October 11, 2011, 7:08 p.m.

I jumped again when, at 7:08 p.m., Katherine sprang through the door.

"What happened?" Katherine asked, wide eyed, as she surveyed the new room. "They said at the office our room had been ransacked. I'm sorry I wasn't here to help you move everything. Are you okay?"

"Well, no, I'm not really okay. I'm worried . . ."

"Don't worry so much, Crissy," Katherine said. "But it is weird to think some dirty rotten bums invaded our world and touched our things, isn't it?"

"Yes, it is," I answered.

"Did they take anything?" Katherine asked, as she searched the room and looked through her things.

"Nothing that I'm aware of," I said.

Once she was satisfied that nothing had been taken, she sat down in a blue upholstered chair by the small round table and began rat-a-tatting her nails.

"Well, there really wasn't much in the room that was worth taking, was there? Are you sure you're okay?" Katherine asked again.

"I'm rattled, but fine," I replied. "A handsome hunk of a neighbor was going into his room as I entered ours. When he realized what happened, he helped with the police reports, and also helped me move things into this new room. Then we had coffee. He was really handsome and gracious, Katherine. You're single. Maybe you should meet him?"

"Why not?" she responded, as she took a jar of cherry butter from her backpack and plunked it down on the table. Answering my unspoken question, she said, "It's made here locally. I picked it up at a farmer's market in the Tlaquepaque center this evening. And I picked up some wonderful coffee liqueur, too. I thought we'd have it over ice cream later. Anyway," she continued, changing the subject to Joe, "I really like spending time with Joe. He's fun. And he's a great dancer." As she looked around the room again, she added, "Are you sure they didn't take anything? If they weren't thieves, why did they break in and trash our room?"

"Katherine, this is serious! If I had been in the room, I could have been injured, or even killed! Jam and liqueur are nice, but . . ." I let my words trail off as I realized Katherine wasn't really hearing me. "Like I said, nothing's gone that I'm aware of. But you should check your belongings yourself more carefully. Everything was a mess. What was there to take that had real value? Dirty clothes? Unless someone wanted our shampoo and makeup, clothes and snacks, they were out of luck, weren't they? I didn't look that closely at what you have, but I only had clothes, make-up, stuff like that, that I'd left in the room. My money, bank cards, jewelry and gun were with me."

"I didn't have anything in the room worth stealing, either. Thank God I was wearing my necklace," she added as she reached up to touch it. "It's irreplaceable."

"It's time to go to the Native American ceremony," I said with a sigh.

Katherine turned her head and looked out the window at the lights that had come on in the various shops. I could tell by the way she avoided eye contact that she didn't really want to go. I could have told her I'd go alone, but I didn't.

After one more long, exaggerated sigh, Katherine picked up her backpack, then said, "I'm not even remotely interested in anything Native American or metaphysical. But I'll go with you."

Even though she wasn't overly happy about it, I was glad Katherine decided to join me. After what had happened earlier, I didn't really want to be alone.

"I know you don't like this sort of thing," I said, "But the search for the sphere was your idea, right? I'm just trying to follow the clues and my intuition, and help you. Besides, if these clues are accurate, we should be led to the sphere."

"Then why all these accidents and problems?" Katherine asked.

"I don't know," I replied. "But often when I know I'm headed in the right direction, all sorts of things seem to come up to sidetrack or derail me. I've learned to suffer through them and follow my intuition and the signs, regardless."

"Fine," Katherine said, as she reached up with both hands and adjusted her blond-streaked golden pony tail.

Chapter Forty-Eight

Tuesday, October 11, 2011, 7:28 p.m.

I accepted Katherine's suggestion we ride together in her Rover. On the way to the ceremony Katherine asked about Joanie, an old high school friend.

"It's a long story," I said. "I don't want to talk about it."

"I thought you'd always stay in touch with Joanie?" Katherine asked, surprised.

"Me, too."

"Well, what happened?" Katherine pressed.

"Like most things, it's a long, long story," I responded, as I turned and looked out the passenger's window, and hoped she'd drop the subject.

"Okay, give me the short version, then," Katherine said again.

With a deep sigh, I continued to look upward at the towering mountains that were bathed in the light of the rising full moon.

"Okay, Katherine. Here's the short version. When I got my Master's degree, Joanie made a comment something like, 'I hope you don't think you're anything special. Don't forget, I know where you've been.' That pretty much ended our friendship," I said. "I had no idea she had felt superior to me all these years. Hers had been a rather cushy life, with her family putting her through college and helping her through graduate school. That she felt superior to me in any way both surprised and hurt me. I haven't spoken to her since."

Katherine asked, "What did she mean by that?"

"I'm not sure," I replied. "But whatever it was, exactly, it wasn't good. Anyway, we're no longer in touch."

For once, it was Katherine who was quiet. As she drove, she turned her head to survey the mountain range. "Well, I wouldn't let it bother you," she finally said. "Don't take it personally. It's her problem."

"I try not to take it personally," I said. "But it sure was a wake-up call. You think you know someone. Then zap! It's taken me a lifetime of study to conclude that we rarely even know ourselves, let alone anyone else."

"Do you know what she's doing now?" Katherine asked.

"I heard from a mutual acquaintance that Joanie had a series of set-backs. Seems she left her husband, then left her well-paying professional job, or lost it somehow. No one knows what happened for sure. Then she lost her rental properties, and even her home. That's all rumor. I don't know for sure. Anyway, that's the last I heard. I have no idea what she's doing now, nor do I care."

"That's really too bad, isn't it?" Katherine responded.

"It is as it is," I replied. "It's probably good for me to know how she really thought and felt about me. Now? It's odd, even to me, but I really don't care what happens to her."

Katherine gave me her now-familiar long, intense look as she drove down a narrow gravel road.

I turned and did what had become my normal response, looked out the window. As I did, I remembered my last painful conversation with Joanie.

When we found ourselves on a gravel utility road, Katherine realized we'd missed our turnoff on Lower Red Rock Loop Road. She made another quick U-turn and, with me hanging onto the door handle as I bobbed around the cab before I was able to right myself, we headed back in search of the turnoff.

When we found our street, we realized the brush and trees had grown so tall they almost totally hid the street sign. That probably didn't bother locals, but it made it hard for us out-of-towners to find the ceremony.

We finally found our way to the right street, located the home at the end of the cul-de-sac where the ceremony was to be held, and pulled into the gravel parking area that over-flowed with cars, trucks and SUVs. We were conspicuously late, so, when we didn't see a place to park in the lot, we parked on the street and quickly walked back to the house.

Chapter Forty-Nine

Tuesday, October 11, 2011, 8:10 p.m.

I had hoped to arrive early to get a feel for the ceremony before it began. Now, though, breathless, I looked for the quickest pathway to where the ceremony was being held.

A dark-haired woman wearing a long denim skirt and pink polka-dot blouse stood at the front of the ranch-style house. She directed us to take the path to the left that led to the back yard. I almost jogged on the freshly mowed grass to keep up with Katherine's long, quick strides.

The large unfenced yard backed up to the creek. A huge bonfire blazed in the center of the large grassy area. The fire was so huge that its heat warmed us even though we were standing near chairs about twenty feet from the flames. About forty metal folding chairs encircled the crackling fire. Embers floated upward into the night sky. A cool evening breeze wafted through the area.

The smell of the outdoors mingled with the aroma of burning wood. It reminded me of long-ago marshmallow and hot dog roasts on the beach. I glanced around at the people in attendance. The glow from the fire reflected off faces of happy, chattering participants. By the time we arrived, all the chairs were already occupied.

The Chief was seated across from us and watched as we considered where we would sit. Almost immediately the woman in the denim skirt appeared and walked quickly toward us carrying two small wooden folding chairs. When she arrived, people moved their chairs outward to expand the circle and make room for Katherine and me. I blushed. Katherine sighed.

The Chief continued to silently watch us. Although I tried to be inconspicuous, every eye had turned to watch us until we were finally settled. The Chief wore a full head-dress. I saw him clearly through fingers of flames that now reached high into the night sky. I was relieved the ceremony hadn't already begun. I exhaled and relaxed.

That was when I noticed the gurgle of the nearby creek. The sound was like soft relaxation music. If one listened, the creek could be heard above the crackle and pop of the bonfire and the hum of the participants as they continued to laugh and carry on noisy conversations.

All attendees seemed happy and upbeat. All except Katherine. She sighed, swung her crossed leg, and tapped her nails on her chair as she glanced around the circle.

On our way around the house to the backyard, we had passed two young Native American women who watched us as they talked in low, intense whispers. I now turned to look at them again. They continued to whisper and look in our direction.

A tall handsome young Native American man stood erect at the right side of the Chief. He wore faded jeans and a green plaid shirt. His long black glistening hair fell over his shoulders and cascaded halfway down his back. He was somber and quiet—as serious as the Chief. They continued to wait and observe the attendees.

A coyote howled in the distance. I looked at Katherine. She didn't appear to have heard it. She continued to tap her nails on the wooden chair and scan the other participants.

Chief Joseph Spotted Eagle spoke slowly and clearly. The group finally became quieter. Most looked to the Chief when he spoke. He introduced the young man behind him as his nephew, Sam Yellow Horse.

Sam Yellow Horse, too, watched intently and quietly as some of the people continued to talk and laugh among themselves. Something about him indicated he had greatness of soul—a mahatma. I remembered that Native Americans consider it rude to talk too much; they believe it a sign of an unsettled mind. I wondered if the other participants understood the leaders were waiting for them to become silent and attentive. I felt humbled in the presence of the Chief and bowed my head in reverence and respect.

Katherine continued to loudly express her dislike of all things Native American and metaphysical by sighing constantly, flipping her foot, turning in her chair, and tapping her nails. She began to talk. The more she talked, the louder she became. People turned to watch and listen.

I know Katherine. Why did I encourage her to join me? Alone, I could have relaxed and experienced the full impact of the ceremony.

Even the melodious sound of the nearby gurgling creek, the crackling fire, and the gentle breeze didn't quiet Katherine's complaints. When a coyote suddenly howled a second time louder than before everyone stopped and listened. Katherine stopped complaining, but soon began impatiently tapping her artificial nails on the arm of the folding chair again.

I turned and looked toward the creek when I heard a dog lapping water. The gentle evening wind stirred the nearby trees along the creek causing their leaves to softly cascade to the ground. Some fell on the creek and were gently whisked downstream. The light of the full moon played on the softly churning, bubbling creek creating gold and white shimmering disks here and there.

I was startled and my attention was abruptly drawn back to the circle when a hand softly rested my left shoulder. When I turned and looked up to face the woman, I recognized her as one of the two young Native Americans who had whispered and watched us as Katherine and I passed them earlier. Her low, soft voice politely asked, "Are you Blue Eagle?"

Wide-eyed, I slowly stood and turned to face her.

How could anyone possibly know my Native American name? I wondered. I felt especially self-conscious since Katherine now stared angrily and quizzically at me. I knew she'd expect an explanation on the drive back to the room. *That's just great! I don't want to have to explain anything else to Katherine. We live in totally different realities. And how can I explain this encounter to her? I don't even totally understand it myself.*

"Yes," I replied to the young woman. "I'm Blue Eagle."

"Will you please follow me? My friend has a message for you," she said.

I walked behind her silently until we reached the other woman, who was also young, slender and pretty.

From somewhere close by a coyote howled a third time.

"My name is Mary Star Blanket," she said. "This is Misty Rain Shadow. She has a message for you from Great Spirit."

I listened. I glanced back at Katherine. She craned her neck and turned completely around in her chair to watch me. My face grew warm. I blinked, then turned back to talk with Mary and Misty.

Mary was dressed in light blue jeans, cowboy boots, and a green and yellow paisley shirt. Her delicate perfume seemed familiar. Was it Ysatis? The breeze ruffled Mary's long black bangs as she turned and took a couple of steps back toward the fire. Having stepped away from me and Misty, Mary turned her face upward to look at the full moon. Both Mary Star Blanket and Misty Rain Shadow were silent for what seemed an eternity.

Misty was dressed in jeans, too, but had on a white cotton eyelet blouse with a ruffle that cascaded down the front and wafted in the gentle breeze, giving her an air of delicacy and femininity. She smelled of musk perfume. Her sandals were covered in silver and turquoise. Long delicate turquoise pierced earrings hung to her shoulders. A turquoise necklace cascaded down her blouse and peeked through the ruffles.

I silently waited.

Misty Rain Shadow took a long, deep breath, and began to quietly speak to me. Her voice was so low that I had to lean forward and strain to hear her. As I listened attentively, light from the fire reflected on her shiny braid.

"I believe Great Spirit wants me to tell you something," said the young woman with the large, soft doe-like brown eyes. "I was given word from Spirit last night that you would be here. I was instructed to give you the piece of the legend that has been passed down in my family for many generations." She stared at me silently for another minute before adding, "I expected you to be Native American. You don't look Indian. Are *you* really Blue Eagle?"

"Yes," I replied. I didn't explain how I was gifted with my Native name.

Taking another soft breath, Misty Rain Shadow turned and looked toward the creek. Then she turned back toward me, and said, "Here is the clue that I was told to give you. It will help lead you to what you seek, and what is seeking you."

She handed me a sheet of pastel lavender stationery with the carefully scripted words:

When the moon is full and the stars are soft in the night sky
Go to the place where the cards tell you who, when, where and
    why.
That is the place where you will be told
Where to find Me—the sphere of magic and gold.

"Along with instructions to share this message with you, Great Spirit informed me you were to make an appointment with Allison Vargas tomorrow night for a tarot card reading. Locals call her Alli. You can find her shop across the parking lot from Inner Light Spa. She'll be expecting your call to set up an appointment for tomorrow night. She has your next clue." With that, Misty held out a slender, well manicured hand, and said, "Goodbye."

I took the paper, shook her hand, thanked her, and said, "Goodbye."

She turned and walked to where her friend stood waiting. Then both women walked silently to the far side of the healing circle. They stood quietly, close to where Chief Spotted Eagle sat and looked from one attendee to the next, in clockwise order.

Both women watched me expressionlessly as I rejoined Katherine.

I put the note in my backpack, then slipped back into my seat. I waited. Almost immediately, the ceremony began.

My backpack rested on the green grass at my feet. Once I had made sure it was safe and secure, I sat up and intently watched the Chief.

As I stared into the hypnotic flames of the bonfire, I wondered again how they had known my Native American name. Then I cringed knowing Katherine would expect a full report.

The ceremony lasted a little over an hour. During that time, everyone considered what healing he or she most needed. Then each fetched a piece of wood and mentally transferred his or her healing needs onto the twig or stick. Next, each person made a full circle around the fire. In the end, the wood that now represented the healing need was placed into the flames, and the attendee returned to his or her seat. All the while, the Chief observed and gave instructions. I sensed he also prayed for the needs of the attendees.

During the entire ceremony, Katherine continued to loudly sigh, twitch, tap her foot, tap her nails, and roll her eyes. She turned her head and body this way and that as if she couldn't quite get comfortable. No one had to wonder whether or not she was having a good time.

I became distracted every time her artificial nails tapped on the wooden chair, which was probably her intent.

I sighed with relief when Chief Spotted Eagle dismissed the group with a solemn Indian blessing. I was glad Katherine could now leave the ceremony, although I would have liked to have stayed to talk with the other attendees. People appeared relaxed and pleasant as they stood and began to walk around. A few people sauntered toward the parking area. Most walked toward the fire and visited.

Chapter Fifty

But the moment the ceremony ended, Katherine jumped up from her chair as if bitten by a snake. Without a word, she turned and strode back toward the front of the house and through the parking area. Normally gregarious, she didn't stop to socialize with one person along the way. Not one. Especially me.

Me? I stood and watched Katherine stomp away from the circle before she turned the corner toward the front of the house. Then I picked up my backpack, took one last look around at the attendees, then gazed at the fire for a few minutes. When I looked over to where the Chief had sat, the chair was now empty. I glanced around the yard, then noticed the Chief stood at the back of his GMC SUV where he carefully and reverently packed his headdress into a large container in the back of his vehicle.

I decided Katherine was already so angry that things couldn't get any worse if I spent some more time at the healing circle. So I changed direction and walked back to where Mary Star Blanket and Misty Rain Shadow stood.

When she turned and acknowledged me, I said to Misty, "Why me? Why would Great Spirit tell *me* these things?"

Misty smiled slightly. Her large olive-shaped black eyes seemed to look through me then grow sad. She said, "I would have liked Great Spirit to have chosen an Indian. But who really knows the way of Great Spirit? Who can question? It is as Great Spirit wishes it to be." She then nodded a farewell to me, turned and walked to where the Chief talked with, or mostly listened to, the last of the attendees.

When I reached Katherine's Rover, the engine was already running. Her jaw was clenched. Both hands tightly gripped the steering wheel. She didn't wait for me to buckle my seatbelt before she slammed her vehicle into gear. Wheels spun and gravel flew as Katherine made a quick, sharp U-turn. Once again, I clung to the grab-bar and bobbed around the cabin of her Rover as she sped toward Upper Red Rock Loop. She flew away from the healing circle just as quickly as she could manage on the narrow dirt road that was lit only by moonlight.

"I take it you didn't like the healing circle?" I casually said, tired of her fits of temper.

"Crissy, I don't understand how you can you waste your time on these things," Katherine fumed. "It's all such nonsense!"

"I told you, Misty Rain Shadow and Mary Star Blanket had another clue for me. You're the one who wanted my help finding the sphere. I thought you'd be glad . . ."

Katherine cut me off. "Fine, Crystal. Can we discuss this later? And what's this about you being called 'Blue Eagle'? You're not Native American. Well, are you?"

My mind began to feel numb. I took what felt like my hundredth deep breath since Katherine and I had reconnected. I thought about how best to make a clear and *short* response. I replied, "Well . . . while in graduate school, I studied the Native American Vision Quest. When I finished the study, I was given my Native American name, along with an explanation of its meaning. I like it—*a lot*. It's very private and sacred to me." I paused and waited. When Katherine didn't respond, I changed the subject. "You seem different. Sort of distant. Are you alright?"

"I'm just disgusted," she snapped. Katherine made a sharp left that threw me into the car door. We were almost back to our room. I was ready to rest. "You know, Katherine, if you throw me into the door like that many more times I'm going to have a permanent nasty bruise."

Katherine didn't respond.

While Katherine zoomed down the highway, I thought about the new clue. Then I reflected on the peace and natural beauty of the sacred ceremony. Katherine's reaction to it puzzled me. But I didn't dwell on Katherine's attitude toward Native American healing and spirituality. Instead, my mind turned back to the clues. I wondered what the next clue would reveal. I also wondered why Katherine seemed so disinterested, even angry, that I was receiving a steady stream of clues.

When we were almost back at the motel, Katherine broke into my thoughts, and said, "Joe loaned me his cell for the evening. I called him on Manny's cell while I was waiting for you. He and I are going out for drinks and dancing as soon as I drop you off. I know you're still upset after our room was ransacked, but I'm sure you'll be fine. Besides, I need to get away from all this Indian woo-woo stuff."

I paused, then said, "You aren't interested enough to ask about the clue I got tonight? You haven't even wanted to read or study any of the clues, for that matter." Then I realized that since Katherine had met Joe, she had wanted to spend all her time with him. She was probably sorry she had asked for my help. I felt like I was in her way. She still wanted to find the sphere. But it had taken second chair to her time with Joe. And she really didn't want to have to deal with me in the evenings. She felt she should be with me, since she'd asked me to join her to help search and get reacquainted. But since she had met Joe, she really *wanted* to be with him. Not me.

I wondered if I should tell her I had been feeling led to spend some time in the desert, and specifically Sedona, long before her call. I decided she would simply dismiss my leading like she did everything else metaphysical. I remained silent.

Finally, I responded, "You're leaving me alone after what happened last night in our other room? If you hadn't told so many people about the sphere, we probably wouldn't have been ransacked."

Then I caught myself and decided if she wanted to go out with Joe, she wanted to go. I was disappointed, but I could take care of myself. In fact, I would appreciate some more time alone to think about all that had happened and what the clues meant.

My breath slowed as I measured my words, and said, "You know, Katherine, a woman stopped me at the ceremony, just like Elke said she would. She knew my Native American name. Only a handful of other people on planet Earth know it, and they don't live in Arizona. She gave me another clue. Aren't you even remotely interested?"

Katherine's head snapped around. Her green eyes flashed briefly, then she said, "Of course I am! But I don't take the clues you've been getting all that seriously. I think it's a joke. With your help, I'll find that sphere by searching for it in the formations, gullies and valleys. You know I don't believe in all that 'other world' nonsense that you seem to have gravitated to lately."

I turned and looked back out the passenger window for a minute before I said, "What is it about Joe you find so interesting? You've liked him from the moment you met him, haven't you? You meet men all the time who try to get your attention and get you interested in them, and you normally ignore them. What's so special about Joe?

"I don't know," Katherine responded. "I just like him."

Obviously. But are these guys safe? Or do they just want to get more information about the sphere?

I dropped the subject and pondered the message from Misty. When I looked back out the window, the full moon reflected off the Sedona rock formations and surrounding countryside. I rolled down my window to enjoy the magic of the night sounds and the cool breeze.

Before long, I was unceremoniously left—or was it dumped?—at the foot of the stairs, backpack in hand. By the time I was at the top of the landing, Katherine had pulled out of the parking lot. Sophie walked up to me, rubbed on my leg, and purred. I stopped and stroked her for a couple of minutes, then turned and slowly walked up the stairs. Sophie trotted at my side.

I cautiously entered my new room. It was quiet and peaceful and *undisturbed*. Everything was as I'd left it.

Relieved, I put my backpack in the chair, then pulled the new clue out of the side pocket. I read and reread it. Then I arranged all of the clues on the table next to the Shaman Stone. After a few minutes, I picked up a banana, walked to the night stand, and called Trevor. I knew he would like to hear about the Native American ceremony. The clue? I would think about it some more later.

Between my room being ransacked and the Native American Healing Ceremony, I was so exhausted that when I finally slipped into bed I quickly fell into a deep sleep.

Chapter Fifty-One

Wednesday, October 12, 2011, 5:30 a.m.

I awoke in the pre-dawn hours to the sound of the shower running. Katherine had returned. Normally a light sleeper, I had slept so soundly I hadn't even heard her enter the room. Steam escaped from under the bathroom door. The smell of Katherine's raspberry-scented shampoo filled the room.

I cracked the patio door for fresh air, but made sure the screen door stayed locked. Then I made coffee for myself and hot chocolate for Katherine. While the coffee brewed, I munched on a piece of day-old bagel, slathered in cherry butter. Since I almost never ate bagels, it was a small vacation indulgence that I totally enjoyed.

While I laid out my white jean shorts and olive green T-shirt, I mentally reviewed the three clues I'd been given. They didn't tell me anything concrete. Just where and when to get the next clue. *Why do I spend my days hiking, and my nights running around Sedona getting strange clues from unusual people? And why am I being followed? What's going on? Actually, what am I even doing here?*

The aroma of fresh coffee seduced my attention. I added milk, then sat down on one of the upholstered chairs at the small brown table and pulled the three clues out of the side pocket of my backpack.

I read and reread each clue.

Katherine stepped out of the bathroom and said, "So, Little Buddy, what's up? It's almost light. Are you about ready?"

"I'm reading the clues," I said. "And, no, I'm not ready. I haven't even finished my coffee or showered. About the clues, they don't seem to really tell me anything, except where to get the next clue."

Katherine drank her hot chocolate and peeled an orange. Then she put on fresh tan hiking shorts and a soft teal T-shirt.

I took a quick shower. I had abandoned my jeans. One pair was ruined. The other pair was difficult to hike in because it bound my legs when I hiked. Besides, I wanted to save my last fresh pair of jeans for the drive home.

My eyes burned and the bones in my face ached as I sat at the table and finished my coffee, ate the last of the bagel, and peeled a banana.

While I took my vitamins with orange juice, Katherine walked over to join me at the table. When she did, she spotted the small tattoo on the inside of my left ankle. She gasped, grabbed my ankle, and twisted my foot to get a better look.

Startled, I jumped and spilled juice on the table. I almost knocked over my coffee. "What are you doing?" I said, as I pulled my foot free from her grip.

"What have you done? Does that wash off?" she said.

"My tattoo? No, it doesn't wash off. It's permanent," I replied.

"How could you do such a thing to your body?" she wailed as if I'd become "the illustrated woman."

I took another long, slow, deep breath, sighed, looked toward the ceiling, and pondered a way to quickly answer her question and change the subject. *How can I best explain this?* "Well, Katherine, it's another long story. Perhaps it's best saved for later?"

"Give me the short version," she quickly rejoined.

I took another long, slow, deep breath and wondered how many explanatory "short versions" I would give Katherine before I left for home. Then in a low voice, I said, "Well, okay. Here's the short version. Did you see *What The Bleep Do We Know?* when it came out a few years ago?"

"No," Katherine said, as she stood firmly in place in her military pose and unsmilingly watched me.

I had to deliberately work to not squirm under her intense gaze. "Okay," I said. "Then have you read the work of Dr. Emoto that was highlighted in the film?"

"No," she said, as she continued to stare at me, arms crossed over her chest, brow furrowed.

"Okay then. Well, here's the short version. I saw *What The Bleep Do We Know?* and I was so impressed with Dr. Emoto's work about the impact of emotions on water that I purchased and read all of his books. As I read about the effect words and thoughts have on water, my excitement and enthusiasm grew to the point I designed this tattoo as a way to permanently communicate my deepest desires and intentions to my heart, mind, body and soul. There. You have the short version. Now can we get on with our plans for the day?"

"Your mother would have been so disappointed," she said.

Surprised she would bring up my mother, I replied, "No, she wouldn't. She would have approved and been pleased."

Katherine was obviously dissatisfied with my response, but appeared to accept it as final. She spun around on her bare heel, stomped back to her bed, and began digging through her backpack. As she re-packed, she seemed to calm down.

I had long ago realized how quickly my anger could escalate when fueled by negative exchanges, so I let go of my feelings of invasion and of Katherine's continual disapproval by taking deliberate deep breaths. At the same time, I calmed myself further by mentally counting backward from ten to one.

After a brief strained silence, I asked, "What do you *really* think, Katherine? Do you think we're any closer to the whereabouts of the sphere? Do you think there's a chance there might be something to these messages?"

"I don't think we're any closer to the sphere," she answered. "But at least we know where not to continue to look. And I certainly don't believe there's anything to the weird clues you've been getting. But I don't know," she added. Brow still furrowed, she walked to the sink and adjusted her thick golden ponytail. "Being around you again has been bizarre. I watched your wounds heal by themselves after your horrible fall down the mountainside the other day. Now you're getting these odd puzzle pieces of clues from strange people. Our room was ransacked. I don't know . . . I just don't know."

Katherine turned and looked at me, then added, "Maybe there *is* something to this metaphysical stuff you talk about." After a short pause, she smiled, slapped her right palm on the table, and said, "But I really don't think so. But Joe's right," she smiled. "I shouldn't make so many negative remarks about you and your beliefs. Right?"

I was so surprised by Katherine's change of heart and near-apology that I couldn't think of anything to say other than, "It's okay, Katherine. No harm done." Then I added, "You say negative things to Joe about me?"

She ignored my question.

We decided we'd search Deadman's Pass at first light. If we didn't have any luck there, we'd change our search to the Devils Bridge area. As I looked on the map, I realized that would take us closer to another major vortex near Boynton canyon. I again decided not to say anything to Katherine about vortexes. I wanted to silently absorb the experience.

While I ate another half of day-old bagel, I sipped on a second cup of coffee. I hoped it would help energize me.

Katherine had gotten ready in record time and was obviously eager to start the search even though it was still dark. As I ate and drank, she paced and tapped her fingers on whatever surface was available. When she sat down, she tapped her nails on the table. The more she fidgeted and darted around the room, the more I wondered what kind of day we were going to have.

Chapter Fifty-Two

Wednesday, October 12, 2011, 6:05 a.m.

Suddenly, Katherine stood and dashed to the sliding glass patio door. She looked outside, then turned back to face me and, almost sweetly, proposed something out of the ordinary. With the lights of Sedona as her backdrop, she said, "Why don't we go into town for an early breakfast before we start to hike today? We can get a nice hot breakfast, then start our search. I'm sure the café we went to Sunday night is open for breakfast. My treat."

Thrown off-guard by her sudden transformation, it took me a couple of seconds to respond. "Why not? It will be fun. Maybe a change of pace would be good for us," I said, "As long as we take separate vehicles. Breakfast out does sound nice, Katherine."

Katherine perked up and seemed much happier as she said, "Great, Crissy. Are you ready?"

"I just need to tie my hair back," I replied. I quickly pulled it back and tied it. I put on what had once been new white tennis shoes, and picked up my old faithful faded red sweatshirt. After closing and locking the patio door, I picked up my backpack and followed Katherine out of the room.

When I stepped onto the landing, I was instantly invigorated by the cool, crisp high-desert morning air. The motel was still. Not even the javelinas stirred. Only a few birds sang in the early morning. I turned when I heard a soft noise to my right and spotted Sophie as she padded up to the base of the stairs. I stroked her, then stepped into the parking lot. Sophie rubbed her soft furry body against my bare leg, then turned and stepped between my tennis shoes as she stroked her multi-colored tail against my ankle. She looked up, meowed softly, then trotted up the stairs and walked down the landing.

Katherine stood by her Land Rover and smiled. "That cat must really like you. Ready?"

"Sure. I'm ready," I replied. "I have the maps and some guide books to check out over breakfast."

Katherine paused, then looked away before she got into her Rover and headed out of the parking lot.

While I drove, the cloudless morning sky turned light grey. The usual slight breeze played through the bushes and trees. Leaves fell. When I stopped at a red light, I looked upward toward the tops of surrounding rock formations. The air was liquid and heavy. I sighed. All was well.

The stir of another new day began. Lights in shop windows went off. The earlier unexpected storm had passed as quickly as it had come, leaving Sedona fresh and clean. The day promised to be another perfect 74 degrees. I absorbed the wonder of Sedona in the still of morning.

When I pulled into the already near-full parking lot, the first thing I noticed was a shiny new black Hummer. My chest tightened and my head began to ache. *She wouldn't have done this deliberately?* I slowly drove by the Hummer and checked out the license plate. Manny! *After Casner Canyon, she wouldn't dare have set this up,* I steamed. My face grew hot and my back tightened. As I walked toward the front door where Katherine waited, I again tasted blood. With each step, my heart rate increased. I took deliberate deep breaths to calm myself. It didn't work. I felt my face continue to heat. I knew it was crimson. Blood throbbed in my temples. The second jolt of pain from my upper lip let me know I had bitten it yet again.

As I charged toward Katherine, I opened my mouth to speak. But before I was close enough to say anything, she turned and headed into the restaurant. Once I was inside, she turned toward me, and said, "Hey. Look. Joe and Manny," as she quickly made her way to their booth. Smiles and laughter ensued.

I stood by the door and wondered if I should just leave them there. The happier they seemed, the angrier I became. I turned and looked back out into the parking lot toward my Jeep. *Should I just split and spend the day around Sedona on my own?*

Joe's voice broke into my thoughts. "Hi, Crystal," he called from across the main dining room that was filling with early morning tourists and locals. "We're glad you could make it. Come on. Join us." By their posture and body language, I suspected that they had been talking about me.

Never one to make a scene, I reluctantly walked toward the booth to join them. Even my arms felt hot. When I reached the booth, both men slipped out and stood while I slid in next to Manny. I glared at Katherine, who was already snugly nestled beside Joe. She averted her eyes, smiled at Joe, and bantered about this and that inane topic.

Everything within me screamed in protest, yet I submitted myself to what seemed an almost inescapable trap.

As I stared blindly at the menu, Manny again put his arm behind the back of our vinyl booth. "What kind of plans do you two have for the day?" he asked. My anger toward Katherine grew as I evaded Manny's question and continued to stare at the menu.

Although furious with Katherine, I noticed that Manny's intoxicating spice and musk cologne permeated the air around our booth and competed with the nearby aroma of pancakes, fried eggs, and bacon that wafted through the room. He had changed from his trademark black T-shirt into a deep golden-brown T-shirt that brought out gold flecks in his soft brown eyes. His coffee brown cargo pants and hiking boots looked new.

I didn't like that my focus swayed more toward Manny than breakfast. I decided I had better eat quickly, then leave. Manny's charm was as intoxicating as his cologne. *I'll bet this is how women feel around George Clooney*, I mused.

I forced my attention across the booth to where Katherine laughed and chatted with Joe. I liked Joe. Even so, I was certain he was not a salesman. Neither was Manny. I was sure of it.

So who are they? And why did they lie to us about their professions? Why do we continually bump into them? Is Joe just interested in Katherine? Or is it the sphere they are interested in?

My poached egg on toast and coffee arrived quickly, along with the rest of our order. Katherine had pancakes, eggs, and bacon with hot chocolate. Joe had steak and eggs with coffee. Manny had what I had ordered—poached eggs on toast with a side of fresh fruit and coffee.

The small talk at the table was amiable, but I was eager to leave.

This time, I didn't try to pay. I sat mutely by and watched when Joe reached for the bill. Then I thanked him for breakfast, gathered my belongings, and left the building.

Katherine and Manny continued to sit at the table and laugh and chat while Joe made his way to the cash register.

I hoped Katherine would not invite Joe and Manny to join us, or even tell them where we would be searching. But I had given up. What she did, she did. It was her search. Her call.

By the time I reached my Jeep, my face still burned and tears of anger flooded my eyes. To be deliberately misled by someone—betrayed—especially by a long-time friend for whom I had sacrificed significantly in an effort to help her, played havoc with my mind and emotions.

I slammed things around in the back of my Jeep as I rearranged supplies. When Katherine approached, I turned to confront her. "You knowingly lied to me, didn't you? You knew Joe and Manny would to be here. Isn't that right?"

"I didn't really lie," Katherine said, slowly. She looked past me into the window of my Jeep. "I just didn't want to upset you. You wouldn't have come if you knew they were going to be here."

"That's right. I wouldn't have. Knowing that was all the more reason you should have told me up front," I spat at her. I felt my outrage grow with every word. "You know, Katherine, to tell only one part of the truth is to deliberately lie. I can't believe you'd be so deceitful, *especially to me!* There's no other way to look at it. I thought we were friends, but you deliberately deceived me. In my book, that's not a friend. I would never have thought you of all people would do such a thing."

Katherine scowled. Her eyes looked weary as she reached up to touch her necklace, then said, "You're too serious, Crissy. You need to get out more and have more fun. You could be more friendly, you know."

That did it! I would have exploded if I hadn't noticed Joe and Manny walking up behind Katherine. I tried to keep my voice low, but I continued to tell Katherine what I thought about what she had done. "You set me up, Katherine. You were dishonest. What a betrayal. How could you?!"

Joe stepped up and put an arm around Katherine's shoulders, which put an end to our conversation. As he did, he said, "We didn't mean to upset you, Crystal. Really. We didn't. We just wanted to have a nice breakfast, then hike."

"We?" I said. "When, exactly, did you become a part of this equation?"

"When Katherine invited me to breakfast," he said, as he slipped his arm down around Katherine's waist.

"Katherine invited you to join us today?" I asked, astonished.

"Well, yes," Joe said, as he glanced at Katherine.

Joe and Manny's embarrassment paled in comparison to my growing anger.

Manny, who had stood nearby, silent, his head slightly bowed, stepped forward and said, "I think we're in the way here, Joe. There's obviously been a mis-communication someplace. We'd better leave."

"You're right," Joe answered, as he backed away from Katherine.

Katherine glared at me.

I said, "You know, I don't really feel like hiking anymore, anyway. Why don't you guys stay and hike with Katherine. She'd obviously appreciate your company."

"We're gone," Joe said, then added to Katherine, "See you tonight?"

"Absolutely," Katherine said.

"I hope to see you later, Crystal" Manny added. Then he turned and followed Joe.

As they left, I said to Katherine, "I'm out of here," and left Katherine standing in the parking lot.

Chapter Fifty-Three

Wednesday, October 12, 2011, 7:15 a.m.

I headed toward Deadmans Pass. My skin was prickly, my hands shook, and my head felt light as I drove down Highway 89. My vision blurred as tears began to slip down my hot cheeks.

I arrived at Deadmans Pass slightly after 7:30 a.m. Katherine was close on my bumper. I was relieved to see no other vehicles had followed her up to the trailhead.

I parked, grabbed my torn and dirty backpack, checked my Beretta, then stomped up the trail at warp speed.

Katherine parked, then called for me to wait up for her.

I ignored her and walked on. It's amazing how betrayal and stone-cold fury can energize a person. I was in full-throttle by the time I heard Katherine yell, "Crissy. Crissy! Will you stop!?"

I continued to ignore her and kept going, almost jogging, up the narrow trail.

When Katherine caught up with me, she brought up the fiasco at breakfast.

"I refuse to discuss it any further," I snapped. "I'll talk with you about it later, *maybe,* when I'm calmer. *If* I'm ever calmer."

"Okay, Crissy. But I think you're making way too much out of this."

I suddenly stopped, spun on my heel, and said, "Frankly, Katherine, I no longer care what you think!" Then I spun back around and continued walking.

Katherine trailed behind.

After an hour of silent hiking, we hadn't spotted anything that looked even remotely like a place where a sphere could be hidden. So we decided to switch locations and search nearby Devils Bridge.

Once at Devils Bridge, we re-parked. The name should have given me a clue as to what I was in for, but it hadn't dawned on me until that moment that it was probably a challenging hike to the end of the bridge.

First, we climbed rock formations, searched alongside trails, and slid down into gullies. The shrubs, cacti and small trees were a welcome change from the sparse vegetation where we'd just hiked. The sky had turned a soft robin-egg-blue with sprays of softly threaded white clouds. I was embraced by a soft breeze. The morning sun warmed my skin. Quail and lizards scurried and chattered around us.

Katherine broke into my reverie when she suddenly stopped in front of me.

I slipped my hand into my backpack to retrieve the Beretta as I walked closer to where Katherine stood motionless. Then, as suddenly as she'd stopped, Katherine started to walk again. Relieved, I returned my gun to my backpack, and walked on.

It was time to stop. Sweat soaked through my thin blouse. My breathing was labored. I needed a rest and a snack. Katherine wanted to continue to hike and search. "We can't waste daylight," she said, as she marched onward.

I didn't follow her. *'Waste?'* I thought as I sat on the red earth. *Since when is it a 'waste' to rest, eat and revive oneself?*

I ate half an almond butter sandwich and drank a bottle of water. Once refreshed, I stood and dusted myself off. Then I again followed Katherine over, around, and up the dusty red landscape.

I kept a few yards between us as we climbed toward the top of yet another incline. We stopped periodically to search behind shrubs, around trees, and down gullies and ravines. Then we came to Devils Bridge.

I froze when I saw it.

The countryside had lost none of its splendor or enchantment, yet for me it seemed to disappear as I focused on the task at hand—getting across Devils Bridge.

"Coming?" Katherine called.

"Soon," I replied.

Katherine thrust her camera in my direction and said, "You don't mind, do you?" Then she jogged out to the center of the high, narrow overpass.

By the time she was positioned—legs firmly planted, head held high, shoulders back, hands thrust into the air in a victorious Rocky pose—she faced the morning sun that reflected off her radiant smile. Her golden hair glistened in the bright sunlight.

I aimed the camera, but the edge of a cloud glided in front of the sun. I waited for it to pass. Then I took a couple of pictures while Katherine pranced and posed. Apparently satisfied, Katherine once again thrust her arms into the air and exclaimed, "*This* is my church!" Then she turned and confidently strode to the end of the formation.

This view, these rock formations, and whatever it is that is in the air, do all conspire to bring one closer to the Divine, I mused, as I surveyed the panorama of red rock formations, valleys, sky and clouds.

All too soon my thoughts turned back to the Bridge. *To try, or not to try? That is the question. God, first, I had to contend with my claustrophobia. Now, it's my fear of heights. This looks dangerous to me. One slip . . .*

Katherine broke into my thoughts, "Come on, Little Buddy. What's the matter? It's a piece of cake. You can do this."

"Have you forgotten my dislike of heights," I said, as I eyed the bridge. "One of us is a risk-taker. The other is not."

"It's not that steep or narrow," Katherine challenged.

"Maybe not to you," I said. I put Katherine's camera around my neck and took small and careful steps onto Devils Bridge. As I advanced on the narrow, dusty red rock formation, I slipped and slid forward on pebbles. I looked down as I struggled to regain my balance. *How does one maintain a sense of dignity while negotiating this terrain?* More pebbles cascaded downward into the gully. My heart beat faster. Finally, I made it across the narrowest part of the bridge.

Katherine watched me edge forward, then said, "Great job! You're doing it! Come on. Keep walking. You can make it. Lots of people wouldn't even try."

Once I'd reached the far side of the bridge, I exhaled, and surveyed the view of distant mountains and valleys from my new vantage point. It was definitely worth the effort.

As I looked out over the high desert valley at trees, brush and red rock formations, I felt an unusual energetic rush—as if in synch with the universe. Once I'd regained my equilibrium, I said, "You know, Katherine, if Native Americans had patron saints, I think yours would have been the Skeleton Man. He was said to have taught the Native people not to fear death. You obviously don't give safety or death a second thought when you're in nature or on an expedition."

Katherine listened as she searched the small patch of earth and rock she stood on. I stood still and absorbed the positive energy of the area.

We found nothing, so we decided to head back.

Katherine practically jogged back over the bridge. I walked as fast as I could, which meant I took small, deliberate steps.

Once on the other side, I sat and rested. I could hear Katherine's voice, but couldn't make out the exact words. Her words seemed strange, as if filtered through an atmosphere liquid and thick with positive energy.

Chapter Fifty-Four

When we reached the parking area, we decided to have lunch at a small Mexican restaurant we'd passed on the way out of town that morning. When we entered, the interior looked old and well-worn. The blue fabric booths were torn and patched. I was so tired I melted into a lumpy seat, then stared glassy-eyed at the cars that whizzed past in front of the restaurant on 89.

Ready for another shower and nap, I began to long for the comfort of my room. After the waitress took our orders—mine, a cheese enchilada with flan and coffee for dessert; Katherine's, a hungry-man burrito and cola with an ice cream sundae for dessert—we sat in silence. The morning had challenged us both.

When our food arrived, I reminded Katherine about our appointments with Alli for the tarot card readings that evening.

I was disappointed, but not surprised, when Katherine told me she had changed her mind, and wanted to cancel her appointment with Alli. Since the moon was full, she said, she had arranged to hike after dark with Joe, then she and Joe would meet Manny for drinks and dancing.

We compromised. There was just enough daylight left to squeeze in a search of Turkey Creek Road. *Another night with Joe? I wonder if Turkey Creek Road was his idea?* "You're not telling Joe and Manny about the messages I've been receiving, are you?" I asked.

"Hey! How about we stop at the chocolate shop when we leave here?" Katherine replied.

Evasion tells me all I need to know. She must have told them. "Sure. I don't mind stopping for chocolate. Does your evasion mean I will not only attend the reading with Alli alone tonight, but also that Joe and Manny know about the clues?"

Katherine turned and looked at me, unsmiling. Then she said, "Well, I did share a little bit about the clues with them, but I don't think they take the clues any more seriously than I do." She changed the subject, and said, "If you don't eat chocolate or sugar or meat these days, what *do* you eat?"

"I guess I have changed a lot," I replied. "I didn't realize just how much until this week here with you. To answer your question, I eat all sorts of things." I knew Katherine was basically disinterested in my diet, so I dropped it.

Chapter Fifty-Five

Wednesday, October 12, 2011, 12:13 p.m.

After the stop at the chocolate shop, where Katherine stocked up on chocolate candy and I got a cherry-filled truffle, we headed to Turkey Creek Road. I drove my Jeep; Katherine her Rover. I refused to risk another of Katherine's tricks.

During the drive, I mused, *I wonder how much of this my body and nerves can stand?*

After parking at the trailhead to Turkey Creek Road, we hiked a short distance. We quickly decided there was nothing to be found along the trail. So, although it was peppered with buildings and homes, we decided to cross Oak Creek and take a look on the other side.

Walking on the crisp fall leaves that blanketed the creek bank was a refreshing change from the dry and dusty trails we'd just explored. At the edge of the stream, the lush flora made a welcome spongy cushion under our tennis shoes. The soft sunshine filtered through trees and glittered as it reflected off slow-moving water that bubbled and gurgled over rocks, around a dead tree branch, and over the sandy creek bottom. The cool crystal clear water sparkled in the bright afternoon sunlight like a blanket of slow-moving crushed diamonds. It felt good to breathe in the cool dampness. I stopped and looked up when I heard the unique song of a Cardinal coming from the willow or cottonwood trees. I spotted him! He sat on a low branch that hung over the stream. The sun reflected off his brilliant red plumage. His mate, less brilliant, but no less beautiful, flew down to join him. The moment was magic. *Why does he seem so much redder and brighter than most Cardinals? The clear air? The high desert elevation? The vortexes?*

In the majesty of the moment, I had forgotten about Katherine, the sphere, and everything else.

All of a sudden, I was gripped by dread. I gasped and could hardly breathe. I knew something awful awaited me. I wanted to turn back, but Katherine had already crossed the creek ahead of me and was nearing a dilapidated abandoned shack.

I glanced at the Cardinals one last time, took a deep breath, then slipped my feet into the icy water. The pebbles were slick and moss-covered. Once I was finally on the other side of the creek, I put my socks and tennis shoes back on my near-frozen feet, then double-timed it to catch up with Katherine. I knew it would do no good to forewarn her that there might be trouble ahead unless I had proof. I had none. Only instinct and intuition.

My lungs burned. I stopped to catch my breath. When I looked up again, Katherine had disappeared into the old shack.

In spite of my alarm, the surrounding scene was serene. The azure sky was covered with huge white clouds that crowded and bumped into one another. The Cardinals still sat on their branches. The creek glided and tumbled behind me. Yet my sense of danger grew to near panic as I neared the cabin.

I flinched when Katherine stepped out of the cabin and shouted, "Crissy! Hurry!"

Although my body protested, I jogged even faster. When I reached the shack, I realized it had fallen almost totally apart.

Katherine turned and disappeared back inside.

Splotches of dried blood dotted the cement steps. A rancid smell emanated from the shack. I turned my head, took a last long breath of clean air, got the Beretta from my backpack, then cautiously entered the shack.

Maybe cell phones aren't so bad, after all. For the first time since arriving in Sedona, I wished we had Katherine's cell phone. I normally hate being interrupted by cell phones when I hike or enjoy nature. Now, though, it would have been heaven sent.

My heart beat wildly as I slowly made my way inside the shack. The door squeaked and scraped along the floor like fingernails on a blackboard when I pushed it the rest of the way open. I shivered. The further I moved into the shack, the stronger the noxious odors. I gagged. The smell of stale urine and vomit mingled with filth. It repulsed me. Even so, I edged forward to check out the cabin.

I paused and opened the dirty windows, pried open the broken kitchen window, and propped open the back door.

I covered my nose and mouth as I walked toward Katherine's voice.

Fresh air flowed into the shack and diluted the stench, but didn't eliminate it. The shack was so trashed and desecrated that it should have been bull-dozed long ago.

"What's that God-awful smell?" I asked Katherine when she appeared in the livingroom.

"Brace yourself, Crystal, that's not the worst part," Katherine warned.

A piece of the flaking paint from the sagging ceiling landed on my cheek. I shivered, and brushed it away.

Katherine said, "This way."

She turned and walked into a small windowless room that appeared to have once been a storage area, closed off from the rest of the shack. The only access to the room was through a narrow door that opened off the tiny kitchen. I put my gun in my backpack, and followed Katherine into the cramped, dark room. I was almost overwhelmed with nausea.

There was very little room for Katherine to step aside. When she did, I gasped. From the light that came into the room through the open kitchen door, I could see a man tied to a chair. His head rested on his chest. He was covered with bodily fluids. Blood was everywhere. Drool fell from his mouth and pooled on his chest. He had apparently urinated on himself while tied in the chair.

"Jesus!" I said, as I stepped forward to get a better look.

He was alive, but barely.

Katherine dropped to her knees and talked to the unconscious man as she worked to untie his ankles and hands.

I used my backpack to prop the door open so we could see. Then I joined Katherine in her efforts to untie the man.

"Look at his smashed fingers and the gashes on his face," Katherine said. "He's been tortured. Something's protruding from his right side. Blood is still oozing, but I think it's started to clot."

Katherine and I worked as fast as we could to untie the man and get him into the kitchen. I shuddered as I brushed against his mangled body. When I touched him, he slowly opened his one good eye and looked at me. Startled, I flinched, then said, "I am so sorry." *Who could have done such a thing to another human being?*

"We're glad you're alive," Katherine said, as she continued to work the ropes to free him.

I wished I had Trevor's knife handy. *Where did I put it?*

He startled both of us when he hoarsely whispered, "Kill me."

"What?" I said. Then I leaned in a bit closer.

"Kill me. I can't stand this pain any longer."

"That's murder," Katherine and I responded simultaneously. Then we looked at one another over his tortured body.

"No. It's not 'murder,'" he whispered. He tried to lift his head, but it lobbed from side to side. "A blessing. A favor. Not 'murder.'"

I continued to talk to him. Katherine told him we would take him to the medical center as soon as he was untied. My stomach turned in revulsion as I looked at his gashes and other wounds while I worked to free him.

He passed out, then came to briefly. He mumbled, "I . . . don't . . . about . . . a golden orb . . . I've never . . . heard of . . ." He took a shallow breath, then passed out again.

"I don't think it exists. I'm not sure there is an orb," I whispered back to him. But he'd slipped back into unconsciousness.

Once he was untied, we pulled him into the kitchen and put him down on his back on the filthy floor. Katherine put her sweatshirt under his head.

Then, without warning, the same warm gentle breeze with radiating multi-colored diamond-like lights that had healed me, returned. The lights looked like dandelions floating on a summer breeze. This time they radiated mostly shining shades of reds and golds. The warm breeze enfolded the man much the way it had me, then sank into his skin.

Katherine and I were on our knees. We stood up, backed away, and watched, incredulous at what was happening before our eyes a third time.

The man's wounds began to heal.

"I would never have believed any of this if I hadn't seen it with my own eyes," Katherine said.

"I'm not sure I would have, either," I agreed.

When he came to, the man sat up and looked at us quizzically. We looked back at him and waited, silent, as he checked out his fingers, then his side, then reached up and felt his head.

"What happened?" he asked.

"We're not sure," I replied.

When it was clear he was able to stand, we helped him to his feet. He appeared to be about 80. He was as tall and thin as Jim Parsons, the man who plays Dr. Sheldon Cooper on *Big Bang Theory*. He told us his name was Tom Johnson, but folks called him "TJ," he added.

We wanted to get him to the medical center as soon as possible. We also had yet another police report to file.

When we walked him back outside into the daylight from that dark and dingy shack, we were temporarily blinded by the bright light and disoriented for a while. Blinking and squinting, we put on our sunglasses.

Chapter Fifty-Six

Wednesday, October 12, 2011, 2:47 p.m.

A s we walked toward the creek, TJ seemed to gain strength. He said two men, both huge and white, had tricked, then somewhat kidnaped him.

"'Somewhat kidnaped' you?" I asked. "How does someone get 'somewhat kidnaped'?"

TJ told us two men had abducted him. One was a huge, muscular man with a head the size of a small watermelon. He had white-blond hair and blue eyes. The second man was just a little shorter, equally muscular, with brown hair and eyes. TJ said they had driven him to the deserted shack and tortured him for information about the golden sphere.

When TJ described the men, I told Katherine, "The men TJ described were at the Purple Moon Sunday night."

She paused. For the first time, she seemed to regret having been so free with information.

Katherine and I walked on either side of TJ. He talked. We listened.

Although we didn't understand how or why it happened, we had witnessed another miraculous healing. And as TJ walked and talked, we marveled that he was not only alive, but appeared to be totally healed, alert, and well.

TJ was covered with drying blood and filth, much the way I had been before my healing. Yet when he talked, something in his manner suggested he was a professional of some sort. As we helped him, he said, "I should help you women. Not the other way around."

Yep. A gentleman.

Chapter Fifty-Seven

Wednesday, October 12, 2011, 3:03 p.m.

On our way toward the creek, we breathed deeply of the clean, pure air. TJ startled us when he exclaimed, "Wait! Now I remember! I was at Ricardo's bar last night. I had a few drinks. I talked with some people. Everyone's talking about an ancient scroll and a magical golden sphere hidden somewhere around here. That was when the two men offered to buy me another drink. Then they offered to take me to a local bar-and-grill for dinner. I didn't see why not."

"Next," TJ told us, "We talked at dinner. They seemed upset that I didn't know any more about the sphere than what I'd told them at the bar."

"After dinner," TJ continued, "They were supposed to take me back to Ricardo's so I could pick up my car. But, instead, they drove me to the shack. They insisted I must know more than I did about the sphere, even though I kept telling them I didn't know any more than what I'd heard around town."

TJ's hands began to shake. Tears flooded his hazel eyes. Beads of perspiration formed on his forehead. He added, "My home is near Steamboat Rock at the base of Oak Creek Canyon. Can you just take me there? I don't want to file a police report or go to the medical center."

"I'm sorry," I said. "We really don't have any choice here, TJ. You were kidnaped and tortured. Those are serious crimes. We *have* to report it. And you really do need to be checked out by a medical professional."

"The men TJ described hung on your every word the other night," I said to Katherine. "I wonder if they are the ones who broke into our motel room?"

"Really? You think there might be some connection?" she said.

"I think so. That's why I didn't want to joke around about the sphere in public. I didn't want anyone to think that if there were a golden sphere, we might know where it was hidden," I replied.

Katherine became pensive. She stopped and looked at TJ. After a minute, she said, "Those dirty bums are really rotten."

"Yes, they are," I agreed.

Katherine started toward the creek again, but when she realized that neither TJ nor I were keeping up with her, she took shorter steps, then stopped altogether and waited for us to catch up with her.

TJ continued to tell us what had happened. Katherine and I realized that dangerous people not only also searched for the sphere, but they were willing to do whatever was necessary to get it . . . even kill someone.

TJ was skeleton-thin. His western-style shirt was caked with blood on top of previous dirt. His hair was matted; his nails dirty and ragged. A large soiled red bandanna hung limply around his neck.

Suddenly, he remembered his old battered hat. He was sure it had been left in the shack, and he wanted to go back for it. "My wife gave me that hat," he said frantically. "I must have it. It's the last thing she gave me last year before she died."

"I'll go back, TJ. You rest here with Katherine for a minute," I said. I checked the time. Then I looked at Katherine.

She nodded her agreement.

I walked back to the shack as quickly as I could. When I reached the front door, I hesitated. I didn't want to go back inside.

Why did they leave TJ alive? Or did they think he was dead? Weren't they worried about leaving a witness? Evidence?

Finally, I re-entered the shack. Once inside, I quickly spotted the hat and grabbed it. When I turned back toward the door, I noticed an old, torn backpack in one corner. I picked it up, too, in case it belonged to TJ, then ran out of the shack.

I double-stepped back to where Katherine and TJ waited under a Sycamore tree on the far side of the creek. The hat and backpack were so grimy I was sure they must be crawling with bacteria and other germs.

Katherine looked at me and seemed to know what I was thinking. "It's okay," she said. "You'll be fine."

TJ added, "You found my hat! And my backpack, too!"

Suddenly, I felt better about having picked up the backpack.

TJ put on his hat, took his backpack, and we all resumed the trek to the vehicles.

"You're sure I'll be fine?" I said to Katherine. Then I added, "You know, Katherine, I knew we were being followed. I'm sure that feeling I kept getting that we were being watched was accurate."

"Maybe," she said with a furrowed brow as she helped TJ into the back seat of my Jeep. "Maybe you're right. Maybe we *are* being followed."

By the time we were on the main road headed toward the police station, TJ seemed perfectly normal. His wounds had totally healed. "How am I going to explain this to anyone?" he asked. "Who will ever believe what happened? I know I wouldn't!"

Chapter Fifty-Eight

Wednesday, October 12, 2011, 4:28 p.m.

It was almost 4:30 p.m. by the time we reached the police station. As we walked through the now familiar front doors, the American and Arizona flags greeted us. So did Officer Rizzo. "Well. Look who's back," he said, as he stood and watched us walk toward his desk. His manner grew even more serious as he took a long, close look at TJ.

I turned to look more closely at TJ, too. Although his wounds had healed, the dried blood on his shoulder-length grey, greasy hair caused most of it to stick to his head. The rest stuck out in all directions. TJ's straggly beard looked like it hadn't been trimmed in weeks. His soiled, bloody clothes bagged on his skeletal frame. His glasses had been broken, so he squinted. His breath reeked, as did his whole body.

"Well," I sighed. "This might sound unusual . . ."

"Not coming from you," Officer Rizzo interrupted.

My jaws clenched. My face flushed.

Officer Rizzo led TJ to the nearest chair. Then he brought him a glass of water. Next, he asked if we would like anything to eat.

I sank into a nearby chair.

Katherine took over the conversation. She loudly and animatedly told Officer Rizzo about the shack and the torture. She left out the part about the healing.

While she talked, I scanned the room.

Officer Rizzo watched TJ the entire time Katherine talked. Then he looked at me. I nodded that it was all true. So did TJ. Finally, Officer Rizzo took an even closer look at TJ. "Mr. Johnson? Is that you?" he said, apparently recognizing TJ as a local.

"Yes," came the subdued reply. "Yes, it's me."

"Just a minute," the officer said. "I'll get Detective DeSena. He's here from Phoenix. This looks like something he should know about."

About ten minutes later, a dark-skinned man of about fifty with deep brown eyes, a goatee, and wavy hair that was so dark brown it seemed almost black, walked from the back of the station into the room where we were waiting. He strode in front of Officer Rizzo. His loosely cut hair fell onto his forehead and over his collar. He set his coffee mug down with a thud next to where I sat.

When I looked at his cup, he almost growled, "Want a cup?"

"No. Thanks. I wouldn't," I said, as I stood to talk with him. "We're here to report that we stumbled upon this man. He had been kidnaped, beaten and left to die in an old shack. I'm Crystal O'Connor. This is my friend, Katherine VanDyke. We are here for the week, sight-seeing and hiking. Mr. Thomas "TJ" Johnson here was almost dead when we found him. Anyway, we'd just like to leave him with you to do whatever it is you need to do. It's late. We assume you'll have someone escort him to the medical center. Here are our business cards if you need to get in touch with us."

As I talked, Detective DeSena watched me while he slowly sipped his coffee. Then he removed the stir-stick and dropped it in the nearby trash can. The room became still. He continued to watch us. I began to feel uncomfortable.

Finally, raising my eyebrows and picking up my backpack, I said, "Well, then, goodbye, TJ," then turned to leave the station.

"Wait just a minute, Ms. O'Connor!" Detective DeSena slowly ordered in a booming voice. "You come with me. Ms. VanDyke, Officer Stampos will take your report. Mr. Johnson, I'd like you sit here, please, and rest. Officer Rizzo will talk with you. Then we'll take Mr. Johnson to the medical center."

I didn't want TJ to feel uncomfortable, but I began to sputter in protest. "We've done a good deed here, Detective DeSena. Really. Is this necessary? Can't you just call us at our motel later if you have any more questions? Or ask us to stop back by, preferably after dark when we're not out hiking?"

Detective DeSena was unmoved by my protest and request. After a pause, he said, "You, Ms. O'Connor, follow me."

"To you," I almost hissed, "It's *Dr.* O'Connor!" I turned and looked at Katherine. Her clenched jaw and military stance mirrored my own feelings. Her arms hung at her side, her face flushed, and her green eyes flashed.

An officer had handed Katherine a cup of instant hot chocolate. She slammed it down on the counter so hard its contents sloshed over the edges of the paper cup.

We exchanged glances a second time as I marched into the room where the detective now held the door open for me. Pain shot through my upper lip and I knew I'd bitten into it yet again. *I'm not going to have an upper lip left by the time I leave Sedona!*

When I entered the small, cramped, blank-walled room, Detective DeSena stepped in after me. *Even a poster on the wall would help,* I thought, as Detective DeSena lowered the blinds that cut off my view of the main room.

As the blinds fell, I could see TJ. He sat on the chair next to a wooden desk. With his shoulders slumped over his lap, he looked like a discarded rag-doll.

Miffed, I decided not to challenge Detective DeSena further—at the moment. I turned toward him, and said, "You know, like I said, we're in a real hurry. It took us a couple of hours to get TJ here. There's still a bit of daylight left. We want to be out in it."

Detective DeSena ignored my protestations. He took another sip of coffee, frowned, then swished the contents in his cup.

The longer I waited, the hotter and redder my face flushed.

"So, what brings you to Sedona?" he finally asked.

"What difference does that make? What does that have to do with someone torturing TJ?" I asked.

He stared at me.

I realized I had to calm myself, lower my voice, and answer his questions or I might be detained even longer. I crossed my legs and flipped my foot as I stared toward the blinds.

I could hear Katherine railing from the adjoining room. She was even angrier than I was. She loudly complained and protested being detained. We both made the same point to the officers who detained and questioned us. We had done a good deed, and now we wanted to leave.

It seemed the more we protested, the slower the detective and the officers moved. I decided to be quiet. A headache pounded at my temples and threatened to work its way into a full-blown migraine. I sat—silent—and focused on lowering my heart rate. I asked for a glass of water and searched my backpack for aspirin.

Finally, I took a pain pill from my backpack and, showing it to the detective, swallowed it with the glass of water. I answered his earlier question, and said, "Katherine and I are old friends. She asked me to meet her here. That's it. If you want more information, I want an attorney."

Detective DeSena continued to stare at me.

I stared at the wall.

Finally, he said, "Okay. You can go."

I snatched my backpack with such force it just missed slamming into the wall. That didn't slow me down. I stormed through the door and out of the cramped room. As I did, I saw that an ambulance had arrived to transport TJ to the medical center. When he saw me, TJ stopped. His eyes teared.

When I waved goodbye to TJ from the doorway of the stuffy room, detective DeSena said, "Who would guess that man is wealthy and had been a CEO of anything? How could he have fallen so low?"

"Wealthy? A CEO?" I said. "Are you sure?"

"Sure I'm 'sure,'" Detective DeSena growled. "In fact, the man's a genius. He had a full scholarship to Harvard. Went on to run a couple of major companies. Turned them around from near-bankruptcy into successful, highly profitable businesses without downsizing even one person. He created jobs for hundreds of people in the process. It's too bad, though. His only child, a son, got hooked on heroin and disappeared. TJ looked for him for years, but never found out what happened to him. Then last year, his wife suddenly died. Cancer, I think it was."

"That is so unfortunate," I said, as I watched TJ leave the station.

Turning to face me, Detective DeSena said, "You know, it's too late for you two to hike anymore today. Why don't you stick around and we can grab some dinner?"

I was stunned. When I'd recovered, I said, "No. Thanks. We need to leave. And you shouldn't rule out Katherine hiking by moonlight." Then I turned, walked toward Katherine, and added, "If you think the darkness or dangers of night dissuade Katherine from what she wants to do, you're wrong."

As I waited, Katherine took the last sip of hot chocolate, tossed the paper cup in the trash, and joined me. Then we walked in unison toward the door.

Detective DeSena stopped us and said that while we were being questioned, he had an officer drive out and examine the shack. It was now officially considered a crime scene and a forensic team was being dispatched from Phoenix. "So," he added, "We'd like you two to stay away from the shack."

"Don't worry," I said. "Nothing could get me back there."

Thanks for your help," he added.

Chapter Fifty-Nine

Wednesday, October 12, 2011, 6:09 p.m.

S till angry that we had been detained for so long, I walked toward the door. Then it hit me. With a sense of mischievous satisfaction, I turned to Katherine and quietly suggested, "You know, Katherine, you shouldn't waste this opportunity to tell the officers what you do. I'm sure they would all benefit from learning more about the flora and fauna, and the local formations and geology that surround them here. Don't you agree? You could even arrange for private lectures for police personnel. It could be really helpful and informative . . ."

I didn't need to say more. Katherine cut me off and enthusiastically said, "That's a great idea!" She lit up, took some business cards out of her backpack, and handed them out. All the while, she did what she loved to do best, tell others about the natural wonders of the desert, and Sedona, in particular. She was animated, alive and enthused. I watched, unable to stifle a smile of pure satisfaction.

As Katherine passed out her business cards, she spontaneously came up with ideas about tours, lectures, and outings that she could lead to teach local police and other service personnel more about the desert.

To conceal my growing delight, I turned my back toward the detective and looked out the window.

I knew Katherine was a free spirit who didn't think much of the police, their procedures, or protocol. Even so, it was easy to see that she would be the ideal candidate to educate personnel about Sedona and their desert surroundings. Her innate love of nature oozed from every cell of her body and radiated with every word.

Officer Rizzo and Detective DeSena both looked at Katherine, then me. I smiled, and looked away.

Within a few minutes, the initial look of shock and "Oh, my God!" had faded from Detective DeSena's face. He pulled himself together and tried to get some order and control back into the station. As he did, he gave me a look that could have melted a glacier.

Finally, as he walked closer to me, he lowered his head as he lowered his voice, and said, "Okay. You've made your point. You can both go, *now*. Would you get her out of here?"

"Sure," I said. "But she really would be a great asset to your group. She's a professional. She organizes and leads expeditions into natural settings, especially desert areas like Sedona, all of the time. You should take her suggestion seriously."

"Fine. I will. Just go," he replied.

"Okay. Great. Bye," I said.

Katherine and I slung our backpacks over our shoulders and headed toward the door. Detective DeSena walked alongside. I was surprised when Detective DeSena said TJ was sixty-three. I had guessed him to be closer to eighty-three. The detective said that while we were being questioned, they had learned TJ had begun frequenting a local bar shortly after his wife died. According to the bartender at Ricardo's, that's where TJ had been the night before last when the two burly men befriended him. Although the bartender said he wondered about Mr. Johnson leaving with the men, he felt he couldn't interfere without good reason.

Katherine seemed to have warmed up to the police personnel and was reluctant to leave, but I could hardly wait to walk back out the station house doors.

Katherine turned around to ask the detective who she should call to set a date to return and present lectures and lead excursions. She was told Detective DeSena or Officer Rizzo would be in touch. She waved. They nodded. We were free to go.

Officer Rizzo said, "We'll put out a BOLO (be on the lookout) for the two men who tortured TJ, but there's little hope we'll find either of them."

Exhaustion suddenly flooded over me. I needed to sit down, have something to eat, and rest. "Let's stop for dinner on the way back to the room," I said.

"Dinner?" she replied. "I don't know if we have time for dinner. The sun's setting. We could still search." Then Katherine's conversation changed to the types of lectures and excursions she could present to the Sedona Police Department.

"If we're going to get to the tarot shop in time for our readings and to get the next clue, Katherine," I said, "We have just enough time to grab a fast bite.

I don't want to risk missing the next clue. You don't either, do you? We've been hiking most of the day. I'm tired and need a shower."

Katherine's frown told me volumes. She slowed, then finally stopped altogether. Facing me full-body, she said, "Crissy, I can't believe you take those notes seriously. Someone's probably just messing with you. And, besides, you know I'm not interested in that metaphysical stuff. And another shower? What's with you and all these showers?"

Once again, I was disappointed, but not surprised. I replied, "If you really don't want to go, don't go. I plan to go, even if I go alone."

I rode with Katherine to the Subway for veggie-burger sandwiches, then we went back to our room.

Katherine suddenly decided she would go to the tarot shop with me, after all. So we ate, showered, and prepared for the evening ahead.

I opened the sliding glass door. Then I paused and watched the last tip of the carnelian sun dip below the horizon. In its wake were rays of burgundy, gold and teal. Katherine joined me on the patio. We sat at the picnic table and silently watched the last of the red, orange, yellow and gold fingers of the sunset fade until there was only a faint glow of gold, rose and amber in the sky. The moment was too brief. Soon, the sky turned a dark blue, then charcoal.

Yes. Selecting Kings Ransom was the right decision. That they suggested we take an upper room was never more appreciated.

I had hoped for a sign, or strong inner knowing, perhaps, about why I had received clues from strangers about the sphere. But no answer came. So my only option, if I wanted to get closer to the sacred mystical sphere, appeared to be to gather the clues, and continue to go where they led me.

Chapter Sixty

Wednesday, October 12, 2011—6:43 p.m.

"You didn't tell anyone at the police station about what TJ said concerning the sphere, did you?" I finally asked.

"Of course not," Katherine replied, "But a couple of cops had already heard about it and they were telling me."

"Great," I said.

"It doesn't matter what they know or think," Katherine added. "We all have an equal chance of finding the sphere. Right? Besides, you might be right. It could all just be an old legend. Even if there is a sphere, it might not be magical or powerful. Probably just a crystal plated in gold, or maybe it is pure gold. But magical? Powerful? I don't think so."

I wonder.

We decided I'd drive to the tarot shop.

After a couple of minutes on the road, I said, "I assumed you'd have mapped out a plan for this week. Since you plan and organize expeditions, I thought you probably had the entire week programmed."

"Nope," came the quick reply. "I made some plans, but I have no idea where the sphere could be, and neither does anyone else. You know as much as I do."

That tired-to-my-face-bones feeling came over me again. I said, "I see. Okay then. Well, Misty Rain Shadow said I'd get another clue when I see Alli for a tarot card reading tonight. I don't know how she knew I was looking for something, or would get another clue, but maybe something will happen tonight? I don't know. What do you think?"

As I pulled into the parking lot, Katherine said. "You know I don't believe in any of that off-beat stuff, Crissy. I'm a scientist and, in case you've forgotten, so are you. How can you go along with this nonsense?"

"Katherine," I said, "You're a geologist. You believe in reason, facts and hard science. I'm a social scientist and an energy healer. Really two totally different worlds and disciplines, don't you think? It's natural for me to consider and explore the metaphysical. Besides, with everything we've experienced this week, I'd have thought you'd have mellowed in your views a bit."

"Right, Crissy. Sure," Katherine replied.

I turned off the engine and turned to look at her.

"Well, let's go," she said. She grabbed her purse from the floorboard. "Time to face the music." The door slammed, and Katherine strode toward the building.

It wasn't until that moment that I wondered why we hadn't picked up a disposable cell phone earlier while we were out. *Why didn't I just stop in somewhere and grab a new wrist watch, too? Oh, well. I have Trevor's Expedition, and there's a clock in the room. And I'll only be here a couple more days.*

Chapter Sixty-One

Wednesday, October 12, 2011, 7:45 p.m.

By the time I walked into Alli's, I had a mild headache. I had followed my inner leading to venture to the desert. I had also made a commitment to Katherine to help her search for the sacred golden sphere. I felt committed—obligated, really—to stay.

The colorful old building housed five small businesses. Next to Alli's Mystic Light & Shadows Tarot Shop was a rock and mineral store with beautiful specimens highlighted in the window. As I looked at the long row of businesses, Katherine spotted a sign with an arrow that indicated where someone offered free food. She perked up immediately and began to walk in the direction of the arrow. She suddenly stopped when she realized the arrow led to Alli's tarot shop.

I followed Katherine. As I walked, I heard the crunch of leaves on asphalt. I turned. When I did, a large muscular man stepped into a nearby shop. All I had seen of him was his outline and the glow from the tip of his lit cigarette. I pulled my backpack forward for better access to my Beretta.

I caught up to Katherine and told her, "Someone followed us."

This time, she didn't say, "You really need to chill, Little Buddy." Instead, she turned and looked in the direction of where the man had disappeared into the shop, and said, "This is beginning to get downright eerie."

When we reached the doorway to Mystic Light & Shadows, I turned to look again for the man. He was gone.

We walked through the narrow midnight-blue door and glanced around. The shop appeared to be empty. Soft music played and the scent of citrus flowed through the air. A single yellow candle burned on top of a nearby glass display case.

We looked through cards and books while we waited for Alli. Within a couple of minutes, a tall, slender woman with strawberry blond hair entered the room from between curtains that separated what appeared to be her reading room from the rest of the shop. She introduced herself as Alli Vargas, and welcomed us.

Some people look *at* you. Others look *into* you. Alli stood for a minute and looked into both of us respectively. I looked back at Alli. Katherine paced around the tiny shop. When Alli asked us questions, Katherine looked the other way and gave Alli short, crisp answers.

Alli was in her early 40's with a thick loose braid that hung down to her waist. Her olive skin had a light golden tan. She was dressed casually in a long flowing multi-colored skirt and a softer-than-lemon-yellow T-shirt. She wore multi-colored flat sandals covered in glitter that twinkled in the soft light when she walked.

The tarot shop smelled of a blend of potpourri, incense and a citrus-scented candle that burned on the counter. The enclosed glass case was filled with crystals and jewelry. Soft lights glowed from overhead, as well as from Tiffany table lamps. Small spotlights near the ceiling were trained on a variety of crystals and minerals that glowed and sparkled under the glass counter. As I waited to see how Alli wanted to proceed, I turned and watched the flicker of the candle flame.

Katherine got my attention when she said to Alli, "The sign outside said there would be free food."

"Really? I'm sorry. I thought Joan had taken that sign down," Alli responded in a low, soothing voice. "We have had an open house with discounted readings all day. The food's been gone for quite some time."

Katherine frowned, then turned her back to us and resumed looking through the books and postcards.

Alli asked if we had a preference as to who would have the first reading. After a brief discussion, it was decided Katherine would go first.

As she marched into the reading room, Katherine gave me an angry glance.

I went back outside. The evening had turned cooler. A gentle breeze had picked up. The light from the full moon filtered through the trees casting moving shadows everywhere. Even the competition of street lights and business lights didn't distract from the beauty of the bright moonlight on the nearby red rock formations.

I breathed deeply of the clean high desert air with its magical feel. Tired, I stumbled over a crack in the pavement, righted myself, then walked on.

The atmosphere in Sedona felt liquid again—as if it had an intelligence of its own.

There was no sign anyone had followed me. After half an hour, I turned around and headed back to the shop. The temperature had dropped even more while I strolled along the sidewalk, so I stopped at my Jeep and picked up my red sweatshirt. When I re-entered the shop, the warmth felt good against my chilled cheeks.

Katherine's reading hadn't ended. As I waited, I sat and looked through books. When her reading was over, Katherine stomped past me without a word, then left the shop.

Alli stood at the curtain that separated her reading room from the rest of the shop and watched Katherine storm out into the parking lot.

She turned her attention to me and motioned me into the room. Not having had a reading before, I was nervous as I walked past the curtain and into her room. She pulled the curtain closed, then closed an inner door for additional privacy.

The room was semi-dark. It had two windows, both of which were blocked by removable boards. A floral cloth covered a small square table on the left side of the room. A tiny table lamp gave off just enough light to see the large well-used and frayed tarot cards. Alli talked slowly and softly as she shuffled the cards. Then she asked me to shuffle the over-sized cards two or three more times. They were rough, well-worn, and about twice the size of a regular deck of playing cards.

When I'd finished mixing the cards, I was asked to spread them across the table. I did. Next, I was asked to select seven cards. I was to turn each card face up, then hand it to Alli. She then placed the cards in formation between us on the table.

Alli studied each card that I gave her. Then she grasped her braid with her right hand and brought it forward over her right shoulder. Then she began my reading.

She asked, "Do you have a particular question? Is there anything special on your mind that you'd like to know more about?"

"Not really," I replied. "I've never had a reading before, so I don't know how this works. The reason I called and made this appointment—the reason I'm here—is last night Mary Star Blanket said I should come here tonight and talk with you. She said you would have a message for me. So I'm here."

"Mary Star Blanket?" Alli asked, as she glanced up at me knowingly.

"Yes," I replied.

Alli flipped her braid back over her shoulder. "Before your reading begins, I do have a message for you. It is from Spirit. I'll give it to you now to make sure I don't forget." Alli stood and searched in the pocket of her floral skirt. When she found the scrap of torn, soiled, wrinkled paper, she unfolded it and read the note to me.

> The cards hold no clues for you, it is true
> Because you're told by Spirit what is in store for you.
> I'm glad you'll be getting your next clue soon
> For I want to be with you, and freed from this gloom.

Alli handed me the small piece of paper and sat back down.

I reread it, then put it in my backpack with my other clues.

She said, "I believe Spirit is telling me to tell you that your final clue will be at the Chapel of the Holy Cross. You are to be there at 8:00 a.m. tomorrow morning. The final clue to the sphere's whereabouts will be given to you then and there. You're almost finished. Don't allow yourself to be stopped or sidetracked no matter what happens. All of that is out of your hands. Your job is to follow the clues that will lead you to the sphere."

I wrote the time and place on a notepad, and slipped it into my backpack.

"Now, as for your reading," Alli said. She studied the first card. Then she began to tell me what it meant. During the reading, she said something about life not being as random as it seemed, my luck would soon change, and I would become increasingly intuitive. I didn't really hear much of what Alli said because my mind was on the clues, my latest instructions, and the mystical way the events of this week had unfolded.

When the session ended, Alli blew out the single lavender candle that burned on the small table. Then she clicked off the desk lamp.

"Thank you for the reading, Alli, and for the clue," I said, as I stood and gathered my belongings, then turned to leave.

"My pleasure," Alli replied. She walked me to the door, pulled back the curtain, and said, "Here's my card. Call if you need me, okay?"

"Okay," I said, and turned to walk back out into the main part of the shop.

Before I got to the main entry door, Alli called out and asked me to step back into her small reading room. Surprised, I turned and followed her. The extinguished lavender candle still sent a small circle of smoke upward. Alli asked me to select another card. I did. It was the Four of Cups.

"That's what I thought," she said. "I'm to give you another message."

You might feel confused or uncertain about what you're doing here. Turn inward. When uncertain about which direction to go, stop, be still and re-evaluate. Then follow your intuition. Don't get forced or rushed into anything. Take time to explore *all* your options. You will be confronted with a new situation very soon. It will puzzle and confuse you. Meditation and contemplation *now* will serve you well *then*.

I didn't understand what the message meant, exactly, but I thanked Alli for the additional information, then walked back through the curtains and toward the door. As I reached for the handle, I heard Alli add, "You are where you are supposed to be, Crystal, and you are doing what you are supposed to be doing. Everything will turn out well."

Once I was back in the parking lot, Katherine asked me what Alli had to say.

"Before I get into my reading," I said, "how did yours go?"

"Not good," Katherine responded sharply. "I don't believe in all that stuff. I don't even remember most of what she said. I think it's ridiculous. What bull! Anyway, what did she say about the last clue?"

"I thought you didn't believe in the clues," I said.

Her sharp look let me know she didn't appreciate my comment.

I pulled the clue out of my backpack, then looked down at the crumpled note with information about when and where I would be given the last clue. I took a breath, then said, "My reading went well, but I don't remember much of it. I couldn't get my mind off the clue and the sphere. Alli said I'm to be on the patio of the Chapel of the Holy Cross tomorrow morning at 8:00 a.m. She said the sphere won't be there, but the last clue will be given to me then. So . . ."

Katherine cut me off, "You expect me to go to a Catholic Chapel?! I'm not going in. So what do you expect *me* to do while *you're* at the Chapel?"

My face grew warm. "Katherine, surely you can entertain yourself for a few minutes while I'm at the Chapel," I snapped. "Besides, what do you think I do while you're out with Joe?" I added, "You can go or not go. I really don't care one way or the other. But I plan to be there. With or without you, I *will* go."

Katherine slammed her car door. My Jeep shuddered. I buckled my seatbelt and slowly eased out of the parking lot onto H-89.

"Besides," I continued, "I may not be Catholic, but I have benefitted a great deal spiritually from a lot of the things I've learned through their organization."

"Really? Like what?" Katherine demanded.

"Yes. Really," I replied. "Like novenas, the Divine Mercy, chaplets, the Miraculous Medal, books about the lives of the saints. All kinds of good and helpful information. It may not be for everyone, but it has worked really well for me."

"Well, nature's *my* church," Katherine said, as she reached into her purse and pulled out a box of Milk Duds. I would hear Katherine say that nature was her church a few more times before I left Sedona. But I would never tire of it. For truly nature was often my church, too.

On the drive back toward our motel, I did what had become my norm—absorbed the mystical, magical beauty and feel of Sedona by moonlight. Fingers of wispy clouds played across the face of the moon. I thought about the fragments of information I remembered from my reading with Alli. *What will the next clue reveal? When and where does Fate end and Free Will begin?*

Katherine broke into my thoughts, and said, "I'll go with you tomorrow. But I won't go into the Chapel. I don't get anywhere near anything Catholic."

"Fine," I said. "I assume you're still going out tonight. Right? So if you're not back and ready by 7:00 a.m. in the morning, I'll have breakfast then take off without you. How's that? I'll assume you'll meet me at the Chapel at 8:00 a.m. But if you don't make it, that's fine, too. Are you good with that?"

"Okay," Katherine agreed. "That works."

The full moon cast a silver glow over Sedona. The air felt as if it were tinged with magic.

Suddenly, Katherine turned toward me and said, "You know, we could still search tonight. It's so light, we wouldn't even need a flashlight. We could drive to uptown and search the area behind the shops."

"Are you serious? There's no way I'm going out in the middle of the night to look for anything. Besides, I think we've been followed more than once. And I don't go out in unfamiliar territory after dark. We could come across all sorts of spiders, or bears, or even mountain lions. And there are those odd little pig-like creatures. I've been told they can be pretty aggressive, and night is when they're out feeding. Full moon or no full moon, I'm through for the day." After a short silence, I added, "When we get back to the motel, go if you want to. You're used to camping out and being alone in the desert day and night. I'm not."

"That's a good idea," Katherine said.

"You know, Katherine," I ventured. "Do you ever wonder where all that energy of yours comes from? Or why you rarely sleep?"

"Nope," she answered.

We avoided the topic of our readings as we drove the rest of the way back to Kings Ransom. I dropped Katherine off at her Rover. Just before she left, Katherine said, "I'm going to call Joe and see if he wants to join me."

I just looked at her, and headed toward the parking lot by the stairs that led to our room. When I was inside the room, I locked the door, put my backpack on a chair, and opened the patio door for fresh air.

Katherine left the way we'd come in. I watched as her tail-lights quickly disappeared around a corner of the parking lot, then darted back onto the highway.

Alone again, I gathered all four clues and arranged them in the order I had received them. I had dated each one, and indicated where I was when I received it, and from whom. I studied them. But, finally, I gave up. There was nothing in the clues that indicated where the sphere might be. Only where the next clue would be given. I put the Shaman Stone on top of the clues, closed and locked the patio door, then collapsed on the bed.

I had almost fallen into another deep sleep when I heard noises on the patio that sent a chill sparking down my spine. *Javelinas?* I wondered. *No. They couldn't get up here. Or could they? Or is it something or someone else?*

Dread mixed with fear caused my skin to feel clammy. I shivered. The hair raised on my arms and at the nape of my neck. I walked to the chair where I had left my backpack and pulled out my Tomcat.

I turned off all the lights, then gingerly picked my way barefoot across the carpet. The street and parking lot lights illuminated the patio. Even so, I flipped on the patio light. When I heard another noise, I looked onto the patio to the left. I couldn't see any activity. So I quietly unlocked the door, slid it open, and stepped outside to get a better look.

As I walked out onto the cold cement, I heard the noise again. This time, it was below me, to left. The neighbor's patio was empty. When I looked down to where the noise was emanating, I saw a large figure walk into the shadows toward the office. *Don't make a mistake. You can't relax. While you're in Sedona, you must be constantly vigilant.*

When the stranger had disappeared, I went back into my room, then closed and locked the sliding glass door. Chilled, I sat on the edge of the bed, stared at the drapes, and wondered if I were safe. Even though I was exhausted, sleep wouldn't come.

Chapter Sixty-Two

Thursday, October 13, 2011—5:30 a.m.

I dozed off and on before dawn and awoke to a quiet and empty room. Katherine hadn't returned. My head buzzed and my eyes burned as I plugged in the coffee maker. The scent of freshly brewed hazelnut coffee lifted my spirits. After a quick shower, I did some yoga stretches, snacked on fruit and yogurt, then braced myself for another day.

I slipped into my Tuscan-red shorts and off-white V-neck T-shirt while I considered the events of the past few days—sleepless nights, injuries that were instantly healed, an infusion of energy and strength whenever I needed it most. Mostly, I puzzled over the messages and the messengers who had given me the clues.

My mind drifted to the constant eerie sense of being followed. My brow furrowed. I shivered. Who would want to follow me? Joe and Manny? Patrick Bailey? Maybe the huge blond man with the greasy face and stringy blond hair? Or his sidekick? The more I thought about it, the more fatigued I became.

Katherine was gone so much I wondered whether I hadn't wasted my time in coming to Sedona to help her. But then there was the "knowing" to visit Sedona. As I picked up my old red sweatshirt, then put my backpack over one shoulder, I thought, *Two more days. If I've made it through all of this so far; I can surely make it a couple more days.*

I'd called Trevor the night before. Everything was fine at home. I thought of my home, husband, cats, yard overflowing with flowers and trees and birds, and my work that I loved—all waiting for me. I liked my life in Austin. Thinking about it caused me to relax. The more troubles and challenges I encountered in Sedona, the more I appreciated my "real" life back in Texas.

I had also called Jody at the vet's office. Pedro was doing well. No one had claimed him. It looked like I would be taking him back to Austin with me Saturday. I liked the idea of enfolding Pedro into my life, but I wondered how our three cats would take to it.

185

On my way to my Jeep, I again paused to absorb the natural beauty of the red rock formations, trees, clear skies, and fresh air. I decided that since the vet's office opened at 7:00 a.m., I would stop by and see Pedro before I headed to the Chapel. It would be a good time to bring my bill current.

Exhaustion played havoc with my nerves; my vision blurred. A headache danced between my temples. I took an Excedrin. Even yoga and floor exercises hadn't helped me totally unwind.

A fresh infusion of energy engulfed me on the way to the vet's office. The headache disappeared. I inwardly began to hear the sound of distant drums, rattles, and chanting. At first, I looked around to see where the sounds were coming from. But before long, I began to sing the words of a song in a language I didn't know. I tapped my steering wheel in time with the tempo. When I pulled into the parking lot at the vets, the unusual music faded.

When I turned off the engine, the chanting disappeared altogether. I was calm, relaxed, and focused. The dark circles had disappeared from under my eyes which were no longer red and swollen. Bones and joints no longer ached. A sense of heightened mental clarity flowed through my mind. This time, I didn't question it.

Walking into the office, I smiled. *It's almost over. I can do this. Only two more days, then I head for home.*

Jody was at the front desk. She recognized me immediately, smiled, and exited into the back of the building. Within a couple of minutes, she returned with Pedro trotting at her side. I spoke to, then played with Pedro. He wagged his tail and put a paw on my leg.

After a few minutes, Jody took Pedro back into the boarding area. When she returned, I brought the bill current, then left for Chapel of the Holy Cross.

It was early for my appointment at the Chapel. The sun had risen. The town was coming alive. Golden leaves cascaded to the ground all around me. Small whipped-cream-clouds dotted the Persian blue sky.

Because the Chapel, which was constructed on the site of a minor Vortex, had been built onto and next to red rock formations, the drive up to the Chapel was short, steep and narrow. As I slowly drove toward the highest section of the rugged parking lot, a covey of quail ran across the street right in front of my Jeep. I slammed on the brakes. Then three red Cardinals flew across the road in the opposite direction. As I resumed the drive upward, the Cardinals turned and flew toward the Chapel. *A very good sign.*

Since the Chapel didn't open until 9:00 a.m., the parking lots were almost empty. After a short hike up a steep incline, I reached the spacious concrete patio of the Chapel. It was 7:49 a.m.

Breathless from the climb, I leaned against the low concrete wall that encircled the patio to catch my breath. Then I walked over and checked the double entry doors to the Chapel. They were locked. So I sat on the ledge and enjoyed the peace and sacredness of the area surrounding the Chapel. I waited.

In the early morning light, the view was incredible. Red rock formations were dotted with green, red, orange and golden trees. Shrubs filled gullies and crevices. The sky had turned a deeper Royal blue as more clouds formed in the west. The air once again felt liquid. Heavy. An unusual peace and tranquility settled over me. When I gazed in the direction of the Verde Valley, my eyelids grew heavy.

I heard a soft scraping noise and turned to look toward the doors of the Chapel. A young man with ebony skin and dread-locks that fell over his shoulders came out of the Chapel, then walked to where I sat. "Are you Crystal Rose?" he asked.

After the Native American Healing Ceremony and the women who knew my Native American name, I should not have been surprised. But I *was*. I replied, "Yes. I'm Crystal Rose. But how did you know my middle name?"

He smiled warmly, but ignored my question. He held out a large, strong hand, then said, "I'm Brian Jones. You're a shaman, aren't you?"

"Me? A shaman?" I stammered, more to myself than to him. "Well, if you're asking if I study and practice alternative healing, then, yes, I guess I am," I replied, surprised, again, by his question. "I was told to come to this patio at this time," I said. "And that someone would have a message for me. Are you that person? Do you have a message for me?"

Brian again ignored my question, and said, "I understand you work with Spirit to help people heal, to put them back together. You've had more than one major life challenge, and have been on the brink of death more than once. After each, you've had another leap in spiritual growth. A deeper spiritual awakening," Brian said.

Feeling uncomfortably invaded, I stared at him in silence, and squirmed.

"Follow me," he said, then turned and walked back toward the Chapel.

I followed Brian into the Chapel. As I stood in the foyer, I noticed that on either side of the huge front windows and doors, votive candles flickered in small red containers. They gave the Chapel a warm red glow. The burning candles made the air stuffy and warm.

Brian smiled again, and said, "To answer your question, yes, I do have a message for you." A thick gold chain supporting an equally thick gold cross hung around Brian's neck. He wore a black polo shirt, black slacks, and black loafers. "Wait here a minute. I do have a message for you, and also a gift."

While I waited, I walked to the front of the Chapel to inspect the huge cross that had been built into the front windows. Through the panes of darkened glass I could see the distant red rock formations. The darkness inside the Chapel made the scenery outside seem especially vivid and bright.

A donation box was conspicuously placed at the entry to the Chapel. Pews lined the small room, and wooden benches faced the heart of the Chapel.

Brian had gone down a small, narrow windowless staircase at the left of the foyer. A sign read "gift shop."

When he returned, he said, "Here's the message Spirit said I was to give you." He handed me a square sheet of onion-skin paper upon which was written a note in block-print. It read:

> Tomorrow at noon, follow the sound of a bird that sings
> brightly,
> Until you're standing in the spot where the sun shines through
> lightly.
> That's where you'll find Me, or, rather, I will find you.
> After I have found you, I can start My work anew.

After I'd read the message, I looked up. Brian's dread-locks were just about to disappear below the railing again when he looked over to me, and said, "Please don't leave yet. I have something else for you. Besides, you need to know where to go tomorrow."

"Okay," I responded. Then I walked back to the front of the small Chapel, picked up a long, thin stick, lit it on a burning candle, then lit three candles, one for each of my prayer requests:

> That we would find the sphere if we were meant to find it;
> That my friendship with Katherine would survive this reunion
> turned ordeal;
> That all would go well with Pedro.

I turned and walked back toward the foyer, enjoyed the vista, and waited.

Shortly, I heard Brian whistling softly as he jogged up the staircase. I stood. He held a small bright-red metal bird the size of my Shaman Stone in the palm of his huge right hand. It was the identical shade of red as the Cardinals I'd seen earlier. I smiled in delight and reached for the gift.

Brian said I should keep the bird as a reminder that a Cardinal's call would guide me to the sphere. Then he told me a Cardinal would lead me to the entrance of Shaman's Cave, and I was to be in the middle of the cave at exactly 12:00 p.m. noon the next day—Friday.

I cupped the bird in my palms and gently closed my fingers around its cool slick metallic body. Then I searched inside my backpack, found an old, soft T-shirt, and wrapped the bird before nesting it inside my backpack.

Just then, I heard a bird singing. Brian and I looked at one another. "That's the song of the Cardinal," he said. "The sound you should listen for tomorrow. When you hear the song, look up. You will see the entrance to the cave. Now, it's time to leave."

As he unlocked the door, I thanked Brian, then stepped out into the bright sunlight. I quickly spotted the singing bird. It was the largest, brightest red Cardinal I'd ever seen. As I watched him, he turned, looked at me, and continued to sing.

Brian stepped back inside the Chapel. While he closed the door, he said, "When you awake tomorrow morning, you will be at peace about the climb to Shaman's Cave. When you arrive at the base of the mountain, a Cardinal will appear far above you at the cave entrance. It will be a sign that you are where you were meant to be, at the time you were meant to be there. At high noon, you need to be in the center of the cave. If you are, you will find the sphere. But remember, you're supposed to be there at 12:00 p.m. Noon. Not sooner. Not later. If you're late, you will miss your chance to find the sphere."

"Okay," I said. "Thank you, again, Brian."

He closed and locked the doors to the Chapel.

I turned and walked back to my Jeep Liberty thinking, *Great! Another mountain to climb and a cave!* I groaned. The Cardinal continued to sing.

Chapter Sixty-Three

Thursday, October 13, 2011, 8:29 a.m.

It was almost 8:30 a.m. by the time I reached my Jeep. As I put my backpack in the passenger's seat, I noticed more people had arrived. The parking lot was almost full. The sun shone brightly on the surrounding high desert landscape.

Suddenly, I heard, "Hey, Little Buddy! Find anything interesting yet?"

I smiled with relief, then turned and slowly walked toward her as I watched Katherine jog up the incline to meet me. We talked as we breathed in the fresh morning air and watched the area come alive. I told Katherine about the three red Cardinals I'd seen on my way to the Chapel, my meeting with Brian, the clue, the gift he'd given me, and the huge red Cardinal that sang to me when I left the Chapel.

"I saw and heard the Cardinal, too," she said. "I've never seen a Cardinal that big before, and I've never heard one sing."

"Me, neither," I responded. "And I love red Cardinals. I even feed them in my backyard at home."

We rolled down the windows and sat in Katherine's Rover while she read the last clue.

"I'm calling that huge Cardinal Big Red," I said.

Katherine looked at me and smiled, then resumed reading the note. "Well, let's go to the cave and find that sphere," she said.

"We can't go to the cave now. Brian instructed me to be inside the cave at precisely twelve noon tomorrow. So that's what we have do," I replied. "Brian said not to be early or late. We have to be exactly on time."

"Okay," Katherine said. She handed the note back to me, then she turned to survey the surrounding mountains.

"Why don't we locate the cave on the map, though," I added. "We can find out where it is so we won't have trouble finding it tomorrow. Then we can hike and search someplace else today just in case this has been a wild goose chase. What do you think?"

We looked at one another, eyebrows raised. We agreed that we'd hike into the cave the following morning long before noon, but today we'd explore other areas.

"You and these clues," Katherine said. "It's really been strange."

"Well, yes," I said. "But who really knows how the Divine works?"

Katherine looked past me at the red rock hillside.

"It seems that this magical, mystical sphere, if it does exist, might have a mind and will of its own. Perhaps, if we do find it, we should allow for that," I added.

Katherine turned and continued to silently stare at me.

I grew silent, too.

"Maybe," Katherine finally muttered in an uncharacteristically low voice. "Maybe."

I remained silent, waiting to see how Katherine wanted to handle the new message, and what her plans were for the day.

"You said I should have it, if we find it? Is that right?" she asked.

"Of course," I replied. "This was *your* idea. *You* invited *me* to join you and asked me to help you. Right? I'm here to help. That's all."

"Right. Well, then, what do you want to do with the rest of the day?" Katherine asked.

"Why don't we check out the Broken Arrow Trailhead area? Then, if we have time, we can tackle Little Horse? They're both nearby. And if these clues I've been getting are accurate and are really leading me to the sphere, then we'll be led to the actual place where it's hidden and we'll find the sphere tomorrow. If they're not, and we didn't search more today, we'd be sorry we slowed down and didn't search harder in other places. Agreed?"

"Agreed. Sounds good. Let's do it," Katherine said.

"I'm glad you haven't given up finding the sphere on your own," I said. "Actually, unless these clues lead us to the sphere, I think it's hopeless. Who could find it here unless . . ." I let my thoughts trail off, wondering if there really was a magical, sacred golden sphere.

"Yes. We should search as much as we can. At the very least, we'll have some great hiking and exploration behind us when we part on Saturday," Katherine said. "I don't give up easily, but without some guidance, how can anyone find a sphere that's hidden up here? Well, unless they stumble over it, like the students in Yosemite stumbled over the scroll, or like you stumbled over the stone in the mine shaft. There are just too many places it could be hidden."

Chapter Sixty-Four

Thursday, October 13, 2011, 8:56 a.m.

"**B**efore we head out," I said, "I have a few more questions for Brian. I know you don't want to go inside the Chapel. But they open in a few minutes, at 9:00 a.m., and I'd like to go back and find Brian. Do you mind?"

"No. Go ahead," she replied. "We have all day. I'll hike around here a few minutes. If you're not back soon, I'll check your map for the road to Shaman's Cave for our hike tomorrow. I think I heard the cave is about a half-hour hike from where we'll park our vehicles."

"Half an hour *up* I'll bet," I said. "And if it takes *you* half an hour to hike it, we'd better plan on an hour for me."

We exchanged looks before Katherine said, "Maybe you're right. We'd better plan on an hour. We can start around 9:30 a.m. tomorrow morning, and that should give us plenty of time to drive there, hike up the mountain, and be inside the cave long before noon."

"That sounds good," I said. I covered my backpack with my red sweatshirt then climbed back up the walkway to the Chapel. "I'll be back soon," I called back to Katherine.

"Fine. No rush," Katherine said as she headed into the nearby gully.

I arrived at the doors to the Chapel right at 9:00 a.m. A smiling woman dressed in a long floral skirt and pastel teal blouse greeted visitors as she unlocked the front doors. I let the two dozen or so tourists walk into the Chapel. Then I followed them inside.

When I stepped back inside the dark, cozy interior, I again marveled at the view of the valley through the glass front of the Chapel. The red glass candle holders continued to give a soft red glow to the front of the Chapel. As people lit more candles, the red hue deepened.

I scanned the Chapel for Brian. I didn't see him anywhere.

The woman who had opened the doors had started to walk down the same narrow enclosed staircase Brian had used earlier. I made a quick left and followed her. I tried to get her attention, but she walked quickly to the narrow door and into the gift shop. The door clicked closed behind her.

I entered right behind her. Inside the gift shop, a cash register rested on a glass counter. I called to her as she walked past the counter and went into a tiny crowded office alcove. As she turned, two coworkers looked up. Although she smiled faintly, something about her manner was aloof and condescending. She ambled to where I stood by the register. She was over six feet tall.

Her eyes were small, like dark grey marbles. Her artificial smile was quickly replaced with a scowl. When she moved, her thin floral skirt billowed behind her. Her silk blouse added an air of femininity that didn't mesh with her stern expression. Her jet-black dyed hair was pulled into a tight bun.

She glowered down at me. I introduced myself and explained I had been at the Chapel earlier that morning. Then I added I had met with Brian, and had a few more questions for him, but couldn't find him. I asked if she could tell me were he was, or call him for me.

"Brian?" she echoed, as she turned her head to one side as if she looked for someone. Her brow furrowed. "I volunteer here two half-days a week and don't know anyone who works here by that name. You must be mistaken. Just to be sure, though, I'll check with Joseph, the manager. What does Brian look like?"

"Thank you," I said. "He's a young black man, about twenty-five, long dread-locks, and warm, penetrating light golden brown eyes."

Something about the way she looked at me made me feel out-of-place in my faded navy blue hiking shorts and scuffed tennis shoes. Even my favorite blue and white floral blouse suddenly seemed shabby and out-of-place.

She sighed, then slowly turned toward the tiny alcove where her cohorts sat, drank coffee, and chatted. She took her time asking them about Brian. Neither of them knew anything helpful.

I felt disoriented and frustrated. The first tentacles of a migraine wrapped themselves around my temples. I tried to recall some bit of information from my time with Brian that would help them locate him for me, or convince them I had been with Brian in the Chapel earlier. Nothing came to me.

The woman sauntered back to where I stood, looking me over head-to-foot. As though talking to someone far beneath herself, she raised her eyebrows when she said, "I'm sorry. No one named Brian works here. Our janitor, Martin Small, has been here since 7:00 a.m. He said he hasn't seen anyone in the Chapel. Neither has anyone else."

I was so taken aback that I continued to stare at her, open-mouthed, while what she said sank in.

"Is there anything else I can help you with?" she sneered.

"No," I said. I turned, left the gift shop, and climbed the stairs to the Chapel.

I sat in a pew, opened my backpack, and took the red metal bird that Brian had given me. I rubbed its cool metal surface and stared at it in wonder.

Finally, I numbly walked out of the Chapel. I sat on the patio for a few more minutes as I tried to absorb what had happened. *Brian? Where are you? Who are you? Where did you go?*

Chapter Sixty-Five

Thursday, October 13, 2011, 9:29 a.m.

When I looked at Trevor's Expedition, I noticed it had been half an hour since I'd left Katherine. I walked down the path in the bright sunlight of a crystal clear October morning. A stiff breeze greeted me. It caused me to look up into a liquid sky filled with large butter-cream clouds. I took a deep breath, then continued my walk.

About the same time I reached my Jeep, I heard, "Hey! Over here!" I turned to watch as Katherine scaled the adjacent rock formation.

"I don't think people are supposed to hike so close to the Chapel," I called back. "It's posted 'No Trespassing.'"

"Okay. I'll be back in a few minutes," she said, as she turned back around and continued her ascent.

What must it be like to have that sort of aliveness and energy?

I had been at my Jeep a few minutes when Katherine jogged to her Rover and stashed her backpack before walking in my direction. She asked me how things had gone with Brian. Not knowing what to say, I told her, "I'll tell you later. Are you ready for Broken Arrow?"

"Sure," she replied," as she turned back toward her vehicle.

The clock in my Jeep reflected it was nearing 10:33 a.m. when we reached Broken Arrow. Before leaving the trailhead, we looked around to make sure no one had followed us. We were alone. We explored every nook and cranny close to where we parked our vehicles. Nothing looked even remotely promising. Nothing. Hunger and fatigue caused us to take a break. We pulled bottled water and dried fruit from our backpacks. Katherine had M&M's and a squished chocolate candy bar for dessert.

Next, we started up the trail into Little Horse. We searched along the side of the red gravel trail as we hunted for anything that looked like a marker, or a possible hiding place for a sphere. Nothing.

I no longer even tried to keep up with Katherine. She sprinted up inclines and dashed down into ravines far ahead of me. She turned periodically, waved, or called, "Good job, Little Buddy," and then dashed off again.

When we stopped to take another break, I pulled a squished banana from my backpack. As I looked at the mangled mess, I was glad I'd put it in a plastic baggie. I was hungry enough that I ate what I could, then put the rest back in my backpack.

Katherine ate her sandwich, banana, a box of Red Hots, half a box of Dots, and drank a Gatorade.

While she ate, she glanced around the new terrain. Then she asked, "How are things with Trevor's daughter these days? The one who created so much conflict. What's her name?"

"Oh. You mean Nadia," I said as my voice grew deeper and my back and neck began to tense. "It's best not to ask. Let's change the subject."

"Whoa!" Katherine said, as she turned toward me full-face. "What's that all about? If I didn't know better, I would think you disliked her."

"I don't think 'dislike' is the right word," I replied. Blood throbbed in my neck and temples, and warmth spread across my face. "I think despise is more like it. Let's change the subject. But I will say that there are two people on planet Earth I despise. One is Nadia. The other is her equally evil mother. And, no, I don't want to discuss either one."

"I take it Nadia never did apologize for slandering you, or commit to being pleasant?" Katherine asked.

"That's right. She refused to apologize and she also refused to commit to being 'pleasant and cordial' in the future. Then her husband, Klaus—keep in mind they are still married and living in Germany and he's a natural-born German citizen—wrote us a terse note in which he told us that we Americans and our insistence on apologies was the *real* reason for WWII. His reasoning? He said that since the U.S. insisted the Germans apologize for starting WWI that angered and humiliated the Germans so much that it was the underlying real reason there was a WWII. As you can imagine, Trevor and I were so incensed that we cut off all contact after a couple more attempts to work with them. Now I'm dropping it," I said. "Glad you asked?"

Ready to end the conversation, I stood and shoved the remnants of our lunch back into my backpack. With a clenched jaw, I realized for the first time I still got angry at just the sound of Nadia's name.

Katherine continued to study me. I was relieved when she finally stopped asking questions about Nadia and helped pick up the debris.

Before leaving, we looked around the area to make sure we hadn't missed any clues. Then we continued our hike.

Katherine slowed down and walked beside me for a few minutes. As we walked, she said, "I hope you don't let them get to you. They're not worth it. If you get hurt or angry that makes them the winners."

"I know," I said. "Life's way too short to dwell on people like that. And I've learned . . . well . . . when people are intentionally combative, or aggressive, or slanderous, I simply have no use for people like that in my life."

"I've never seen that in you before, but I'm glad you're not putting up with Nadia or her Mother's or husband's stuff," Katherine said. Then she stepped up her pace and was soon far ahead of me.

My heart raced, my face flushed, my head ached. I was glad for the solitude.

As we walked, we came across a big sinkhole labeled Devil's Dining Room. I was alarmed by the name. Katherine was as mesmerized by the opening as a teenager at a fair. She became even more animated as her fascination of experiencing a new geological novelty grew and absorbed her interest. "I should bring one of my classes here," she exclaimed.

I became nervous as she skirted the hole, peering into its depths.

I took a step backward, took a deep breath, and glanced toward the heavens.

Katherine returned to where I stood, slipped out of her backpack, dropped it by my feet, and resumed her exploration.

The wooden sign near Devil's Dining Room indicated the site was about thirty feet across and seventy-five feet deep. It was fenced off, which didn't stop Katherine as she walked to its mouth and looked down into the blackness.

I knew it was impossible to deter her. But as she explored, my chest tightened and I realized I had once again begun to hold my breath. I reached in my backpack for Excedrin and water. Then I spread my sweatshirt on the ground, sat down, took the pill, and waited for Katherine.

When she glanced at me, Katherine said, "Crissy, you really must learn not to worry so much!" At her admonition, my face flushed and my jaw clenched. I turned away and looked toward a far mountain range. When I did, I tasted fresh blood, and realized I was once again biting my now-raw upper lip.

I turned back to where Katherine continued peering over the edge of the sink hole. She picked up a pebble and tossed it into the blackness. When she did, I heard a slight cascading sound as it tumbled into the abyss.

"What are you doing?" I asked. "You're not . . . you wouldn't . . . you plan to stay up here, right?"

"Well, it might be a good place to hide something," she answered.

"Don't do it, Katherine!" I said. "No one in their right mind would even go near the edge of that hole, let alone try to go in it."

I waited.

I watched.

Katherine edged closer to the sink hole. Then a little closer. Then still a little closer.

I watched, wide-eyed, and realized I had stopped breathing.

Suddenly, her right foot slipped on the loose red dirt and she fell onto her fanny and began to slide. As she did, she grasped and held onto a nearby shrub.

"Jesus, Katherine! Are you alright?" I screamed, as I bolted upright.

Finally, Katherine righted herself. She slipped on loose gravel again as she carefully inched her way out of the mouth of the hole.

I watched, not sure what I'd do if she slipped again. Katherine scrambled as she emerged from the mouth of Devil's Dining Room. She dusted herself off, then walked back around the fence. Finally, she stood next to me on the trail.

I exhaled.

A minute later, Katherine strode off down the trail as if nothing had happened.

After another half-hour of hiking, I walked around a curve in the trail and noticed Katherine was in the shade leaning against a boulder. She absentmindedly tapped her nails on the rock as she rested.

When she saw me, Katherine paced, checked her watch, and said, "We only have about another four hours of daylight. We'd better pick up the pace."

Something moved on the boulder above Katherine. When I looked up, I saw a mountain lion slink around an incline just out of Katherine's view. The lioness moved silently toward Katherine in a slow, low, crouched position. Since mountain lions are usually shy and stay away from people, I was surprised to see the lioness stalk Katherine in broad daylight. *She must be starving or protecting cubs somewhere nearby*.

I yelled to Katherine, "Don't move," and quickly slid my backpack to the ground, grabbed my Beretta, took aim right below the orange lioness, and pulled the trigger. The bullet rang out then ricocheted off a rock. The lioness darted behind the boulder.

Katherine jumped. Then she turned back toward me, fire in her eyes, apparently angry I shot at something near her. Her anger morphed into shock when the mountain lion jumped onto the pathway between Katherine and me. The color beneath Katherine's tan paled and her eyes grew wide as she stood erect and watched the lioness.

The mountain lion now stood still as she looked at Katherine, then at me. I shot below the lioness again. I hoped she would take off. She did. When she had gone about twenty yards, she turned and looked back toward us. Then she lay down, and watched us.

Katherine slowly walked to where I stood, Beretta at my side in case the lioness changed her mind and decided to return.

"I've had it for today," I said. "I'm heading back. What about you?"

"Sure, Little Buddy. Let's go," she said. Then, looking at my gun, she added, "Maybe that's not such a bad idea, after all."

We walked back down the trail to our vehicles with an eye on the lioness until the lioness was out of sight. "I thought mountain lions only came out at dawn and dusk," I said. "I wonder if she has cubs around here? Maybe she doesn't have enough to eat? Do lions get rabies? That would explain her odd behavior."

"I don't know, but I'm ready to leave here, too," she said.

We walked in silence back down the trail toward where we had parked.

It was unusual that Katherine was so quick to call off the search so early in the day, but I was more than ready for a meal and a nap. *Besides, we're either going to find the sphere by following the clues, or we're not going to find it at all*, I thought.

Chapter Sixty-Six

Thursday, October 13, 2011, 2:23 p.m.

Katherine insisted she treat us to a nice Mexican luncheon at The Elote Café. Since it was built into Kings Ransom, and had a great reputation among locals, I decided it was a wonderful idea. I accepted.

We were back in our room at 2:34 p.m. After we'd taken quick showers and changed, we walked to The Elote Café. Katherine's offer fell flat when we realized that the café didn't open until 5:00 p.m. for dinner. No luncheons.

When we turned back from the front upstairs door of the restaurant, I noticed someone watching us from a distance. He was too far away to make out who it was, but he appeared large. I shivered.

Katherine hadn't noticed him as she brain-stormed alternative options for lunch.

I interrupted her. I told her I was tired and just wanted a quick bite and then to rest. When I alerted her to the man under the pines, she turned to where he had stood. But he had disappeared.

Katherine suggested lunch at a nearby brewery and grill. Since it was within walking distance of Kings Ransom and was built slightly above the banks of Oak Creek, it seemed like an ideal choice.

Over a pleasant lunch of creamed pasta and artichokes, we discussed our experiences. We reviewed the clues, then considered how best to tackle the climb to Shaman's Cave in the morning. The gurgling creek at our side lulled me, but it didn't Katherine. She quickly ate her lunch and was too soon ready to resume the search.

I was surprised when Katherine suggested we return to our room around 4:27 p.m. With two hours of daylight left, I thought it strange that she was ready to call it a day. I assumed it was a combination of our lack of success in finding the sphere on our own, the stress of our encounter with the mountain lion, and the disappointment of the Mexican restaurant being closed.

I was growing eager to see what would happen when we reached Shaman's Cave. I knew our only hope to find the sphere was to follow the last of the clues I'd received. Then, with or without having found the sphere, I had to call it an adventure well lived, and head for home.

I warmed to the idea of Katherine and I spending a low-key night shopping and visiting. We could spend some time together while we got better acquainted with the town of Sedona. "Perhaps we could go see the Sacajawea statue at Sacajawea Mall, or the shops at Tlaquepaque?" I suggested.

"Well, Crissy," Katherine said in a low, slow tone that let me know she had other plans. "I'm getting together with Joe again tonight. I know you'll be leaving soon and that we haven't seen much of each other in years, but I've made other plans for tonight. I hope to see Joe when I'm back in Prescott. You don't mind if I leave you here tonight, do you?"

I was hurt. "Katherine . . ." I began, but quickly gave it up. "Okay."

When we got back to the room, Katherine changed into soft brown slacks, mini-heels, and a silky light tan blouse with purple, blue, red and pink flowers. A soft ruffle encircled the neck of her blouse. The short sleeves fell in lovely folds along her tanned arms. Her gold and emerald earrings brought out her tan and complimented her yellow-flecked green eyes.

Katherine stood and headed for the door.

I said, "If we haven't connected by 9:00 a.m. tomorrow, I'm heading to the cave without you. I plan to drive myself, either way, anyway. So if you come back tomorrow and I'm not here, I've taken off early to see some of Sedona. Then I'll meet you at Shaman's Cave."

"That's fine," she said, as the door closed.

Chapter Sixty-Seven

Thursday, October 13, 2011, 5:56 p.m.

Around 6:00 p.m., I decided to take a short walk and then check for messages at the office on my way back to the room. It was 6:30 p.m. by the time I walked up the incline that led to our room, preoccupied, per usual. This time, I was thinking about what I would find in Shaman's Cave. *Well, one thing's for sure. Not much else could go wrong. Things can't get much worse.*

I was wrong.

In the parking lot, I stopped to get my sweatshirt from the Jeep, then headed toward the stairs. At the top of the stairs, just as I stepped onto the landing, a woman screamed in a frantic, shrill voice. My eyes widened and my heart raced as I turned to watch her.

She ran toward me. She had a jar in her left hand. As she ran, she screamed obscenities, apparently at me. Her long slightly wavy red hair flew out behind her in all directions. She was tall and model-thin. Something about her and the entire scene seemed vaguely familiar.

I stood transfixed and kept my eyes on her.

The parking lot lights reflected off her dangling diamond earrings, a number of rings, and a long gold and diamond necklace.

Then it hit me. *The dream!*

By the time she had loped to the top of the steps, I could see the rage in her crazed brown eyes. With her right hand, she unscrewed the lid off the jar. When she was just a few feet from me, she made a motion as if to throw the contents of the jar onto *me*.

Reflexively, I grabbed my heavy backpack with both hands and swung it as hard as I could toward the woman. It caught her mid-section. She doubled over, almost collapsed, and then tumbled backward down the stairs. As she fell, the jar and its contents flew upward, then came back down. The jar hit the woman in the middle of her back; the contents cascaded all over *her* backside.

When she landed on the concrete path at the base of the stairs, she screamed, and writhed on the hard walkway as she tried to get the liquid off her back.

A large drop of the liquid had landed on my left forearm. I cringed in unbelievable agony.

A passerby had immediately called 9-1-1. Within a couple of minutes, I heard sirens. With my backpack in one hand, and my Beretta in the other, I slowly walked down the stairs toward the woman. She continued to roll on the ground, swearing and shrieking.

People began to congregate, but no one went near her. The jar of liquid had rolled to a nearby flower bed. No one touched it.

I stood a few feet from the woman and watched.

Out of nowhere, Ralph ran to the woman, bent over her, and cried, "Kate? Kate?" As he tried to talk to her, Ralph's composure crumbled.

When she heard Ralph's voice, Kate tried to sit upright, but couldn't. She screamed and cried. Her left arm wrapped around her body as she tried to brush the liquid off her back. As she did, she spread the liquid over more of her back, legs and arms. The more she spread the liquid over her body, the more her hysteria grew.

The police and the ambulance arrived simultaneously. They flooded the whole area in headlights. As the medics worked with the woman, the police moved the witnesses back away from the area. They began taking reports.

I told them how the woman had come out of nowhere and tried to throw that horrible liquid on me. As I angrily told the officer what had happened, Ralph ran over to me, clutched my arm, squeezed it tightly, and told me it was all a horrible mistake. "Kate's my fiancée," he said. "She just misunderstood our having coffee the other night. That's all."

"Misunderstood?" I screamed, as I jerked my arm away from Ralph. "And so she tried to disfigure—and maybe even kill—*me*?!" I took a step backward so I could turn and face Ralph. Then I continued, "If she's upset, that's between *you* and *her*. What's that got to do with *me*? If she wants to punish or disfigure someone for *your* behavior, she should throw that stuff *on you*, not on *me*!"

When my voice grew more shrill, the officer stepped between us.

That didn't stop me or slow me down.

Ralph changed his attitude as quickly as a light comes on when someone flips a light switch. His face contorted into an ugly mask as he glared at me. It was hard to believe this was the same man who had so recently charmed me. For an instant, I couldn't think of how to respond.

Then before our eyes, he morphed back into the man of a few nights before and said, "Please don't press charges, Crystal. It's just a misunderstanding. Kate needs medical attention. It won't help anything if you press charges."

"Kate needs a shrink!" I spat back at him.

I sensed that rare feeling I have grown to hate. The feeling that something inside of me—some sort of innate control—has given way, and part of my personality that I don't like has just been released.

Side-stepping the officer, I hissed, "It will help ME, Ralph. Me!" I immediately worked to regain control, but it was too late. "She could have killed me. Or at least disfigured me! What would you have me do, Ralph? Just blow this off and pretend it never happened? What if she'd been successful? *I'd* be the one writhing on the ground right now—disfigured and disabled for the rest of my life—that's what! For me, that would have been worse than death. My future would have been hopeless. I'll tell the authorities the truth, no matter what happens to *her.* I hope she spends the next year in court, then spends the next few years in a dark, dank, solitary prison cell—the uglier, the better. Or a psych ward."

I stood my ground and glared back at him as Ralph stepped toward me. Officer Reese quickly placed his body firmly between us, one hand on his weapon. He told Ralph, "Stand over there, Sir. Next to the light pole. Now!"

Then the officer turned to me and pointed to the base of the staircase. I snatched my backpack, glared at Ralph one last time, and walked to where I was instructed to wait. Once there, I sat on the bottom step and watched the paramedics and police.

The EMTs quickly prepared Kate for transport to the medical center. The police interviewed the witnesses. I sat and steamed in silence.

Suddenly, my head began to spin. I felt incredibly dizzy. Then I heard an inner Voice say, "You were forewarned this would happen. You handled it just as you were instructed to. Let it go. It has nothing to do with why you are here. It was meant to derail you. Don't let it." I looked around, but no one else seemed to hear the Voice. Then I felt that same breeze that calmed and healed me before as it soaked into my body and did its magic. I relaxed.

Officer Reese returned to re-interview me. I had cooled down. He sat next to me. Once the report was completed, he folded his notepad and turned to walk away. He paused mid-step, then turned and looked back at me. "You look almost delicate," he said, "but you must have a backbone of pure steel." He paused, then added, "Be sure to get to the medical center as soon as you can. That arm needs attention."

"Okay," I said. "I'll go now." I felt hot tears flood my eyes.

I shivered slightly, then stood, and walked on shaky legs to my Liberty. My wounded arm burned as if torched, and I shivered as I put my backpack in the Jeep.

Was someone watching me? I turned and looked into the crowd, then at the nearby trees, then into the pool area. I didn't see anyone watching me. Yet my skin crawled and chills ran up my spine.

The ambulance that had taken Kate to the medical center was the first to leave. The officer assured me Kate would be charged. Ralph had gone with Kate. I followed the last police Jeep out of the parking lot and drove myself to the medical center.

When I walked into the medical center, I heard Kate screaming. *Better her than me*, I fumed.

My wound was treated and covered with a thick gauze. I was given ointment and bandages, as well as instructions on how to treat the wound. *Why isn't it healing like the other wounds did?* I wondered. *I'm sure to have a scar to the bone.*

I drove back to my room. Once through the door, I collapsed on the floral bedspread, grabbed a big, soft pillow, and buried my face in it. The small digital clock on the nightstand reflected 7:53 p.m.

It was 9:52 when I awoke, startled by another noise. I got out of bed, turned off the lights, and picked up my Beretta. *This feels too familiar*, I thought as I tip-toed to the patio. I didn't see anything when I pulled the drapes aside. I listened. Nothing.

Barefoot, I again slipped outside onto the cool patio and looked around. A few guests were returning to their rooms. I didn't see anyone else.

Relieved, I went back into the room, picked up what had become my staple—an orange juice and a fresh bagel—and returned to the patio. I sat in a chair by the light of the waning full moon and looked out over Sedona. The night grew quiet. Peace and stillness engulfed me.

When I returned to my room, the light on the phone flashed. I called the office. The receptionist said flowers had been delivered while we were out. We hadn't answered the door, so the flowers were left at the office. She said someone would bring them now, if that was agreeable.

It was.

Soon, a large floral arrangement was delivered. Two dozen deep velvet-looking red roses were arranged in a stunning crystal vase with etched frosted roses encircling it. Queen Anne's Lace and tiny purple flowers were mixed in with the roses.

I placed the stunning floral arrangement in the center of the table. A strong, lovely scent from the fresh roses filled the room.

An envelope was tucked in among the roses. It wasn't addressed and, when I opened it, the card was blank. It had the name and address of the florist. No other note. No indication of who had sent the roses.

Joe must have sent Katherine flowers. But why no note? And why didn't he have them delivered when he knew she would be here, or when she was with him?

The velvety crimson-red roses were beautiful, but they somehow added to my anxiety. Even though the arrival of the roses unnerved me even further, I returned to bed, and fell into a fitful sleep.

Chapter Sixty-Eight

Friday, October 14, 2011—morning

After a restless night of tossing and turning, I had two cups of strong Hazelnut coffee, then took vitamins with orange juice, and prepared for whatever the day had in store for me. A cold shower helped to wake me. Then I changed into pastel yellow hiking shorts and a white T-shirt. Before long, I sat in the chair by the window and reached for the map. I was as prepared for another day in Sedona's red rock country as I was going to be.

I felt numb.

Katherine's unexpected 5:30 a.m. phone call had jangled my nerves even more. She said she was with Joe, and they were somewhere near Oak Creek in the lower part of Sedona. After they had breakfast, she said, she'd meet me at the base of Shaman's Cave.

"Fine," I had snapped, and hung up.

She didn't ask how I was doing, so I didn't tell her about the fiasco with Ralph's crazed fiancé the night before, the wound on my throbbing arm, my exhaustion, or that my eyes felt on fire with grit and grime no matter how many times I washed them out with cool water.

Katherine was so excited and happy when she spent time with Joe that I tried to relax and let her have fun without creating feelings of guilt related to how she was, or wasn't, treating me. This was my last day in Sedona. *Tomorrow I will head for home.*

A dull headache now plagued me most of the time. The pain medication I had been given at the medical center had worn off, so the wound on my forearm burned and pain shot outward in jagged lines of agony in all directions like tiny daggers piercing my arm. *Why hasn't this healed miraculously, too? And why are my lips still cracked and swollen?*

The morning grew lighter. I sat by the table with the lights off and the drapes open and watched the street lights of Sedona begin to click off knowing I'd never tire of watching night slip into day in Sedona.

Katherine had assured me she would meet me on time to hike up to the cave.

I had reminded her if she weren't on time I would begin the climb without her.

Chapter Sixty-Nine

Friday, October 14, 2011—9:30 a.m.

I was surprised when Katherine bounded into the room a little before 9:00 a.m., the time I had planned to take off for Shaman's Cave. I had just returned from breakfast and was gathering my things.

The red roses delighted her. She quickly picked up the note and, when she saw it was blank, asked me what I thought.

"I have no idea," I said. "I assumed the roses were from Joe, for you."

Katherine was radiant.

I was worried.

After a quick shower and fresh make-up, Katherine dressed in army green hiking shorts and a lime green T-shirt. Her Moonstone earrings glimmered in the morning light. "Ready?" she asked, even more energetic than when she'd breezed into the room. The more I watched her, the more tired I became.

"Oh," I said. "Remember the dream I told you about earlier? It came true last night."

"Really?" Katherine said, as she reached over and touched a crimson petal. "What dream?"

"Never mind," I replied. I locked the doors and followed her to the parking lot.

We drove separate vehicles to Shaman's Cave. We traveled mostly on gravel and dirt roads, around puddles and pot holes, and over rocks.

At one point close to the base of the mountain, terror gripped me. Then I remembered reading that the Native Americans felt this was a sacred site and that many people felt fear as they neared the mountain.

I drove on even though hyper-vigilant and fighting panic.

The chill morning air cooled my bare legs as we began the climb to the cave. I stopped and pulled on my old red sweatshirt, positioned my backpack, and stood for a minute looking up at what appeared to be a near perpendicular rock formation. As I looked upward, a large red Cardinal flew into my line of sight, singing loudly, then sat at the opening to the cave.

That was the sign I had been told would lead me to the entrance. My heart raced and chills ran up my spine.

I called to Katherine. When she turned around, I pointed out the Cardinal and the cave entrance. We looked at one another, eyebrows raised.

When we began our climb, a warm sparkling breeze engulfed me. My energy increased.

Birds of all kinds—quail, swallows, sparrows, towhees and Cardinals—either raced up the incline with us or flew before us. A hawk circled above the entrance to the cave. Energized, I made my way up the side of the formation.

Sections of the path were worn into the slippery rock. Water from inside the mountain oozed down the side and over the path making it a treacherous climb.

"Katherine, I'm not a rock climber," I yelled, as I secured the toe of my tennis shoe on a narrow piece of damp rock. I wished I'd worn my hiking boots. I had decided to follow Katherine's lead and wear tennis shoes, so my boots were at the motel.

"You'll be fine, little buddy. You're doing great," Katherine called back to me as she strode up the side of the mountain.

The fifty foot drop and damp, slippery rocks slowed my progress as I inched my way along the narrow path.

In spite of the difficulty, before long Katherine and I both stood on a small ledge at the mouth of the cave.

Katherine was covered in a light film of dust and was slightly winded.

I was covered with dirt, grime and grit that stuck to my sweaty body. My chest heaved and my eyesight blurred. When I caught my breath and could see again, I looked at the Expedition. It was 11:33 a.m.

We clicked on our flashlights and made our way into the mountain. We soon realized, though, that the cave was so shallow that we didn't need extra light. It went nowhere. There was no tunnel.

A low wall had been constructed at the entrance to the cave; a fire pit was in the center.

The cave was the size of an average American livingroom. There was a small side-room that wasn't very deep. We clicked off our flashlights and put them in our backpacks.

A few minutes before 12:00 p.m., we stood directly by a light that came into the cave from a second smaller opening at the right side of the mountain next to the entrance. We agreed that we were where the clue instructed us to be. We looked around in all directions. We paid special attention to the area lighted by the bright sunlight that now shone through the two openings.

"Let's turn our flashlights back on," Katherine suggested. "It's pretty light in here, but perhaps if we move the light over the surface of the cave we can see if anything stands out or glitters. The sphere is supposed to be gold, so it should show up."

"Let's try it both ways," I said as I clicked on my flashlight.

We stood behind the light that poured through the openings. We slowly turned around in place. The light from the sun shone on one side of the cave floor. Suddenly, a slight sparkle caught my eye. "Katherine, look!" I said in whispered awe. I cautiously walked over to the mostly buried object. The tiniest curve of glittering gold was visible. I brushed away dirt from on top of the object, then began to dig the object out with my bare hands. Katherine fell to her knees and joined me.

"No wonder we were to be here at exactly 12:00 p.m.," I said. "That's when the sun entered the cave through the smaller opening, lit upon this tiny exposed piece of the sphere just right, and caused it to glisten."

"You know," I added, "If we hadn't been in this spot on this day, the sun wouldn't have been just right to cause it to reflect off the sphere. Maybe that's why no one has found it before now?"

Katherine was too busy digging to answer.

I stopped digging long enough to pull Trevor's Swiss army knife out of my backpack. I didn't want to nick or scrape the sphere, but I had to loosen the soil around it. It worked. When enough of the soil was loose, the sphere moved. I closed the knife and continued digging with my hands.

Katherine stopped digging and unpacked her collapsible shovel. In a flash, she assembled it, then gently positioned it under the sphere. I stood back. She added gentle pressure to the handle of the shovel. When she did, the sphere popped free of the earth!

Once the sphere was unearthed, I let Katherine claim her prize. We examined it in awed silence. Katherine said, "Whoa! This is really heavy." It was smaller than we had expected—a little larger than a softball—but much heavier.

Even so, the sight of the sphere as it softly glimmered in the afternoon sunlight was mesmerizing. We both stood silently and admired it.

"What now?" I finally said. "It's really heavy. How do we get the sphere out of here? Will you carry it in your backpack? How can you get it out of Sedona without anyone knowing?"

"I'll carry it out of the cave. Then I'll just pack it in with my clothes and drive it home to Prescott with me," Katherine added, as she turned the orb over and over in her hands. "Let's take it to the entrance to get a better look."

With the sphere nestled close to her chest, Katherine turned and walked the few steps to the entrance.

I carried both backpacks. They felt oddly light.

At the mouth of the cave, the bright sunlight momentarily blinded me. Then, suddenly, I was stopped cold in my tracks and chills began to race up my spine when I heard a deep male voice demand, "I'll take that."

We had been so totally focused on the strenuous climb up the mountain, then the search for the sphere, that we hadn't paid close attention to anything else in that remote location.

Oh, God, no! Don't let this happen. My joy quickly morphed into terror.

Too shocked to respond immediately, Katherine, too, stood motionless. She clutched the sphere as she looked in the direction of the voice.

"I said, hand it to me!" he demanded again.

A second voice ordered, "Now! Hand it over!"

Rex, the huge blond man with icy blue eyes, waited for us on the right side of the cave.

I froze.

They were covered with dust and sweat. Hank's tan T-shirt looked as if it had been sprayed onto his muscled body. *How did they follow us up here? Why didn't we hear them?*

I considered trying to bolt down the mountainside, but my body wouldn't move. My heart-rate skyrocketed.

Katherine, clutching the sphere, remained silent behind me.

Hank repeated, "Hey, Goldie, thanks for finding the sphere. Now, hand it over!"

Katherine still didn't move or respond.

My mind spun as Hank stomped past me toward Katherine.

Rex noticed when I slowly slipped my hand into the backpack for my Tomcat. His expression sent chills racing violently down my arms, back and spine. In one fluid movement, he lunged toward me, kicked my backpack across the cave, then backhanded me. I heard my walking stick crack as the bag fell to the cave floor. Then his huge hand locked around my neck. I couldn't breathe. His rancid breath gagged me. He lifted me off the ground by my neck with one massive hand, then squeezed. I felt like a rag-doll in the grip of a Rottweiler. I began to lose consciousness, his face an inch from mine. He smiled.

Just as I was about to pass out, he opened his grip. I dropped to the ground with a thud.

Then he turned toward Katherine and said, "You. Get out here where we can see you better."

Katherine silently took a step forward.

Rex repeated, "For the last time, hand me that sphere."

Katherine stopped walking forward, took a step backward, and shouted, "You bums are evil!" She was about to say more when she heard me gasp. Her head snapped to look at me. Then she saw what had startled me. Hank had a gun pointed at her head.

I trembled.

Katherine's eyes blazed with rage.

My legs grew as weak as if made of warm wax. I groped for the nearest rock with my free hand and held on. As I did, I told Katherine, "Don't argue with them. Give them the sphere. It's not worth dying over."

Katherine glared at Rex as she clutched the sphere even tighter to her chest. Even though the sphere was mostly covered by her arms and hands, the bits of it that were visible sparkled and gleamed in the warm fall noonday sun.

"Katherine! Give that thing to them!" I yelled.

Hank stepped toward her and pressed the gun barrel hard into Katherine's temple.

I watched, silent and motionless. I hoped Katherine would let go of the sphere before one of them had to pry it out of her cold, dead hands.

"Katherine," I said loudly, "Let . . . it . . . go. It's not worth it. There's no way we can win here. Give them that sphere. Do you hear me? Let it go."

The men looked at Katherine the way a cat watches a mouse. "That's right. Listen to your little friend and hand over that sphere!" Hank demanded.

Rex watched the sphere reflect the afternoon sun. He said, "I *was* right. You *have* found the sphere. It was well worth following you this week. *Well* worth it." His yellow-toothed sneer frightened me even more as I tried to think of a way for Katherine and me to come out of this alive. Sphere-less, perhaps, but alive.

For the first time in all the years I've known her, Katherine looked defeated. Then she slowly unfurled her arms and held the sphere in Rex's direction.

His huge hand encircled the sphere and he snatched it out of her hands. Staring at the sphere, Rex walked past me to the landing. When he did, he shoved my left shoulder so hard I gasped as I fell back onto the protruding rocks along the side of the cave entrance.

While I struggled to stand, Hank struck Katherine so hard with his massive elbow she screamed and flew sideways. She landed on her back about three feet inside the mouth of the cave entrance.

I tried to regain my footing and get to Katherine to help her, but I couldn't move. She lay crumpled and motionless. Relief washed over me when she began to stir. *At least she's alive and doesn't appear to be paralyzed.*

Katherine shook her head. She appeared to be alright. Dazed and angry, but okay.

When she tried to sit up, though, she fell back onto the dirt. She put her hands on both sides of her head and moaned. I started to crawl toward her, but Rex put his enormous boot between me and Katherine and said, "You stay right there."

I stopped, frozen. My head spun and my shoulder still throbbed from hitting the wall of the cave. Rex stood close to us. He reeked of such a rancid odor that I quickly became nauseous.

Katherine's whole body sagged.

I tried again to get up, but my legs gave out and I slid back down the wall of the cave.

Katherine continued to hold her head in her hands and moan.

"I've searched for this sphere for thirteen years now. Long before the scroll was found," Rex gloated. He talked more to himself and the sphere than to us.

He added, "Hank, take them to the pit and tie their hands tight enough they can't get loose anytime soon. That will stop them for a few hours. By the time they get untied, we'll be out of the state, if not out of the country." Rex focused his icy blue gaze on me.

I shivered, even though I had begun to feel the warm gentle breeze that glistened with radiant tiny diamonds of various colors once again encircle me. This time, Katherine didn't seem to see it. Neither did the men. Confused, I tried to focus on what Rex was saying. I wondered why the men didn't seem to feel the breeze or see the lights.

How can this be happening? Will Katherine be alright? We're losing the sphere, and . . . All of a sudden my thoughts stopped. It was as if someone had pulled the plug on my brain. Chills ran down my spine. I began to shake.

Rex's gaze grew even icier. I was suddenly even more sure he planned to kill us.

Then he turned his back to us, and sneered, "Thanks for your help, ladies. It's been a pleasure. Now get moving toward that pit over there." With that, he looked back down at his prize. He tossed his filterless cigarette on the dirt then ground it out with the heel of his black hiking boot. He laughed a loud, crazed laugh that ricocheted and echoed throughout the cave.

Katherine tried to struggle to her feet.

"Don't try to stand, Katherine," I said. Just crawl toward the pit.

I again tried to get to her, but Hank grabbed my shoulder and sunk his fingers into my flesh so hard I winced. My knees buckled again. My eyes blurred. I fell.

He then clutched my arm exactly where the bandage covered my wound, and squeezed with all of his strength. The pain was so severe I almost passed out. I couldn't even scream.

Apparently satisfied with the degree of pain he'd inflicted, Hank grabbed both of us by the back of our T-shirts as if we were toys, and shoved us into the cave. We were too dazed and disabled to fight back.

Hank half dragged, half pushed us toward the pit.

We stumbled and tripped.

Rex had begun his descent down the mountainside. He talked to himself and laughed so loud we could hear him as he descended all the way down to the parking area.

The warm glistening breeze continued to dance around and soak into me. Now it bathed Katherine in its radiance, too. It infused us with peace, strength and courage. I could tell that Katherine finally saw it, and felt it, too.

Hank continued to savagely drag and shove us toward the pit. We didn't have a chance against him unless I could get to my gun, and I couldn't.

Hank tied us together, back-to-back, with our hands behind our backs. Next, he tied us to a large boulder.

Oh, God! I don't want to die in a cave in the desert! I inwardly screamed.

Then he left.

I was surprised he'd left our backpacks behind.

A couple of minutes passed while Katherine and I adjusted to being left alone. Strangely, I remembered the time my mother insisted I crawl under the house, with all the dirt and spider webs and debris, to fetch a new litter of kittens because I was the smallest. That same sense of horror and dread overtook me now.

Katherine mumbled words about "bums," "evil," "jerks," and "rotten."

I took that to mean she was recovering and would be fine.

"I'm furious with myself for being so stupid," she ranted. "I walked right into those two bums! I should have listened when you said you thought someone was following us."

With an intensity that startled even me, I said, "I feel just as disgusted with myself for being caught off-guard! What cowards they are! Lying in wait for two women. Well," I continued, "It's a moot point now, isn't it? They are long gone, and *they* now have *your* golden sphere. I'm just glad they didn't kill us outright. I was sure they were going to, weren't you? I thought for a minute they were going to kill us just for the fun of it."

My concern over our getting untied and out of the cave as quickly as possible over-rode everything else. "I hope you have some kind of plan to get us out of here," I said. I felt as if I were floating underwater. In spite of the breeze and the lights, I slipped in and out of consciousness as I continued to fight to stay alert. The world seemed to move in slow motion around me.

Katherine and I both worked to loosen the rough ropes that bound us to the rocks, and to one another.

Then, simultaneously, we spoke. I stopped so Katherine could tell me what she had in mind. She said, "Why don't you sit still. I'll work on my ropes. That way we won't be working against one another. The way we're doing it now the ropes seem to be getting tighter."

"Okay," I said. "The more I try to loosen my ropes, the more numb my hands get."

It seemed like Katherine worked the ropes forever.

Finally, I said, "I think I feel blood on my wrists and hands. I'm losing the sensation in my right hand altogether. I'm not sure how long we can manage this, Katherine."

Katherine stopped her work on the ropes. Then she turned her head toward mine. "Don't worry, Crissy. I got us into this mess. I will get us out of it, too," she said.

"I know, Katherine," I wearily responded.

The now familiar warm breeze that glittered with diamond-like colors increased in intensity and, before long, grew as strong as a Texas wind. Red dust swirled away from us as the colors engulfed us. As the wind blew and danced around us, we both exhaled and relaxed.

"I wish the breeze, or whatever it is, had a knife," Katherine said. Then she added, "I'm getting used to this strange world you live in, Crissy."

The breeze continued to grow thicker and stronger. Before long, the ropes loosened as if they were large rubber bands and Someone was stretching them so we could slip our hands free. My heart danced. For the first time, hope flooded through me. I slipped free of the ropes. Feeling returned to my right hand. As I stood, my legs became stronger. This time, they supported me.

"We're free, Katherine!" I exclaimed. "Free! Are you free, too?"

It took Katherine just a minute to realize what had happened and to get totally free of her ropes.

I was eager to leave. I wanted to race out of that cave.

Katherine's movements were uncharacteristically slow and jerky.

I worried.

"Hold on, Crissy. I'm free now, too, and I've got water in my backpack. Luckily, the bums left them for us!" she said.

We drank water. Then we limped back out of the cave into the bright sunlight. Tears welled in my eyes when I thought of all I'd endured the past week only to have the sphere stolen from us. I couldn't see any sign of the vehicle the men had used. They must have already made it back to the main highway.

I looked at Trevor's timepiece. It was 2:59 p.m.

Katherine reached for her backpack, slipped it over her left arm, and mumbled, "Those dirty rotten bums," one more time, then added, "Well, let's go, Little Red. We're not that far from the police station."

"I thought you hated the police," I said, as I picked up my backpack. "I can't believe you're taking this so well."

"I don't like the police, and I'm not taking this well, but what else can we do?" Katherine responded. Then she turned, looked in the direction of our vehicles, and loped down the mountainside.

Katherine was halfway down the mountain before I started to pick my way down behind her.

With visions of my fall on Monday in Casner Canyon, I took my time as I worked my way downward. It took me twice as long as Katherine to slip, slide, and scoot down to where our vehicles were parked.

When I arrived at my Jeep, Katherine held out a bottle of water that she'd dug out of the ice chest in the back of her Rover.

I took it gladly and gulped down the fresh, clean liquid.

Katherine's normal graceful movements still seemed uncharacteristically rough. Her hand jerked at odd times. I studied her with increased concern, and said, "You know, you need to go to the medical center. We should stop by there before we go to the police station. The report can wait. You need to be checked out."

"No. I'll be fine. I don't need . . ." Katherine's words were cut off mid-sentence by a loud, long blast that rocked the valley.

We both jumped. The ground vibrated.

I turned toward the sound of the explosion. The shock caused me to step backward into the side of my Jeep. Water spilled everywhere as the bottle fell from my hand.

Dust and debris belched out of what had been Shaman's Cave. The face of the cave entrance crumbled and closed in on itself. Shrubs careened down the mountainside. After a few minutes, the dust settled.

It took a couple more minutes before we realized the men must have rigged the cave with explosives. We had barely made it out alive.

Katherine silently stared for a long time at the side of the transformed mountain to where the cave entrance had once been. Finally, she said, "Those evil jerks intended to kill us. The bums meant to blow us up!"

"Yes. It appears they did intend to kill us," I said. I had slid down the side of my Jeep and sat limply, cross-legged, in the red dirt staring at the mountainside.

When I looked at her again Katherine had turned deathly pale, yet still stood, feet firmly planted, as she stared toward the mountain. The last of the pebbles, dust and debris continued to slide and settle.

We didn't cry. We didn't speak. We didn't move. A silent horror had settled over us like an invisible net.

Katherine broke the silence and said, "I'm scared, and I don't get scared often."

"Ditto," I said.

Then, as if jolted with a bolt of electricity, Katherine almost shouted, "I feel like such a jerk! Such a sap!" Her hands shook as she reached up to touch her necklace.

"It wasn't just you, Katherine," I said, as I struggled to my feet.

After a long pause, I finally said, "We were both excited and caught off-guard. The whole time I've been here I knew someone was watching and following us. But when they showed themselves, I was so unprepared that I couldn't even get to my gun. I still can't understand how they followed us up a mountainside without us knowing it."

"Neither can I," she replied.

"I wonder how and why this happened like it did?" I said.

"There isn't a reason," Katherine answered. "It just happened. There was no cause. No *design,* as you would call it."

I wonder.

"I still can't believe I had it in my hands, and then lost it," Katherine whispered.

We continued to stare at the mountain in silence.

Chapter Seventy

Friday, October 14, 2011—3:30 p.m.

By the time we met back at the entrance to the police station, an uncharacteristic gloom had settled over Katherine. Her black cloud didn't help to lift my own morose mood. Even so, we trudged forward to make the necessary police report.

When we dragged ourselves through the double glass doors, Officers Stampos and Rizzo greeted us by our first names. *I think we're getting too familiar with the people at this station.*

When we walked closer to where they stood at the back of the room, their eyes widened. They put down their paperwork and quickly escorted us to chairs.

Without warning, the sudden safety and security of the police station caused tears to flood my eyes. When I opened my mouth to tell them what had happened, the tears slipped down my dirty cheeks. My voice caught.

Officer Rizzo gave us water and told us to take our time.

Katherine had stopped shaking and began to tell the officers what happened.

Fortified with fresh hot coffee that Officer Rizzo brought me, I took a deep breath then joined in as Katherine continued to tell the officers about the two men who had stolen the orb and left us in Shaman's Cave to die.

"I'm sure they are the same men who tortured TJ," Katherine said. "You've got to do something! You can't let them get away with this. They tried to kill us. We barely got out of the cave before the explosion. They left us in that cave to die just like they left TJ in that horrid old shack. They are evil—wicked—bums. *And they have my sphere.*"

We were asked if we could identify the two men. "Once you've seen them under the circumstances we did," I replied, "you could never forget anything about them, right down to their hiking boots and stench."

Three more officers now crowded around us. They were genuinely concerned.

We told them again how Rex and Hank took the sphere from us, then bound us and left us in the cave.

Officer Reese got a camera, took pictures of the fading finger marks around my neck, the disappearing bruises on my arm and shoulder, and the gash on Katherine's head that was almost healed.

The officers told us they had already put a BOLO out for the two men when they attacked Mr. Johnson. Officer Reese added that they'd put an APB out for them, check all the airports. Even though they had attempted to murder us, that was all the police could do. The officers said they had DNA from the shack, but that would take a long time to process. "Besides," Officer Reese continued, "By now they could have boarded a private plane and flown out of the country."

"You know," I said, "I know how this sounds. But there were a series of clues that we followed. They were all accurate. They really did lead us to a large golden sphere the size of a softball. It had a mellow glistening shine to it. It was so beautiful. And heavy. I can't believe we had it, but now it's gone."

"I'm leaving for home in the morning, and it's a two-day drive," I added. "We've both told you all we know. So, are we finished here? We need medical attention."

The officers said they would let us know if they learned anything. I took a last sip of the now thick, muddy coffee.

We were preparing to leave the station when Patrick Bailey walked in. He looked around, then spotted me. *Oh, great! Just what I need!* I tried to wipe away the tear stains from under my puffy eyes, but quickly realized it was hopeless.

Bailey strode directly to where I was gathering my copy of the report and picking up my backpack. A slithery half-smile covered his face.

My skin crawled.

Once again, he glanced at me from that side angle I had grown to hate.

Intercepting what he was about to say, I said, "Mr. Bailey, you're just about the last person on planet earth I want to have to deal with right now. Leave me alone." Everything about him annoyed me.

The room became so silent you could hear a spider walk.

An exaggerated look of mock-hurt furrowed Bailey's brow and his mouth turned downward.

Repulsed, I turned to make my escape.

Just then, Officer Stampos said, "I didn't think you knew Mr. Bailey."

"I don't know him. Not really," I responded. "I've just had the misfortune to have bumped into him a few times. He's followed me and pestered me ever since I arrived in Sedona."

"'Pestered'? Oh, come now. Really, Ms. O'Connor," Patrick Bailey said in a mocking civility that exaggerated his accent. He slithered closer. I noticed that the bright lights in the station highlighted his greasy coal-black hair and light aqua-green eyes causing them to stand out all the more. *He's like a shiny cockroach.*

I noticed that the more sinister Patrick seemed, the uglier he appeared. The correlation between a person's character and how he is perceived—handsome, or ugly, or somewhere in-between—struck me once again.

Pain shot through my mouth alerting me that I had once again bitten my upper lip. I looked away so I wouldn't get entwined in a conversation with Mr. Bailey. I could feel that old primitive *fight or flight* response well up inside me. I began to feel alarmed. I needed to get away from Bailey, and soon.

Officer Stampos asked, "Did you know Mr. Bailey represents the heirs of Dunluce Castle?"

I stopped, inhaled sharply, and turned to face Bailey. "No. I didn't."

Bailey smiled arrogantly as he rested an elbow on the surface of the old wooden counter over-flowing with papers, reports, and equipment.

"I definitely did not know," I repeated. I inwardly turned even colder toward Patrick Bailey while my skin grew hotter. *Why didn't he just tell me who he was in the first place? Why follow me?* My head felt like it might explode.

Bailey straightened the collar of his forest green jacket, then said, "Your suspicions about me were correct, Ms. O'Connor. I have followed you. I wanted information about *my* golden sphere. You know, the one you have managed to lose. Isn't that right Ms. O'Connor? The sphere is now gone? It's in criminal hands again thanks to your bumbling. That's what I have been told, anyway." Blame and contempt oozed from Patrick Bailey the way slime oozes through a strainer.

"You know, Mr. Bailey," I said in a low, slow, deliberately clear and modulated voice, "I have a low threshold for people like you. I always have. I need to warn you, I don't get angry and lose my temper very often, but I'm

on the verge of losing it right now. I suggest you back off and leave me alone."
Then I added, "And I did not *lose* anything."

"Really?" he said.

"Yes, 'really,'" I responded. "It was *stolen* from us. We were manhandled,
tied up, and left in a cave to die. We nearly *did* die." With every word, my
breathing grew more ragged and my focus more intense—warning signs I'd
grown to recognize all too well.

"Besides, if you are so adept," I continued, feeling my self-control slip
further away with every new word, "why didn't *you* find the sphere and
reclaim it? While I'm at it, why didn't you just introduce yourself in the first
place and say why you were in Sedona, and explain why you followed us?"

As my voice grew louder, Officer Stampos and Officer Reese began to
walk closer to where we stood.

Every slicked-back hair in place, his black shoes spit-shined to perfection,
Patrick's eyes narrowed into ugly slits and his smug grin changed to a sneer.
He replied, "If I had told you whom I represented, and that I intended to
claim the sphere if you found it, how hard do you think you would you have
looked for it?"

I felt myself turn crimson.

Katherine took a step backward.

The officers stepped closer.

The more Bailey talked about the Northern Ireland Environmental Agency
that now managed Dunluce Castle as a National Monument in state care, the
angrier I became. I couldn't believe it when he held out his business card and
told me to get in touch if I heard anything more about the sphere.

I didn't take his card, so he set it down next to me on the desk.

"Those of us who are patriotic by nature and have a respect for history
and archeology just might have returned even a priceless treasure to its
proper owner or country," I countered. "If asked."

"Of course. Of course," he responded, sarcasm dripping from every
word.

"Are you calling me a liar?" I said.

"No. No. Not at all," Bailey replied, with a smirk that said he was doing
just that.

Why am I always just on the edge of losing self-control around this
guy?

He started to leave, then, halfway to the door, turned, strolled back to
where I stood, and said, "If you're ever in Antrim, look me up. I'd be glad to

give *you* a personal tour, Dr. O'Connor." Chills of repulsion trickled along my spine.

Then he reached out to put his hand on my shoulder.

"Do *not* touch me!" I warned.

Bailey smirked, then put his hand on my shoulder, anyway.

I stood my ground. In an explosion that I don't recall, Patrick Bailey's body flew across the room and slammed into the wall by the double glass entry doors. The impact rattled the doors.

He slid to the ground. He stared in shocked disbelief. So did everyone else in the room. Bailey radiated hatred the way a furnace radiates heat. "You . . ." he seethed, then caught himself. The veins in his neck bulged.

"Go ahead, Mr. Bailey. Touch me again," I said.

He glared.

I waited.

No one went to help him.

He finally struggled to his feet.

Officer Reese walked to where Patrick Bailey now stood, glaring at me, and asked him, "Are you alright?"

"I will be," Bailey snapped, as he straightened his jacket.

"Then you should leave," the officer said.

After a long, weighty silence, someone asked, "Do you want to file a report, Mr. Bailey?"

Patrick Bailey remained silent.

"If you do," Officer Reese said, "You can. But there is a room full of police officers and other witnesses that watched you provoke and then accost Dr. O'Connor. She had the right to stand her ground and protect herself, and she did. But if you want to file a report, we can do that."

"No. I do not want to file a report," Bailey growled. He squared his narrow shoulders. "Call me," he said, more to the room than to anyone in particular, "if you learn anything new about the sphere." Then he turned, picked up his attache case, and slammed through the glass doors.

"Well, aren't you the surprise of the year?" Officer Reese said to me.

I stood in place, trembling slightly after the adrenaline rush of my encounter with Patrick Bailey.

Katherine seemed more shocked than anyone else. Finally, she walked closer to me. In a low, conspiratorial voice, she said, "I've never seen you pushed that far before. Good for you. He deserved it. Are you ready?"

The office came back to life with movement and chatter. Officer Reese continued to watch me. "There's no reason for you to stay," he finally said. "You're free to go. You should both pay a visit to the medical center."

Without responding, I took the card Patrick Bailey had handed me and, with shaking hands, shoved it into my backpack.

"You wouldn't seriously consider contacting that bum if we ever do find the sphere again, would you?" Katherine asked.

"I don't know," I said. "But I do know I'm ready to get out of here. And even more ready to head for home."

We walked toward the door. Exhaustion settled on me the way dew blankets the morning grass. Katherine called out to each of the officers and staff, all of whom she now knew by first name. She waved. Most of them smiled and waved back.

Me? I watched for a moment, then turned and slowly walked out of the same doors Patrick Bailey had just charged through.

Chapter Seventy-One

Friday, October 14, 2011—5:49 p.m.

Sunset was quickly approaching when we left the police station. Still in a mild shock, neither of us talked.

The physical and emotional exhaustion of what I'd been through had taken its toll. We had hiked every day, sustained injuries, been miraculously healed, watched a man on the brink of death mysteriously recover, dealt with being watched and followed, had our room ransacked, had a prophetic dream materialize, confronted the guilt of a long-ago mistake, followed mystical clues from unlikely sources, and then actually found the sacred golden sphere of legend—only to have it stolen from us minutes later. It was mind-numbing. To have held the mystical sphere then have it taken from us was a shattering experience.

A migraine throbbed behind my left eye.

"What are you doing?" Katherine asked, when she saw me rummaging in my backpack.

"I need something for this headache," I responded.

"That stuff'll kill you," she said, while munching on a handful of mixed Red Hots and Good 'n Plentys.

I took the pill.

We decided Katherine would pick up a pizza, and I would pick up Pedro. Then we'd meet at the Airport Road lookout and watch our last Sedona sunset over the Verde Valley.

Chapter Seventy-Two

Friday, October 14, 2011—6:19 p.m.

I was glad the vet's office stayed open until 7:00 p.m. When I arrived, Jody brought Pedro out from the boarding area. His head was up, his tail over his back, and his step was springy as he pranced at her side. His eyes, one brown and one blue, glanced up at Jody. When she stopped, he sat down at her feet. Jody petted Pedro for awhile. He licked her hand as his tail thumped on the floor.

Jody handed me the lead and went back around the counter. Pedro started to follow her, and seemed confused when he realized I now held the leash.

After I had settled the bill, I thanked Jody, and walked toward the door. Pedro stopped, and turned back toward Jody. After some encouragement, he followed me to my Liberty. I put Pedro in the backseat and headed for the Airport Road lookout.

Katherine had already picked up an especially large, thick, cheesy pizza at one of the locals' favorite places, Pizza Delight. She waited for me and Pedro at the lookout.

I parked in the lot to the left of the main road. Then Pedro and I headed to where Katherine sat near the ledge that overlooked the Verde Valley. It seemed odd to see Katherine sitting so still and quiet. She was so engrossed in her own thoughts that she didn't even hear us approach.

When I got closer, I let Pedro off his lead. He ran and bounded yet stayed reasonably close. When Pedro dashed in front of Katherine, she seemed to snap back to the present.

She forced a smile, although her eyes looked tired and lifeless.

I returned her smile, feeling exhausted and disappointed.

Neither of us spoke as we watched Pedro run.

227

Katherine put large slices of cheesy veggie pizza on heavy-duty paper plates. Then she handed me a Coke Classic and said, "The events of this day call for 'the real thing.'"

"You're right," I said, balancing the pizza on my lap and reaching for the Coke.

The sun continued to sink lower in the west behind clouds that had slowly transformed into myriad shades of reds, oranges, golds, and whites that streaked the evening sky. As we watched, the sky changed from blue to dark blue to grey. Clouds floated lazily in the sky. Sprays of golden light radiated and sparkled as they coated the city and rock formations in a blanket of soft golden color.

Through swollen, burning eyes, I scanned the natural beauty all around me. The bones in my face still ached. My arm hurt. In spite of everything, as I watched the sinking sun, I was calm and at peace. *It's that liquid magic that permeates the air of Sedona. I love it here. I'll be back someday.*

As the top of the sun sank below the horizon, we took our last bites of pizza. The sky had turned a deep purple-black. Gold and silver hues streaked outward from where the sun had set. We silently watched the waning spectacle of nature.

Then, as if I'd been in a pressure chamber but hadn't known it, I suddenly felt free. Colors became more vivid. Scenery seemed more alive. My appreciation of life increased. My thinking seemed crystal clear. All of my senses were quickened. Both the headache and pain in my arm disappeared.

Then I heard a Voice say, "You have done well, and all is well."

I looked at Katherine, but she obviously hadn't heard the Voice. So I remained silent.

Katherine broke the silence and said, "Any chance you would change your mind and stay a little longer? It would be nice to visit and shop over the weekend."

Amazed she would even ask, I said, "You're two hours from Prescott. I'm two days from Austin. Besides, you've been with Joe far more than you've been with me this week. So, no. Thanks. I won't stay. Besides, I really miss my life back in Austin. I'm ready to be home."

The now familiar warm glistening wind flowed around us and embraced us. This time, there were no sparkling diamonds of any particular color.

It was good to end our visit with a gorgeous view of Sedona. Katherine reached up with her left hand and touched her necklace. There was no need to say anything.

Finally, we both sighed, looked at one another, and agreed it was time to leave.

"You know, Katherine," I said, as we started to pick up the wrappers and empty bottles, "It's been some experience, hasn't it?"

Katherine responded, "Maybe there *is* something to all this metaphysical stuff you're into, Crissy. Maybe. But I really don't think so." She smiled.

"Maybe?" I said. "After all the amazing things we've seen and been through this week, and experienced first-hand, you still doubt?"

"Too much has happened this week for me not to at least consider there might be something to your research and work." After a brief pause, she added, "Crissy, don't get upset, but when I told Joe and Manny what happened today, they said they would like to take us both out to dinner tonight. I told them we'd meet them later. You're leaving tomorrow morning, and they'd like to say goodbye."

Amazed, I looked at Katherine for a minute, then mellowed, and said, "Okay. Why not?" I smiled the smile of one resigned, every bone in my face aching, and turned away to call Pedro.

"Good," she said, perking up.

"Don't expect me to stay long, Katherine. Just dinner, then I'm gone. That's it. I leave for home early tomorrow morning. I've already let the staff at Kings Ransom know. If you're not back and checked out by 11:00 a.m., the charges for the room switch over to you. Deal?"

"Deal," she said, smiling the smile of the victorious. She slapped her thigh and headed toward her Rover.

"Come on, Pedro," I called. I put him back on his lead. He trotted alongside me, then jumped into the backseat of the Liberty.

Chapter Seventy-Three

Friday, October 14, 2011—7:33 p.m.

When I walked into our room, the red light on the phone was flashing. There was a message from Jody, the assistant at the veterinarian's office. I noticed the return telephone number was different from the main office telephone number. In her message, Jody said she missed Pedro, and asked me to call her, whatever the hour.

What now? I hope whoever abandoned Pedro doesn't want him back. Or his abuser doesn't want to claim him now that I've had him neutered and treated. I took a deep breath, then dialed Jody.

Jody answered immediately. She said she couldn't get Pedro out of her mind. Then she asked if I would consider allowing her to adopt him. I didn't know how to respond. "Well," I said, "Why don't you give me a minute to think about it, okay? I'll call you back in a little while."

She agreed, but I could tell she was anxious and hopeful.

I was already attached to Pedro. I knew that I would miss him if I left him with Jody. But I also knew that if I took Pedro into our home it would send our three cats into horrified shock.

So I called Jody back and said, "I'll tell you what. If this works for you, here's what I suggest. Why don't we meet in a quiet corner of the parking lot at Tlaquepaque at 7:30 p.m. I'll bring Pedro. I'll let him run free for a minute. Then we'll see who he chooses to go to. If he chooses to go to you, he'll be yours. If he comes back to me and wants to get in the Jeep, I'll keep him and take him home with me. How does that sound?"

"Great!" Jody jubilantly responded. "I'll be there. And I'd be glad to reimburse you for Pedro's vet bill and care if he chooses me."

"Let's see what he does," I said. Then we hung up.

Katherine had entered the room, and I told her what Jody had asked.

We were subdued as we packed. Katherine being low-key was such an anomaly that I wasn't quite sure how to handle it.

Chapter Seventy-Four

Friday, October 14, 2011—7:21 p.m.

Packed and ready to take off at first light, Katherine, Pedro and I left to meet Jody. She was there, waiting for us. When I opened the car door, Pedro bounded out of the backseat and raced over to Jody. He wiggled and jumped up on her, obviously delighted to see her again. As she laughed and played with him, tears formed in her eyes. Tears formed in mine, too, because I knew where Pedro belonged, and it wasn't with me. *Love is such a funny thing. It takes so many forms. They both seem happy, so I'm happy for them.* But a soft sadness came over me because of my loss of Pedro. *At least this pooch will live a good life*, I thought.

Jody and I talked. I gave her a large paper bag with Pedro's food, water dishes, and toys. Then I handed her his leash. "I think he's found a loving home, here, with you," I said.

Jody put the bag in the backseat of her lime-green VW. Pedro jumped into the front seat. Jody reached for her wallet.

"Oh, no," I said. "It's a gift to me that Pedro has a loving home. Please, accept him as my gift to you." Jody hugged me. Then she turned, got into her car, closed the door, and drove out of the parking lot. Pedro's head bobbed out the passenger window, ears erect in the evening breeze. I watched them drive away.

Chapter Seventy-Five

Friday, October 14, 2011—8:14 p.m.

Katherine and I headed back to Kings Ransom. We were to meet Joe and Manny at the Elote for a Mexican dinner at 8:30 p.m. We'd be a couple minutes late. Now that I knew they hadn't been following us, I felt better about them.

When we met Joe and Manny, I noticed Manny was wearing jeans. "You? In jeans?" I said, surprised, "I didn't think you ever wore jeans."

"I don't. Not normally. But I bought these today for tonight."

Our eyes met. I felt warmth and appreciation toward Manny. I looked away.

Joe ordered a pitcher of margaritas. Per usual, Katherine took center stage as she relayed all of that happened to us at Shaman's Cave. I leaned back into the booth, sipped my drink, and relaxed.

Katherine suddenly remembered the dozen large-stemmed deep red perfectly shaped velvety roses. She turned and thanked Joe.

"You're welcome, but I didn't send them," he said, as he and Katherine locked eyes.

"Well . . . then . . . who did?" she asked.

"There wasn't any writing on the envelope other than the room number," I said, "so I assumed they were from you for Katherine." My voice slowed, then trailed off as I wondered who could have sent them.

Manny said, "Maybe they're from TJ as a 'thank you.' You probably saved his life."

Katherine and I looked at one another. I wasn't convinced. But I said to Katherine, "Well, if you're sure they weren't for you, and if you don't mind, I'll put one in a paper cup and take it home as a reminder of this week. Not that I need much of a reminder."

"Sure. Go ahead," she said.

Dinner was relaxed; the food delicious. I had a cheese enchilada, Katherine had chicken enchiladas, and the guys had steaks with the works.

I glanced over at Katherine from time to time. She seemed happy with Joe's arm wrapped around her shoulder. Then I realized this would probably be the last time I would see Katherine for many years.

While we chatted, my mind wandered, and I wondered why handsome men so often wear black. Black shirts, black slacks, black shoes.

After we'd had flan and coffee for dessert, Katherine slapped Joe on the shoulder with her dessert menu and said, "Hey. Let's go for a walk."

He smiled, said they'd be back in a few minutes, and led her to the door.

Manny and I chatted as we finished our coffee.

"You seem like an unlikely woman to hike all over Sedona, climb rock formations, follow Katherine up mountainsides, and venture into abandoned mine shafts," he said.

"Well," I replied, "Katherine and I have been friends since we were teens. She said we'd hike and look for a sphere. I didn't realize she meant rock climb and 'go where no woman has dared to go before.' We worked together and played together for years. There's a sort of unspoken pact that if one of us ever needs help from the other one, really needs her help, she will be there."

"I guess I'd feel the same way if Joe asked me to help him," Manny said.

"This has been the experience of a lifetime, as it usually is when I hook up with Katherine. This week has increased my belief in the supernatural, and it was pretty strong already," I smiled.

"How about another margarita?" Manny asked.

"How about I say 'goodbye' and head back to my room," I replied.

"I'll walk you out," Manny said. "Joe's already picked up the bill."

I was beginning to feel too comfortable with Manny, which concerned me.

"You know," Manny said, "I think Joe fancies himself in love with Katherine."

"Really?" I said. "I don't see her as the partner of a traveling salesman. By the way, Manny, what do you and Joe *really* do for a living? I don't believe either one of you sells anything."

"Don't tell Katherine," he said. "Joe wants to tell her."

"Okay," I said.

"Joe works for Homeland Security. I inherited a few buildings in New York. I manage my properties and invest."

The thought of Katherine, who disliked government workers in general, and law enforcement personnel in particular, with a man who worked for Homeland Security struck me as just too funny. Maybe it was the margarita, but I began to smile, then laugh. "That's sort of like Karma, or Divine Justice, isn't it?" I said.

As we left the restaurant, I spotted Katherine and Joe, and waved goodbye.

She and Joe both waved back, then walked over to say goodbye. After I hugged Katherine and shook Joe's hand, I turned and headed toward my room. Manny walked with me a short distance.

"Just a minute," he said. "I have something for you. It's in my Hummer."

I was instantly concerned. I wasn't keen on the idea of a man who oozed charm giving me a gift to take home. My mind turned to Trevor and how I would explain a gift from a man I met in Sedona.

When he returned, Manny held a box about the size of a hat box under his arm. He handed it to me, and said, "Open this when you get back to your room. It's a eudialyte sphere. I bought it for you one evening while Joe and Katherine were out. It came from a local shop so you will have it as a reminder of Sedona. I was going to get you a clear crystal sphere because of your name. Then I thought you might prefer this sphere's brilliant purple, burgundy, black and mauve colors. The shopkeeper said eudialyte is rare, and that it's all the rage these days with people who are into the metaphysical. She also said eudialyte spheres this size are especially rare and very hard to come by."

"I know," I said. "I've been looking for one for months now."

I was going to object and refuse his gift, but then decided to just accept it and say goodbye. As I took the heavy box with both hands, I smiled, and said, "I don't think there's any danger I'll forget anything about this week, or Sedona."

When I held the box, warmth coursed up my arms. My mind cleared. The disappointment and anger over the loss of the golden sphere drained away. Any residue from a trying week also slipped away. I was left with a sense of peace, enchantment, and the Divine. The contents of the box felt as if it were a living being with a distinct personality.

The feeling was so overpowering that I lost track of Manny for a moment. Then, as Manny moved closer, it felt as if an invisible cord attached to my naval pulled me toward him—as if we were beginning to meld into one another.

Then the unimaginable happened. A bolt of positive regard leapt from the center of my chest into Manny's. When it did, I flinched, and stepped backward. So did Manny, which made me believe he'd felt it, too.

I gasped, caught myself, and took another step backward. "*I must go,*" I said. "*Now!*"

"I wish I'd met you sooner," Manny whispered in a soft, deep voice. "You're the most beautiful person, inside and out, that I've ever known." Manny started to take another step closer, but I thrust out my hand, and said, "I really *must* leave, and *now.*"

I turned and double-stepped back to my room. Once I was around the corner from the restaurant, I shifted the box to under my left arm and used my right hand to fetch the room key out of my pocket.

Moonlight, margaritas and Manny. Not a good mix for me!

Chapter Seventy-Six

Saturday, October 15, 2011—4:59 a.m.

Katherine hadn't returned to our room during the night, so I was glad I'd said goodbye at the restaurant the night before. I wrote a note and left it in the center of the small round wooden table by the red roses. Then I walked out onto the patio to take one last look at Sedona.

Back inside the room, I stood and took one long last look around. As I did, I remembered the string of events that tied the past week together. I took another long, slow, deep breath. During the week in Sedona I had gained a renewed appreciation of being alive and whole.

I had wanted to visit the Sedona Mago Retreat (Mago, I had learned, meant Mother Earth). But now I changed my mind. I just wanted to be home. And as quickly as I could get there.

I had put on fresh, loose jeans that would be comfortable for driving, went for a short walk in the light of the parking lot, and enjoyed the quiet of a Sedona morning by the light of the waning full moon.

Back in the room, I left my key on the desk, then walked out onto the landing. When I did, I felt a slight sadness when, for the last time, the motel door clicked closed behind me.

I had already packed the last of my things into my now red-dust-covered Jeep. So I headed out of the parking lot of Kings Ransom. When I looked back at the room, Sophie sat in front of the door and watched me as I drove away from Kings Ransom.

I made my way to Highway 179, then headed toward Interstate 17. *It's amazing that Sedona has been able to maintain its charm and rural, small town feel while also being such a mega tourist attraction and such a spiritual hot spot.*

I backtracked all the way to Austin. I had told Trevor to expect me sometime Sunday afternoon. I left Amarillo at 3:00 a.m. on Sunday, and made it home earlier in the afternoon than I'd anticipated.

All the way, I pondered the miracles, mysteries and mistakes of the past week. *And the sphere. How could we have found, then lost, the sacred golden sphere?* I kept asking myself.

Chapter Seventy-Seven

Sunday, October 16, 2011, 5:31 p.m.

I arrived home dazed and exhausted.

I was greeted by my relieved husband. I hugged him, then played with my excited cats who rubbed against my legs and jumped onto the sofa for me to pet them. They "head butted" me and followed me wherever I went.

I told Trevor about some of the events of the past week. "But," I added, "I can't possibly tell you everything this evening. It will have to wait."

The more I tried to explain the past week to him, the more I realized it was impossible to convey it in its entirety. There were pieces that would forever remain unspoken.

Finally, in response to his puzzled expression, I said, "Remember that quote from Viktor Frankl that I often refer to? The message in his book that said 'survivors didn't like to talk about their experiences because those who went through the holocaust and a concentration camp didn't need anyone to explain what they experienced, and those who didn't experience it would never understand what it was like no matter what they were told?' Well, it was like that. I can talk about it forever, and probably will. But I really don't think anyone else would or could quite understand what it was like being in my skin this past week. Not even you." As I talked, I felt oddly detached from what had happened. It seemed distant and unreal, even to me.

While we continued to catch up over one of Trevor's signature sandwiches, mixed fruit and coffee, Trevor asked, "Did you know that the temperature in Sedona dropped twenty degrees the day you arrived, then went back up almost twenty degrees the day you left?"

"No. I hadn't heard," I replied, surprised. "Really? I know it had unexpectedly dropped, which was great. But I didn't know how much. It was in the high sixties and low seventies the entire time," I responded, feeling that odd chill that the supernatural had somehow been involved yet again.

While we chatted, I told Trevor more of the highlights of my sojourn to Sedona. Then I looked around and took in Trevor, our cats, plants everywhere, the soft colors of our home, birds that flitted around in our backyard, the outdoor trees and plants that were losing the last of their flowers and foliage. I suddenly appreciated more than ever my comfortable, fulfilled life.

Trevor told me about his week. As I tried to listen, fatigue overcame me.

After a short nap, I decided to empty my backpack, start a load of laundry, then call it a day. When I spotted my filthy, torn floral backpack in the entryway corner, I decided it would be in the first load of laundry. I took the backpack to the bedroom, emptied the contents onto my white quilted bedspread, then put the backpack in the washer filled with hot water and Tide.

When I returned to the bedroom, the almost forgotten Shaman Stone had rolled off the pillow sham and into the center of the bed. As I watched, it continued to move and shape-shift. Within a couple of seconds, it had become a large radiant translucent golden orb the size of a volleyball with a red vibrating center the size of a golf ball. The orb looked as if it had the consistency of a jellyfish. It began to pulsate. A warm breeze engulfed me. Red, gold, blue, green and yellow beams glistened like crushed diamonds all around me. Some of the colors began to settle on, then melt into my skin.

I backed into the wall with such force I almost knocked a painting off the wall.

I stared in silent amazement. The golden sphere seemed alive—as if a person was in the room with me. Then it telepathically said:

> I summoned you to take Me out of Sedona.
> You did all that you were asked to do.
> We are now partners.
> Your goal is to do good.
> And doing good is My purpose, as well.
> Together, we will accomplish great deeds.

Speechless, I stared at the orb. Then I mentally "saw" a video of the week's events play out in my mind. As my shock dissipated, a gentle peace and confidence took its place. I continued to stand motionless, staring at the golden orb. Finally, I mentally asked, "What was the other orb those vile men stole, then? I thought that was You."

> It was a decoy. You were being followed.
> Others wanted to find Me.
> So I gave them something to distract them.
> Now they will not bother you, or Me.
> Tell no one what has happened between us.
> No one must know. Not even Trevor or Katherine.
> Do you understand?

A feeling of pure joy and celebration flowed through me. Then I realized that the Sacred Golden Sphere of legend had been calling me. *Me.* I savored every second as I gazed at the sphere in wonder and deep gratitude.

I was soon jarred when the phone rang. I flinched. When I turned to answer the phone, the sphere's brilliance faded and it shape-shifted back into a Shaman Stone.

When I answered the phone, I heard Katherine say, "Hi there, Crissy. I just wanted to make sure you got home safely and that we're still friends."

"Yes, and yes," I smiled as I walked back into the bedroom and marveled at the mystical sphere in front of me, now once again masquerading as a Shaman Stone. "But barely on both counts."

"You know," Katherine went on, "There's an annual gem and mineral show in Trona next year. You could fly out and I could pick you up in Vegas and . . ."

"Oh, no . . . no . . . no, Katherine. Really," I quickly said, "I don't see me leaving home for any more adventures for many years to come. But thanks for thinking of me." And with that, I said goodbye.

Upcoming Books
by Sharon O'Shea

Non-Fiction

The Butterfly Series: A four-part series of how the Divine has infused and inspired my life.

Look for:
White Butterflies in 2013
Blue Butterflies in 2014
Yellow Butterflies in 2015
Red Butterflies in 2016

Fiction

Matagorda Bay Mystic—A sequel to *Sedona's Golden Secret*—to be published in 2014

Female Victimization Issues

After watching Half The Sky on PBS in October 2012,
I have decided to include Female Victimization research findings
at the conclusion of this book.
It is, after all, the desire to create independent funding
for a healing and recovery center, Merry Heart Ministries,
that prompted the writing of this book.

Female Victimization Issues

Statistics and Consequences of Abuse

Partial List of Possible Consequences to Victims of Abuse (in alphabetical order)

Alcoholism, anger, borderline personality disorder (BPD), branding (by self and/or by society), decreased parenting ability, decreased self-esteem, denial, dependency, despair, destructive relationships, dismemberment, drop-out or change schools, drug abuse, eating disorders, fatigue, fear, guilt, headaches, helplessness, hopelessness, increased need for counseling, increased need for medical attention, increased risk and spread of sexually transmitted diseases (STD's), increasingly needy, insecurity, isolation, lessened capacity to gain and maintain viable employment, melancholy, migraines, multiple personality disorder (MPD), murder (of victim by perpetrator and/or perpetrator by victim and/or children and/or pets as a means to control the victim), nervous disorders, numbness, obesity, passivity, pessimism, phobias, post-traumatic stress disorder (PTSD), promiscuity, prostitution (because of resultant survival issues), rashes, revictimization (by abusers and/or others in society, such as the legal system, religious organizations, becoming victim of a pimp, and so forth), psychosomatic illnesses, rage, reclusiveness, relocation, sadness, self-devaluation, self-loathing, sexual addictions, sexual dysfunctions, shame, shock, sleeping disorders, stress, substance abuse, suicidal thoughts, suicide, suicide of victim, unwanted pregnancies, world view crisis (world no longer considered safe and secure place; men no longer seen as protectors and providers), wounds.

Statistics

It is estimated that 50% of American women are victimized by 10% of American men (many men have multiple victims). The most severe victimizations are rape, incest, battering and/or prostitution. In many other countries, the percentage is much higher, and can reach 90%, or more.

Determinants of Physical, Emotional, Psychological and Fiscal Consequences

Basic personality of the victim at the time of the abuse; strength of her support network; attitude of members of victim's social structure toward the abuse; duration of the abuse; victim's emotional reaction to the abuse; mental health of the victim at the time of the abuse.

Consequences to Society and Off-Spring

The cost to society in relation to medical costs, legal costs, law enforcement costs, time missed from work, social services, and destroyed lives is enormous. The lives of many children raised by victims are also negatively impacted in that victims are often struggling to survive their abuse and not fully present and "well" enough to focus on child-rearing vs. self-survival.

Some Global Abuses of Women

For information about the global issue of female victimization in relation to prostitution, trafficking in females, and female genitalia mutilation, please read or see (PBS) *Half The Sky* by Nicholas D. Dristof and Sheryl WuDunn.

Made in the USA
San Bernardino, CA
25 August 2018